The Counterfeit Gentleman

This time even Vanessa suspected she had gone too far.

It was bad enough engaging in a carriage race in the park to show herself as capable as anyone in London at handling a team of spirited steeds.

It was even worse to masquerade as a man to enter the masculine preserves of White's, and match her skill at cards with the gamblers there.

But now she had not been able to restrain herself from accusing one of those blue-blooded plungers of common cheating—and now she had to prove herself the equal of a man in yet another way.

On the field of honor—with a pistol in her hand . . . and the knowledge that even should she win the duel, she would lose the man she loved. . . .

THE
IMPULSIVE
MISS PYMBROKE

SIGNET Regency Romances You'll Enjoy

Norma Lee Clark
The Impulsive Miss Pymbroke

A SIGNET BOOK

NEW AMERICAN LIBRARY

NAL BOOKS ARE AVAILABLE AT QUANTITY DISCOUNTS WHEN USED
TO PROMOTE PRODUCTS OR SERVICES. FOR INFORMATION PLEASE
WRITE TO PREMIUM MARKETING DIVISION, NEW AMERICAN LIBRARY,
1633 BROADWAY, NEW YORK, NEW YORK 10019.

SIGNET, SIGNET CLASSIC, MENTOR, PLUME, MERIDIAN AND NAL BOOKS
are published by
New American Library,
1633 Broadway,
New York, New York 10019

First Printing, December, 1984

1 2 3 4 5 6 7 8 9

PRINTED IN THE UNITED STATES OF AMERICA

1

Lord Chance bent a courteously attentive ear to the nearly toothless mumblings of the frail old gentleman beside him as they strolled into Lady Truscombe's ballroom together. The ancient dandy was resplendent in an apple-green satin coat and knee breeches and an elaborately embroidered waistcoat of primrose satin. Two bright spots of rouge, a beauty mark on his left cheekbone, and powdered hair completed this outmoded toilette, which was in marked contrast to Lord Chance's exquisitely cut coat of black superfine, black pantaloons, and plain white marcella waistcoat.

". . . and the dear duchess told me herself that the duke had never been capable of—*mumble, mumble*—and so, of course, what is one to deduce from this but that the boy must be—*mumble*—now what d'ye think of that, eh?"

The ancient snuffled gleefully over this *on-dit* that had been stale news while Lord Chance was still at Oxford. He smiled agreeably, however, turning only momentarily from the swirling couples on the floor, and from one figure in particular who had captured his attention as he entered the door. She fairly shimmered before his eyes, a vision with silver-gilt curls in a gown of spangled, white tissue gauze.

Peter, Viscount Chance, was a squarely built young man of medium stature, but strength was evident in the breadth of his shoulders and his muscular thighs. His dark curls fell carelessly over his brow and his fine gray eyes and regular features drew the eyes of more than one young woman in the room, for not only was he comely, he was also heir to the Earl of Carrisbrooke. There could not have been more than five persons in that crowded room who did not know to within a few pounds the exact extent of the vast Carrisbrooke fortune.

"Well-favored wench," commented the old fellow, holding up his *face à main* and staring frankly at the vision who held Peter's attention. Peter jerked his own gaze away, wondering if the company were being entertained by the spectacle of the two of them rudely ogling a young gentlewoman. He turned away in some confusion and met, over a languidly waving feathered fan, the amused regard of his sister, Lady Ann Chance. He hastily excused himself and made his way around the edge of the dancing floor to her side.

"Well, sister, you are in good looks tonight," he said, bowing with exaggerated gallantry.

"But not so good as Vanessa Pymbroke, it seems," she replied teasingly.

"I am not acquainted with a Miss Pymbroke," he said gravely.

"Not by name, perhaps, but I should imagine your acquaintance with her face and form extensive by now," she retorted, her dark-gray eyes, so like his own, sparkling mischievously.

"Ah, you refer to the young, ah, lady in white, I take it. She did rather catch my eye," he admitted, his own eyes twinkling now at his absurdity. They began to laugh.

"Oh, Peter, I adore you when you become pompous."

"I am never pompous!" he declared pompously, sending her into renewed fits of the giggles.

"Now, now, you are attracting disapproving glances from the dragons with such unseemly mirth. Since you are not engaged, I will lead you out," he offered with condescension.

"How gallant you are, little brother, but I will not put you to the trouble. My reputation would be in shreds if it was thought I could find no partner but my brother."

"All cods wallop, if you ask me. But"—here he lowered his voice and spoke seriously—"why *are* you not dancing—I mean to say, has no one, er, asked?"

"They have, and I have refused. I do not dance this

evening," she said firmly, staring him straight in the eye, her chin lifted proudly.

He returned her look squarely, refusing to allow any pity to inform his regard, for he knew she would scorn it. Lady Ann, at twenty-five a year his senior, was burdened with a delicate constitution. She was as tall as her brother, but of a wraithlike frailty that made her thick auburn hair seem too great a burden for her slender neck.

"Gammon," Peter said gruffly, "trying to make yourself interesting, I suppose. If you do not dance, why are you here?"

"I came up from Falconley to visit a school friend who has just returned from the Continent after years away. She is staying with her aunt and knows no one, naturally, so I am taking her around a bit."

"Damned waste of your precious energy," he said, then bit his lip, knowing she hated any reference to her health. She pretended not to have heard.

"There is her aunt, Mrs. Clarence, over there, beneath the mirror."

He looked as she directed, and saw, seated upon a sofa against the wall, a very large lady in yards of purple lustring and a towering plumed turban. She was obviously feeling the heat of the room, for she fanned herself vigorously while continuously mopping her face with a large handkerchief.

"Good Lord!" Peter exclaimed simply.

Ann giggled. "Yes, she is awesome, is not she? But it is only a facade. She is the most good-natured creature alive."

"And the niece? Why has she been on the Continent so many years?"

"Because of her father. He is of a restless nature, I gather, and when his wife died, he simply bundled the child up and set sail with her. Is not that romantic?"

"Ramshackle sort of way to behave, if you ask me. What sort of life is that for an infant?"

"Oh, she seems to have thrived on it. She missed him dreadfully when he sent her for two years to Madame Beauclerc's school in Brussels, where I met her. We became bosom bows and have corresponded ever since."

"So here she is at five and twenty—"

"Three and twenty."

"—with no friends, no sponsors, no proper chaperonage—"

"Pooh! She has me as a friend, and after tonight I make no doubt, she will have as many as she cares for. As for chaperonage, I think Mrs. Clarence is entirely suitable. She is not much in society these days, but when she cares to go out, she is received. Now, please stop being so bearish and disagreeable, for I want to ask you a favor."

"What is it?" he asked suspiciously, half-suspecting what she was going to ask.

"That you request my friend to stand up with you when I introduce you to her."

"Now, see here, Ann," he protested, "if you are foisting some antidote on me—"

"She is not an antidote. She has nice eyes and a lovely nature," Ann replied, lowering her eyes to hide their glinting mischief.

Peter groaned audibly. "Deadly attributes! Every antidote I've ever known was described in just those terms."

Ann's lips twitched, but she only said sternly, "I count upon you to behave just as you ought. Now, come, I will introduce you to Mrs. Clarence before this set ends."

She took his arm and he had nothing to do but lead her around the floor to where Mrs. Clarence sat. He was introduced and bowed with grave courtesy over the pudgy hand extended to him.

"Charming," murmured Mrs. Clarence breathily, "what a handsome family you Chances are, to be sure. Ann, do you not dance tonight?"

"No, Mrs. Clarence."

"And quite right, too. Monstrously warm for dancin', my dear." She applied her damp handkerchief to her upper lip.

"Allow me, madam," said Peter, taking her fan and waving it before her face.

"Too kind," she gasped, closing her eyes and leaning back gratefully.

The set ended and there was a general swell of conversation and movement as young women were escorted back to their chaperones.

"Well, Aunt, not here an hour and already you have made a conquest, I see."

Mrs. Clarence sat up abruptly and Peter whipped around in surprise at the words, delivered in a deep, rather husky voice, and his mouth fell open.

"Oh, Vanessa, here you are. Allow me to introduce my brother to you. Peter, Miss Pymbroke."

Peter took in the startling blue eyes, the silver-gilt hair, the petite figure in silvery gauze that had so riveted him before, and with a major effort he pulled his shattered wits together and bowed.

"Your servant, Miss Pymbroke." He cast a reproachful glance at Ann, who hid her smile behind her fan. "May I request the pleasure of standing up with you for a set?"

"You may, sir."

"The next?"

"Yes."

Her unusual voice was sending ripples of excitement through him and he wished her answers were not so short. The voice went so oddly with the dainty figure and the, surely, pure Anglo-Saxon coloring. The music struck up and he led her out to the floor, his heart behaving in a most uncomfortable way that seemed to affect his breathing and his ability to think properly. After the prolonged silence that ensued while he tried to formulate a coherent sentence, she spoke.

"Do you enjoy dancing, Lord Chance?"

"Ah, it can be most enjoyable upon occasion," he replied rather stiffly, his efforts to cover his confusion causing him to speak with more formality than he intended.

She raised a quizzical eyebrow at this response but made no further comment.

He cursed himself for his lack of conduct and forced himself to speak. "My sister tells me you have been away from England many years, Miss Pymbroke."

"Yes, I have."

"Dare we hope you will make a long stay now that you have returned at last?"

She cast another look up at him, then lowered her eyes and said demurely, "Oh, that will depend, you see, on how I fare."

"Fare?"

"In the marriage market," she said simply. "Papa would have me married, you see."

"And were there no marriageable gentlemen on the Continent?"

"Oh, Papa became very chauvinistic on the subject. Nothing but an English gentleman would suit him. But I suspect he simply wanted me out of the way for a time while he pursued an *affaire du coeur*." She offered him this somewhat shocking information with the same directness she might use to state "The grass is green."

The pleasure of listening to her strange, husky voice could not prevent a disapproving crease between his brows. He changed the subject firmly. "The orchestra is very fine, is it not?"

"Ah, I have shocked you. I have forgotten the English gentleman prefers to think the *jeune fille* ignorant," she said remorsefully.

"Nothing of the sort," he said stiffly, "it is only that—"

"They should pretend ignorance," she finished for him, "and, indeed, I suppose it does make them appear more virginal, a prime requisite in the marriage stakes. I must remember that from this moment. You have done me a great kindness to point it out." She smiled up at him bewitchingly. "How fortunate Ann is to have a brother to advise her in these matters. Perhaps you will stand brother to me, Lord Chance, and pull me up when I fall into error in future."

Peter was by now in a state of total confusion. In spite of his disapproval of the subjects she spoke of so frankly, he could not deny the eroticism of her voice and smile. Nor was he exactly pleased to figure in her thoughts as a brother. To hide his feelings, he said more coldly than he realized, "Naturally I shall be delighted to be of service to a friend of Ann's."

"Too kind," she said absently, her mind obviously pursuing its own train as the delicate brows drew together. "Perhaps it is my way of speaking that frightens the young gentlemen away. I had thought my lack of dowry explained it, but—"

"Certainly if you make it a habit to explain to your dancing partners that you seek a husband and have no dowry, you might expect it to be in some ways off-putting," he retorted dryly.

"There! You are right, I think. How stupid of me. In future I must not *tell* the rich young gentlemen I am in need of a husband. Of course, they must already know that is what we young women are all seeking, but they prefer not to have it spoken of so openly. It is odd sort of behavior, is it not? Still, I must conform."

"Are these things discussed openly on the Continent, then?"

"Well, I do not know. I was not much in company there. I went about with Papa, you see, and he did not care for balls and evening parties. At least not this sort."

"But surely you had friends who invited you?"

"No. Only Papa's friends, and as their interests marched with his . . ." She shrugged eloquently.

"What were their interests?"

"Oh, Papa was interested in antiquities and mountain climbing and gambling—oh, and food. He was ever in search of good food."

"Good Lord! And you accompanied him in these pursuits?"

"Of course, Lord Chance. Except for my two years at Madame Beauclerc's school, I was always with my father. Where else could I be?"

The set had come to an end and he realized they still stood in the middle of the floor. He had no recollection of the dance or of its end. As for her question, he felt it was not his place to criticize her father, so he only bowed and led her back to her aunt.

Ann had placed a chair for herself beside Mrs. Clarence and smiled up in welcome.

"Oh, Ann, how glad I am that Papa insisted I go to school, for there I found you and now, through you, I have a brother. Lord Chance has agreed to act as a brother to me and advise me on how I am to comport myself in company."

"Has he, indeed?" said Ann, raising an astonished eyebrow at her brother.

"Miss Pymbroke is amusing herself, I think," said Peter stiffly.

"Oh, then you will not advise me, Lord Chance?" cried Vanessa sorrowfully.

He bowed. "Naturally, if I can be of service, Miss Pymbroke, you have only to call upon me."

"There! I knew you would not disappoint me." She lowered her voice and bent closer to him to whisper confidentially, "Here comes my next partner, the heir of Lord Wortley, and excessively rich, I am told. You must observe him and give me your opinion of him. Naturally, I will not confide in him my need of a rich husband, as you have advised. Ah, sir"—she smiled radiantly at the blushing youth who bowed before her—"here you are to lead me out." She took the arm the youth extended to her and was led away, casting a smile over her shoulder at Peter and Ann.

Ann rose. "Perhaps you will escort me to the refreshment room, Peter. I feel the need of a glass of lemonade. May we bring you a glass, Mrs. Clarence?"

"Oh, my dear, yes, if you please. I am fair parched with this heat," gasped Mrs. Clarence gratefully.

"Well, Peter," said Ann as they walked away, "what do you think of my friend? She is beautiful, is she not?"

"Exceedingly," he replied shortly.

"Oh, dear, I thought I detected something amiss. She has not met with your approval?"

"I would not dream of judging a friend of yours, Ann."

"Pompous," she said warningly.

"Nothing of the sort."

"Now, please do not take that lofty tone with me. What has she done?"

"Well, if you must know, I think she should study to be a little less forthcoming in her conversation."

"Less forthcoming! That from you, who have complained this age about missish girls who have no conversation."

"I agree that I dislike missishness, but I would never condemn decorum. I cannot like Miss Pymbroke's manner. It is bound to discredit her in the eyes of those very people she is so desirous of attracting."

"Good heavens, what did she say?"

"That she was sent to England to catch a wealthy husband, that her father wanted her out of the way so that he could pursue an affair, that she has no dowry, that—"

Ann interrupted with a shout of laughter. "Oh, Peter, she was teasing you for sure. You *do* bring that out in people."

"Do you tell me none of these things is true?"

"Well, as to that, I cannot know, but I feel sure she was only funning."

"Then I must tell you I find her sense of humor without taste. I make no doubt she will take in some circles. I suppose such behavior must be attributed to her unorthodox upbringing, and allowances must be made."

Having by this time fetched the lemonade and returned to Mrs. Clarence, Peter handed each lady a glass, bowed, and went away.

Ann watched his disappearing back with some dismay. He was clearly more than a little overset by his brief encounter with Vanessa, and Ann had been infected with that purely feminine disease, matchmaking, as she had watched them dancing together. What a handsome couple they make, she had thought. Still, looks were not as important as personality, it seemed, when it came to partnerships. Ann knew and loved both of them so well it had not occurred to her that they would misunderstand each other.

Vanessa was a high-spirited girl, with many escapades to her credit that Ann knew of from school, where that starchy martinet Madame Beauclerc had been reduced to quivering frustration by her inability to curb Vanessa's mischief. For instance, Vanessa's vow to avenge the cowed, homesick "babies" class, eleven- and twelve-year-old girls ruled over with ice-cold cruelty by Fräulein Heidigger, who took pleasure in humiliating her pupils and watching them cry. One day in the dining room, as Fräulein, with steely eye and razor tongue, hectored her crushed charges, Vanessa, passing with a tray, "accidentally" dislodged Fräulein's wig, to reveal a shining bald head. Her ramrod-straight pupils, eyes fixed firmly on their plates, dared to look up at Fräulein's howl of rage. After a shocked, disbelieving silence, the older girls at other tables began to giggle. Then, as Fräulein snatched up her wig and fled the room, the "babies" joined in, rolling about in helpless merriment and release while Vanessa ran after Fräulein crying out her apologies. Called to Madame Beauclerc's office, Vanessa pled her case with so much remorse there was little Madame could do, despite her suspicions as to the accidental nature of the mishap.

Ann felt sure that if she related this story to Peter he would laugh and enjoy it. He himself had been a notorious ringleader in mischief in his own school days, so why was he being so stiff-necked about what was clearly only a bit of teasing?

Ann looked up at this point and her face lit up with joy and her heart sang, for there was Giles! He scowled about the room, searching for her, tall, dark-browed, and almost unbearably handsome.

2

Raking the room from beneath his dark scowling brows, Giles saw Ann at last and he pushed through the thronging guests with eyes firmly fixed upon her. He had discovered that the best technique for avoiding unwanted encounters was simply to refuse to allow one's eye to be caught, for to acknowledge acquaintances was to be trapped. Why *would* people hold on to one so? Elderly men grasping his arm to keep him from escaping while they catechized him about his family, older women with a firm grip of his sleeve pulling him inexorably in the direction of a marriageable daughter or niece, and the young women themselves expecting him to offer his arm for a three-yard walk across a room, as though they were not strong enough to essay such a distance unaided.

Giles could not bear to be held on to, captive of needs he could not fulfill, being wary that his firmly checked compassion would escape his control and compromise him. He gave his arm freely to only two people: Ann and Oliver. Or at least he would do to Oliver if he— No! I mustn't think of him now.

He forced himself to focus on Ann. Poor old girl looks peaky, he thought. Shouldn't be here, of course. All non-sense going about with that Pymbroke creature, who might look like a Dresden figurine but who was clearly as strong as a farm horse. Oh, she was a beautiful young woman, but he would prefer the china shepherdess. At least one could ad-

15

mire it without having to make stupid conversation with it or offer to stand up to dance with it.

"Come away out of this, Ann. You look like a wrung-out dish clout," he said without preamble, coming to an abrupt halt before her.

Ann laughed. "Charming, Giles, thank you."

"You may laugh, but I doubt you will enjoy it quite so much when you find yourself in your bed for two weeks."

"That will teach me to enjoy myself, won't it?"

"Enjoy yourself? You know you hate these dos and always pay for—"

She gave him a barely perceptible shake of her head and flicked her eyes warningly toward the lady beside her.

Giles saw Mrs. Clarence for the first time and bowed perfunctorily to her. "Mrs. Clarence. How do you do?"

"Very well, dear boy, though I cannot like this heat, which you young people seem not to feel at all. I suppose you have come to lead dear Ann out for a dance, and a very good thing, too. She will insist on keeping me company, but I like to see young people enjoying themselves. Go along, dear child, do."

"Oh, no, I—" Ann began.

Giles cut in abruptly. "Ann should not be here at all, much less be dancing, it is the very worst—"

"Giles, dear, do come for a walk on the terrace," Ann interrupted hastily. "It *is* warm, I find. You will excuse us, Mrs. Clarence?" Without waiting for an answer she walked away before Giles could say anything further.

Giles jerked another bow to Mrs. Clarence and turned to follow her, then turned back to snatch up the shawl from Ann's chair before hurrying after her.

Mrs. Clarence stared at his retreating back. What a very odd young man, she thought, so devastatingly handsome, but so forbidding, somehow, and not, I'll vow, in love with her as she is with him. Mrs. Clarence had little inclination to exert herself physically, but she was a keen observer of the human condition and had not missed the way Ann's face had lit up when she saw Giles Dalzell enter the room. Poor child, she thought with a breathy sigh.

By the time Giles caught up with Ann she had reached the terrace, romantically lit by the candlelight making golden pools on the dark stones at their feet. Giles draped the shawl over her shoulders and turned her around to arrange the soft folds high about her throat. "Idiot. To come out at night without your shawl when you know the least draft will—"

"Oh, please don't fuss, Giles. I am not an invalid, after all," she said crossly, pulling away from his long, delicate fingers, which seemed to sear the skin of her throat and chin where they touched her as he adjusted the shawl. He looked puzzled and a little hurt, but she only turned away.

He had always fussed over her since she was four and he six and had come to live with them. His father was an officer of the East India Company and had been sent out to take charge of affairs there. Since Mrs. Dalzell had died some years previously, Giles was left behind in the care of his godmother, Lady Carrisbrooke, Ann's mother.

Giles had not cared in the least for the rough games of Peter and Robin, Ann's brothers, but Ann herself had appealed to him. She had been a tiny, elfin creature, so frail, so trusting, giving him the feeling of being necessary to *someone*, helping him to forget his loneliness after first his mother and then his father had disappeared so suddenly—and so callously, he felt—from his life.

Ann freely acknowledged to herself that she had given him her heart the instant she saw him, and had never dreamed of loving another man. He had played with her, told her stories, read her his first poems, and worried about her health. She had taken it all for granted and accepted his ministrations joyfully. But then, quite suddenly, at sixteen she had not wanted them anymore. She could not bear his casual, brotherly affection, nor could she bear to appear an invalid in his eyes.

She was not, as a rule, angry as she was tonight, always managing to turn him off lightly, jokingly, for she would rather die than have him guess her feelings. She stared blindly into the massy dark of the Truscombes' garden, her back to Giles, struggling to regain her composure.

He came up beside her and gave her shoulder a friendly pat. "You are out-of-reason cross, Annie, and I make no doubt it is because you are overtired. I knew no good would come of this jauntering about from party to party. I cannot think what your mama was thinking of to allow it."

Ann pulled away from his hand and said lightly, "But I am not in the least tired. Why should you think so? I have done nothing but sit beside Mrs. Clarence all evening and she is excessively restful company. Oh, do listen, Giles, it is the boulanger. Dance a few steps with me." She held out her hands coaxingly.

He scowled, then shrugged and came to take them. He could never deny her anything, though she knew he despised dancing. Oliver loved dancing, but said he had given it up when he realized he was also required to make conversation with insipid females, all bent on starting a flirtation with him. Oh, yes, Giles could well understand that they would do so, for never could they have beheld a more strikingly handsome man than Oliver, with his tight cap of golden curls, his intensely blue eyes and charming smile. Dear heaven, how many heads he must be turning in Italy right at this moment? Will he remember me at all? wondered Giles in an agony of doubt. Will he write to me as he promised?

He recovered himself from these painful speculations and said to Ann, "You know I cannot dance, as well as you know that you should not," he grumbled.

"Oh, pooh, just a few twirls cannot do much harm. It is quite easy, just follow me—you see?"

After a few steps, however, she stopped. He was so exasperatingly stiff, deliberately so, she knew from the stubborn jut of his lower lip, which she remembered as a signal of rebellion from their earliest moments together. He had never given way gracefully to what he did not want, whether through coaxing or direct orders from his elders.

Ann pulled her shawl closer and turned back to the ballroom. "I must go back to Mrs. Clarence," she said shortly. "You will oblige me by not saying anything further about my health in her presence. You know perfectly well I do not like it, and I chose to come up to town to introduce Vanessa around with no coercion on her part. I am not suffering in the least from it, but if I should do so, it is entirely my own affair."

Little spitfire, Giles thought, grinning at her retreating back. Her constitution might be delicate, but she was spirited for all that. He always found her rare outbursts of temper reassuring, somehow. Perhaps they soothed the gnawing fear that he might lose her, as he had lost his parents and then Oliver.

I wonder if he has received the poem yet, Giles thought, and will he bother to read it? Of course he will, he reassured himself, he has always been interested in my work and he will see at once that it is about himself. Reassured by this thought, Giles lounged back into the ballroom after Ann. She was standing before Mrs. Clarence talking with Vanessa and another young woman. As Giles came up to them Ann turned and gave him a ruefully apologetic smile.

"Why, Mr. Dalzell," exclaimed Vanessa, "I never thought to find you here tonight. Ann has told me you do not care for dancing."

"No, I do not," he answered firmly, in case she hoped he would ask her to stand up with him.

"Miss Chamfreys," Ann interrupted smoothly, "you will allow me to present Mr. Giles Dalzell to you."

Miss Chamfreys smiled and extended her hand, which Giles took and bent over perfunctorily, wondering where he had seen her before, for there was something familiar about the triangular face, the brilliant dark eyes, and the rich, black hair.

"I make sure you will have seen Miss Chamfreys' parents last season in *Macbeth*," Ann continued.

"Oh, *that* Chamfreys," Giles exclaimed, remembering at once his enthrallment at the performance and with the almost legendary acting couple. Mrs. Chamfreys had especially haunted his memory with her portrayal of the doomed Lady Macbeth, and her daughter resembled her closely. "Do you act, Miss Chamfreys?"

"That is still debatable," she laughed, "though I have been allowed to try several small parts this season. But you must allow me to ask if you are the poet who wrote 'The Wraith of Worley Vale'?"

Giles felt a flush of pleasure stain his cheeks. "You have read it?" he asked, gruffly, to cover his embarrassment.

"Papa read it aloud to Mama and me. We were all terribly moved by it, and Mama cried. Papa said he hoped you would write a play someday. Do you think you might? I am sure Papa would produce it if you should do so."

Flustered by her admiration, he swallowed several times

before he was able to speak. "Most kind—only too gratified to have pleased you. I fear I know nothing of the art of writing plays."

"I am sure you would do it very well," said Vanessa, "even the critics claim you have a dramatic gift. You should go about more and you would find that your latest book of verse is the talk of London. You are much too elusive, you know. Not the least like Lord Byron. One sees him everywhere."

"I do not care for wasting time with parties," replied Giles severely.

"But then how is one to compliment you upon your work?"

"By buying the book," he riposted succinctly, causing them all to laugh.

A young man approached to claim Vanessa, and Ann seated herself again beside Mrs. Clarence, smiling about brightly to hide her extreme weariness. Why did her body betray her in this way, protesting at the least exertion, causing her chest to tighten with sharp, dabbing little pains and her pulses to race? She dared not even lean back a little for fear Giles would see it and began scolding her again. But Giles, she was astonished to see, had offered his arm to Camilla Chamfreys and was suggesting she might care to stroll about the room with him if she were not engaged to dance. Miss Chamfreys accepted and they walked away.

Ann stared after them, torn between her amazement and jealousy, for she knew how he disliked anyone clinging to his arm. Ann had never known him to offer it voluntarily before to anyone but herself. Suddenly she felt swamped by her exhaustion, and her throat tightened with held-back tears.

Mrs. Clarence saw Ann's head droop forward like a heavy blossom on a too slender stem, and searching the dance floor, she caught Vanessa's eye after a moment and raised an eyebrow at her and indicated Ann with a movement of her eyes. In a moment Vanessa was being escorted back to her aunt's side by her clearly disappointed partner.

"You must simply attempt to forgive me, Mr. Himble, but I felt that one more step and I would drop to the floor. I am not used to dancing so much, you see, for on the Continent my papa would rarely attend balls, and when he did, he would take me away again after three-quarters of an hour.

Oh, Aunt, I hope you will not mind, but I must get to my bed as soon as may be. You will stay with Ann, of course, and I will just slip away quietly and send the carriage back for you.''

"No such thing, I will not hear of it," declared Ann, forcing herself to her feet. "I am quite ready to leave also and I am sure Mrs. Clarence has been ready this age."

"Yes, indeed, child," said Mrs. Clarence, struggling to her feet, "you know balls quite exhaust me."

Vanessa giggled at this as they made their way across the room to bid Lady Truscombe good night. Ann cast a sidelong look at Giles and Miss Chamfreys deep in conversation and quickly looked away. Soon the three women were in Mrs. Clarence's comfortable carriage and Ann sank gratefully back into the velvet squabs and closed her eyes. Vanessa slid a covert look at her as they passed beneath one of the new gas lamps on the street and saw the white face and the mauve shadows beneath the eyes and was conscience-stricken. I should never have allowed her to come to London, Vanessa reproached herself, though in truth, I cannot think how I could have prevented it.

In fact, it had never occurred to Vanessa that Ann would feel it necessary to come to London to take her about. Vanessa had come from the Continent equipped with several letters from her father to various London hostesses of the highest *ton*, any one of whom would guarantee that his daughter had entrée into the best drawing rooms in London. Vanessa was also possessed of a warm, outgoing personality and a great deal of self-assurance and had suffered not a moment's worry about her debut in London. However, her letter to Ann announcing her return to England and her plans to visit Ann after the Season was over had brought Ann to London the very next day, declaring that she intended to ensure that her dear Vanessa received cards to all the important parties and, under Ann's sponsorship, met all the right people.

Vanessa had been overjoyed to see her old friend and delighted to have someone to go about with, which is always pleasanter than going with only a chaperone. All had gone well for several days before Vanessa began to notice signs indicating that Ann's schoolgirl delicacy of constitution had not been outgrown. Then Giles Dalzell had appeared on the scene, looking displeased and dropping scarcely veiled hints that Ann should return to her own home, and Vanessa had begun to be more than a bit worried.

Now, when she made sure that Ann's light was out, Vanessa tiptoed along the corridor to her aunt's bedroom. Mrs. Clarence was propped up by several stout pillows. Her large face and many chins were surrounded by the ruffles of her nightcap, and she was sipping at a glass of port. Vanessa curled up on the end of the bed.

"Aunt, I am worried about Ann."

"I shouldn't be, dear, it never does the least good."

Vanessa laughed. "No I suppose not, but you know very well what I mean."

"She is a young woman with great strength of character who will do what she decides to do. How else could she have persuaded her mother to allow her to come here when it is clear the most exercise she can tolerate is a slow walk through the shrubbery on a fine day."

"Shall I suggest that I am weary of town? I am sure she would ask me to come for a visit with her in the country."

"I shouldn't if I were you, my dear. She obviously desired to come to town. No doubt Mr. Dalzell's being in residence here influenced her, as well as her wish to be kind to you. I very seriously doubt she could credit that you are so soon wearied of society, and she would suspect the truth and resent it. Unwilling invalids detest pity."

"But I cannot simply stand by and allow her to make herself ill. What shall I do?"

"Do nothing. It never pays to interfere. Now do go away, my love. I must go to sleep."

Vanessa kissed her good night and went back to her room deep in thought. Aunt was probably right and Ann's motives for coming to London were more involved than they had at first appeared. If she was in love with Mr. Dalzell, then naturally she would not like to appear as an invalid in his eyes. Still, there was the fact that she was not strong and a Season of parties could do her little good, even positive harm. Oh, Lord, what to do? Perhaps I should have stayed with Papa. But then I should never have met anyone. Until tonight she had met few young men who interested her, and she had begun to think they were as dull and self-satisfied as those she had met on the Continent. Now, she felt very different and found London an exciting place. She would really not like to leave and go into the country.

Lord Chance's disapproving eyes floated before her closed lids and a smile of pure mischief curled up the corners of her enchanting mouth. She burrowed her head into her pillow and drifted into sleep.

3

Ann woke slowly, reluctantly, but lay for some time trying to hold on to sleep, feeling that surely she had only just gone to bed, for she still felt so tired. When it became evident that sleep would elude her, she turned over and opened her eyes, and for a moment thought that she had been right, for the room was still dark and the fire not made up. Then she realized the curtains were still drawn close, but not so close that a sliver of sunlight could not find a way through to throw its shard of golden light across the carpet. She lay staring at it for some time before summoning the will to sit up and ring for the maid.

The girl came in a few moments with a tray, which she put across Ann's knees before crossing to make up the fire.

"Thank you, Ellen. It must be quite late."

"Gone eleven, m'lady."

"Good heavens! Why did you not come to wake me at the usual time?"

"Miss Pymbroke said as how you was to be left to sleep because of the ball last night, m'lady."

"How thoughtful," murmured Ann, though she could not help feeling some resentment that Vanessa should think she needed cosseting. "Has Miss Pymbroke gone out?"

"Bless you, no m'lady. She 'as only just gone down to breakfast herself."

Ann set the tray aside and threw back the bed covers. "I will wear the green muslin, Ellen."

Vanessa looked up in surprise when Ann sailed into the

24

breakfast room. "Now, what are you doing up so early? I made sure you would sleep another hour at least."

"Another hour? Good Lord, I hope I am not such a poor creature that I must lie prostrate on my bed half the day after attending a ball."

"No, no, of course not," Vanessa said hastily. "Will you go out today?"

"I have no plans for the morning, but I believe I overheard you last evening inviting Miss Chamfreys to call."

There was something in her pronunciation of the actress's name that caused Vanessa to look at her curiously. The evening before, Ann had introduced Vanessa to Miss Chamfreys with every evidence of warmth and approval, but now there seemed to be a trace of coldness in her voice.

"So I did. Do you not approve?"

"Why, of course I do," protested Ann, flustered. "What can you mean? I have been friends with Camilla Chamfreys this age."

"That is all right, then. Now, since you have no plans and I certainly have none, we shall spend a quiet day at home, which I, for one, look forward to very much."

"But I had thought you were promised to attend Mrs. Boyington's afternoon salon today."

"I only said I might do so, but I have no inclination for it. In fact, I shall have to give up some of these daytime engagements or I shall not be able to keep up with the evening parties. I plan to spend the time until Miss Chamfreys calls curled up on the chaise in the back sitting room with a book."

"Then I will come with you and write some letters."

They were both absorbed by their occupations when Hay, Mrs. Clarence's butler, came to announce that the Honorable Mr. Robert Chance had called and was waiting upon his sister in the drawing room.

"Robin!" Ann cried happily, dropping her pen and springing to her feet. "Do come and meet my youngest brother, my love. You will like him enormously, I promise you."

"Is this the brother who has entered the Church?" asked Vanessa cautiously.

"Yes. What is wrong?"

"Well, your older brother so obviously disapproved of me, that I fear a vicar—"

"Now you are teasing me. Peter did not— Well, at any rate, Robin is not at all censorious of anyone. Please come to meet him," she pleaded anxiously.

"You pea goose, of course I mean to come," Vanessa laughed, "nothing in the world could prevent me." She linked her arm through Ann's and hugged it as they set off to the drawing room.

The young man who turned away from his contemplation of an awesome painting of Mrs. Clarence in full court regalia, was, though younger, startlingly like his older brother at first glance. Then closer examination revealed that his eyes were blue rather than gray as were Peter's, that his nose was less aquiline, his expression softer than Peter's sterner regard.

"Dear Robin," Ann cried, running into his outheld arms, "what a lovely surprise! I had no notion you were coming to London."

"Nor did I until yesterday. Mama insisted that I come. She said I needed some gaiety before taking up my post, after grinding away at my books for so long. You must be Miss Pymbroke," he added, releasing his sister and turning to Vanessa with a warm smile.

"How do you do, er, do I call you Reverend Chance?"

"You will call me Robin, I hope," he returned, taking the hand she extended and bowing over it. "And I shall address you as Vanessa, if I may, since I have been in the way of hearing you called so by Ann all these years."

"You most certainly may and I will look upon you as a brother as I do Lord Chance."

"Peter?" Robin looked startled.

Vanessa smiled impishly. "Yes, he agreed to give me brotherly advice as to how I must conduct myself in society, though he did not unbend so far as to give me permission to call him Peter."

"Well, he is sometimes a bit of a stickler, old Peter, but if he offered to advise you on your conduct, you may be sure he was bamming you. Odd sense of humor, sometimes."

"Oh, really? Strange. My impression was that he is quite earnest about things. Never mind, tell me of yourself. You are surely very young for a vicar."

"Not really, only very fortunate. I started my studies early and a living in my father's gift became vacant just when I was finished, so I was not forced to wait about being a curate as most young divinity students are."

"Is it a large parish?"

"No, quite small, really. Medford Yatter. Do you know of it?"

"No, I know very little of England, not having really lived here."

While Vanessa acquainted him with her background, Ann was puzzling yet again over Peter's behavior the evening before regarding Vanessa, her thoughts on the subject reactivated by Robin's declaration that his brother must have been hoaxing Vanessa. Ann could not quite believe this when she remembered the scene herself. Which was strange, for in her memory she had never seen him express disapproval of anyone's behavior outside his family. There he *was* a stickler, indeed. For everyone else, however, he displayed only an amused tolerance or a shrug of indifference at the most outré conduct, even of people he quite disliked.

". . . but you must accompany us to the Riddleys' tonight, mustn't he, Ann?" Vanessa said eagerly, interrupting Ann's musings. "I know they will be delighted with an extra young man, for, you know, they have three excessively plain daughters nearly on the shelf. Mrs. Riddley, however, refuses to despair."

Robin laughed delightedly and agreed that it must surely be his Christian duty to keep Mrs. Riddley in good heart.

"That will be lovely, Robin," said Ann, "and I promise to introduce you to some partners who are *not* antidotes."

"Oh, and do come to dine with us first. My aunt would ask you herself if she were here," added Vanessa.

Robin looked questioningly at Ann, who smiled her agreement. "Then if you are sure, I will be delighted. And now I'm to meet Peter at White's, so I had better be on my way."

"Oh, must you Robin? We have hardly visited at all," protested Ann.

"I daren't keep Peter waiting. He does not care for unpunctuality. I shall be here a month at least, dear girl, and you will see so much of me you shall be heartily sick of the sight of me, I assure you.'' He rose, bowed, and strode purposefully to the door, and Ann hurried after him into the hall.

He took his hat and stick from Hay and bent to kiss Ann's forehead. ''Are you being run off your legs, my dear?'' he murmured with a searching look at her face.

She knew at once that her mama had sent him to London to check on her health. She stared back at him steadily. ''Good heavens, no. I have never felt better in my life. I was moldering away down in the country and needed Vanessa and this visit to bring me out of a fit of the dismals.''

''Then I am delighted, of course,'' he replied kindly, ''and I like your friend very much.''

''Oh, I knew you would do so, dear Robin, everyone must like her. How could they not, when she is so charming? Until tonight, then.''

''Yes. Do you dine at seven?''

Just then the knocker was firmly rapped and Hay, waiting to open the door for Robin, stepped forward and opened it. On the doorstep was Miss Chamfreys, the very picture of *à la modalité* in a red velvet spenser over white muslin gown, with a chipstraw bonnet trimmed in red ribands and tied in a fetching bow beneath her chin. A faint touch of rose flushed the cream perfection of her cheeks and her dark eyes sparkled.

''Why, Miss Chamfreys,'' exclaimed Ann, ''do step in. You are just in time. Allow me to present my brother Robert to you.''

''Servant, Miss Chamfreys,'' said Robin, stepping forward at once to bow over the hand she extended.

Ann was not quite sure how it came about that in another moment they were all back in the drawing room and Robin, who had been in such a hurry to leave before, was seated beside Miss Chamfreys on the sofa. Robin made no attempt to monopolize Miss Chamfreys, nor did he cause her to blush by too assiduous attention; nevertheless, Ann watched bemusedly as her baby brother turned from the quiet, shy youth she had known heretofore, into a poised gallant with witty conversation at his fingertips. At one point, while Miss Chamfreys was conversing with Vanessa, Ann asked him if he would not be fearfully late in keeping his appointment with his brother.

"Not to worry," he replied airily, waving the thought of Peter away negligently.

Well, thought Ann, suppressing a smile, our little book-worm has turned.

After wine and biscuits were served and the correct half-hour had flown by effortlessly, Miss Chamfreys rose to take her leave. Robin declared that he too must be off and would be happy to escort her.

"How kind of you, Mr. Chance. I have my mama's carriage waiting. Perhaps I can be of service to you?"

It was agreed that she would take him up as far as White's, and after making his second farewell to his sister and Miss Pymbroke, Robin escorted Miss Chamfreys out to her carriage and assisted her into it. When he was settled beside her and directions had been given to the coachman, she said, "Do you make a long stay in London, sir?"

"Only a month. My new parish awaits me, you see."

She turned her large brilliant eyes upon him, slightly widened in surprise. "Your . . . parish?"

"Yes, I— Oh, dear, I do believe Ann neglected to mention that I am in orders, and I quite understand that I am not everyone's idea of a vicar," he explained ruefully.

"Well, no. Perhaps more a curate," Camilla managed, despite the confusion of mind she was experiencing from this disclosure, for she had been about to invite him to a performance this evening in which she was to take a small role, but was not sure now whether it would be appropriate to do so. He grinned engagingly at her words, however, and she felt so reassured that she smiled back.

"I think you have put your finger squarely upon what will be one of my major problems, Miss Chamfreys. However, I do not intend to face it before I must. I have a month in London and propose to enjoy myself. Do you go to the Riddleys' ball tonight?"

"Unfortunately not. I am a working girl, you see, Mr. Chance."

"A working girl?" He hesitated, thinking she was teasing him, for it was impossible to associate the fashionably dressed young lady driving about the city in her mama's smart carriage with any form of employment.

"Oh, dear, I do believe Lady Ann neglected to mention

that I am on the stage,'' she quipped, parodying his previous words. Then, taking pity on his bewildered expression, she added, ''Only in a minor capacity, so far, Mr. Chance. I am the daughter of Mr. and Mrs. Edmund Chamfreys.''

She looked at him, so clearly expecting him to react that he was nonplussed. ''I fear I am a very ignorant fellow, Miss Chamfreys,'' he apologized, ''whose head, for the past ten years, has been so firmly wedged between his books that he had no notion of what was going on in the world about him. You must forgive me.''

She was disarmed by his confession and said warmly, ''Nonsense, how should you know my parents? Theater people think the world revolves around them, I fear. At any rate, my parents are having some success at the Drury Lane. Perhaps you would care to see the performance tonight? They are doing *Henry the Fifth*.''

''And you are the French princess?'' he hazarded.

''Ah, I see you know Shakespeare, even though you are not acquainted with the stage. But no, I am not trusted with such parts as yet. I am but a 'lady in attendance.' I am the lowliest beginner, you see, and must serve my apprenticeship.'' Her last words were spoken in an amused and faintly mocking accent.

''You are ambitious to move on to more exalted roles?''

''Oh, you must not think me so conceited of my abilities, Mr. Chance, for truly I have not proved, even to myself, that I have inherited any. It is only that I sometimes find it difficult to take the whole thing quite so seriously as my parents feel I should. My papa declares that my attitude in itself speaks volumes to my discredit.''

''One's parents are often harsher toward one than they would be to others. I am sure you could not prevent yourself being an ornament to any stage you graced.''

She blushed and was silent at this warmly expressed compliment and was almost grateful to see they had reached the street where he had asked to be set down.

When he had stepped out onto the pavement, he said, ''I shall come to see the performance tonight, Miss Chamfreys, and then perhaps tomorrow I might call upon you and give you my critique.''

She dimpled with pleasure. "I will look forward to hearing your opinion, sir."

He swept her a profound bow as the carriage moved away and watched her out of sight before turning to make his way to White's. I must send a note to Ann and Vanessa that I must be excused from dinner, he decided. Then I can see the play and explain it all to them later at the ball. They will surely understand that I could not be rude to Miss Chamfreys and refuse her invitation to see her perform.

4

Peter, just coming down the steps of White's and in none too sanguine a temper after having been kept waiting by Robin for over an hour, looked up in time to witness the bow and get a glimpse of its recipient. His annoyance with his brother was immediately tempered by amusement.

"Well, well, you young scamp, not in town above two hours and already an assignation," he said. "Naturally, one's own brother cannot count for much against the charms of Miss Chamfreys."

"Oh, Peter, do you know her?"

"Not even an apology for keeping me waiting, by the Lord! Not to speak of a civil greeting."

"Forgive me, Peter, and how do you do? Do you know her?"

Peter laughed. "I suppose I must make do with whatever crumbs are offered. Yes, little brother, I have met the young lady. She is a friend of Ann's. But where have you met her? I thought, from your note, you only just arrived this morning."

"So I did, and there was some time in hand, so I went around to check up on Ann for Mama, and Miss Chamfreys came in while I was there to pay a morning call. I had not realized that actresses were, well, received, if you understand me."

"As a general thing they are not, but the Chamfreys are very good *ton*. He is the son of a vicar, of all things, and she is from a very old county family. The daughter has led an extremely well-chaperoned life."

"Have you seen her perform?"

"No, for as I understand, she is only just beginning. Her parents are spectacular. You must see them in something while you are here."

"Oh, I shall see them tonight. And Miss Chamfreys as well. She has invited me," returned Robin triumphantly. The way his eyes lit up at the thought gave his brother pause. Lord, the little parson has an actress in his eye, he mused. Now I suppose I shall have to worry about him as well as Ann.

"Well, I wish you joy of it. They are doing *Henry the Fifth*, which I always found rather heavy going myself. Did you happen to meet Miss Pymbroke?" he added casually.

"Oh, yes, jolly young woman," Robin exclaimed enthusiastically, "we went on very well together. I felt I had known her all my life."

"Indeed, she is most forthcoming," replied Peter dampingly. "Too much so, to my mind. I am not sure she is a good companion for someone of Ann's delicate constitution."

"Oh, come now. I think you worry too much. Though I must admit she was looking somewhat pulled. I cannot think what I should say to Mama."

"Tell her Ann is enjoying herself and that we will keep an eye on her."

"But if she should become ill—"

"Leave it, Robin. It is Ann's business. Let her live her life as she chooses for a change." What is left of it, he thought involuntarily and felt himself shiver as a pain seemed to tear through his heart. He loved all his family, but Ann was particularly dear to him, and he could not help half-endorsing his mother's tendency to wrap Ann in cotton wool, while at the same time, for Ann's sake, doing everything in his power to frustrate his mother's inclinations.

He knew that while Ann refused to discuss or even acknowledge her limitations, she was very much aware of them and husbanded her strength carefully. Witness her declaration that she would not dance the previous evening. Though actually this could be laid more directly to her disinterest in standing up with anyone but Giles Dalzell. And there was another worrying thought.

Peter had known Giles, if not as well, at least as long as

Ann. Since Giles had never shown the least interest in playing Pirates or Red Indians or Knights and Dragons, which were the games Peter and Robin most often indulged in, they had never become friends. Nevertheless, Peter felt he knew him well enough to judge his feelings for Ann, and while Peter knew Giles cared for her, he was also quite sure there was nothing of the lover in Giles' feelings for her. On the other hand, Peter had known for some time that his sister was passionately in love with Giles and that Giles was unaware of it. Though Giles had never been known to so much as look at another girl, there was little comfort in this knowledge for Peter, who had been tempted several times in the past few months to give Giles a hint as to the state of affairs.

Until now he had always drawn back because he knew Ann would consider it unforgivable interference, nor could he think of any words of warning to say to her to possibly prepare her for the unhappiness he felt sure lay in store for her. Perhaps he should take the opportunity of seeking Robin's advice. He was young, to be sure, and green in the ways of society, but he was a minister of the Church of England and there must surely be something in the teachings of the Church to help in such a situation.

Young devil, he thought with a sudden surge of pride and affection for his young brother, to think of him trying his luck with Camilla Chamfreys, who was more closely chaperoned than the princess royal.

Robin learned this himself that evening when he went to the Drury Lane for the performance. He had been dazzled by the acting of the elder Chamfreys and enchanted by Camilla's brief appearances as a lady attendant, though they did little to display her histrionic abilities. They did, however, add to his conviction that she was an uncommonly pretty girl.

Carried away by his enthusiasm, he became greatly daring and decided he must tell her so at once. Upon inquiry he learned from an attendant that the Chamfreys received the congratulations of their admirers in the green room backstage and promptly made his way there.

He found Miss Chamfreys seated upon a sofa beside her mother, with her father standing beside her. She dimpled up at Robin and extended her hand, but remained firmly in place. When she introduced him to her parents, they greeted him charmingly and inquired very kindly after his sister, then turned with equal charm to a gentleman who had entered after Robin and was awaiting his turn to greet them.

"Lord Threlfall," cried Mrs. Chamfreys happily, causing Robin to move aside. The gentleman stepped forward and bent to press a reverent kiss upon Mrs. Chamfreys' hand. He was an overly stout man whose florid face was pressed like a balloon between his extremely high shirt points. His mulberry coat strained across his heavy shoulders and he was liberally beruffled and bejeweled across his pouting chest. There was a distinct creaking sound as he bent, indicating heavy corseting.

"Madam, the delight is all mine. You have enchanted us all again with your magic," replied Lord Threlfall. "You were the very embodiment of a queen-to-be tonight, though every night you are the queen of the London stage." He delivered himself of this labored encomium and paused a moment as though in self-congratulation before turning to Camilla. "And here is a worthy princess, whose graceful carriage upon the stage makes us a promise of the greater performances that are to come."

Robin was pleased to note that Camilla did not take this rococo compliment seriously. She laughed lightly and shook her head in denial. "Now you must not tease me, my lord. Even my most ardent well-wisher could find little to base hopes on by tonight's performance, as I am sure Papa will agree." She turned to smile up at her father, and Lord Threlfall, reminded of his duty, bowed to Mr. Chamfreys and began a fulsome praise of his interpretation of King Henry.

Camilla looked at Robin and raised an eyebrow the barest fraction, causing Robin's lips to twitch. He was delighted to be sharing an opinion with her in this unspoken, secret way. However, pleasant as it was, it was clear to even the meanest intelligence that Lord Threlfall was of considerable importance in the eyes of the elder Chamfreys, for they hung on his every word and paid only the briefest attention to their other admirers, who thronged in and out of the room. Presently, when Lord Threlfall began to make elaborate speeches of farewell, Mrs. Chamfreys said she hoped he would honor them with a call on the following morning, when she would be receiving at home.

"I could not deny myself such a pleasure, madam, I assure

you,'' he replied before bending to plant a fervent kiss upon Camilla's hand.

She looked up from it to say, ''And of course we hope you will come also, Mr. Chance, do we not, Mama?''

''Certainly, sir,'' responded Mrs. Chamfreys graciously after only the most infinitesimal hesitation, which Robin did not miss.

Realizing that there was not the remotest chance that she would allow him any private conversation with her daughter, Robin bid Mrs. Chamfreys good night, shook Mr. Chamfreys by the hand, and bowed to Camilla before making his way out of the room.

In the carriage as they were carried home, Mrs. Chamfreys said, ''I think it would be unwise to be too encouraging to Mr. Chance, Camilla.''

''Encouraging? Surely you are not serious, Mama? I was only courteous to Lady Ann's brother.''

''Her younger brother, is he not?'' asked Mrs. Chamfreys significantly.

''Yes, Mama. He has not the title and he does not inherit the Carrisbrooke estates,'' retorted Camilla shortly.

''Please do not use that tone to me, Camilla.''

''I beg your pardon, Mama, but surely it would have been monstrously rude not to ask him to call after inviting Lord Threlfall in front of him. I cannot think such a courtesy could be called encouraging.''

''Very well, child, I will say no more on the subject,'' Mrs. Chamfreys declared and then proceeded to do so. ''I would only remind you that young men are very susceptible at that age and have many misconceptions where actresses are concerned.''

''But he is a vicar, Mama,'' Camilla protested.

A vicar indeed, thought Mrs. Chamfreys contemptuously, for she had no great respect for vicars after having met her father-in-law, a gentle little man of no ambition and no fortune, who had yet fathered ten children to be raised in abject, if genteel, poverty. She dismissed the thought of Robin from her mind and contemplated the degree of attachment Lord Threlfall was evincing toward her daughter. So hopeful was her prognosis that her thoughts went on quite naturally to the vision of her daughter emerging from St.

Paul's in clouds of white lace as Lady Threlfall, Countess of Northwick, mistress of no less than five country seats and a town house in London, and mother-to-be of a son who would inherit a fortune estimated at no less than a million pounds.

These prospects so dazzled her that she was blind to the fact that Lord Threlfall was a less-than-prepossessing man who would fail to appear as a figure of romance in the dreams of a pretty young girl. She was not so lost to good sense, however, that she did not instinctively attempt to shield my lord from the competition of handsome younger men when she could do so.

Mrs. Chamfreys' dreams of an advantageous marriage for her daughter were certainly not uncommon for the times in which she lived, but they were inspired by reasons beyond the usual one of a parent desiring one's child to rise in the world, though that was a powerful one on Mrs. Chamfreys' part. She was also aware, however, that her daughter sadly lacked the gifts she could have been expected to inherit from two such parents. Mrs. Chamfreys had realized this when Camilla was but nine years old and had appeared as one of the young princes in *Richard III*. She had treated the entire experience with the casual aplomb she exhibited at a nursery tea party, with none of the excited, trembling tensions of the born actor.

Mrs. Chamfreys reluctantly, but firmly, put aside her dreams of establishing a great acting family, and set her sights on a brilliant marriage for her daughter. Camilla was educated in every accomplishment to be expected from the wife of a titled gentleman, and raised in an aura of rigid respectability. Having been blessed with enviable good looks and great charm, Camilla was, Mrs. Chamfreys was convinced, destined for a great marriage. Mrs. Chamfreys was not so unreasonable as to hold out for a duke, though Camilla was certainly fit to be a duchess. Still, since none had yet appeared who was eligible, there was no reason to be dissatisfied with an earl.

5

Vanessa drove Mrs. Clarence's open barouche along
expertly, occasionally flicking the lead horse's withers
lightly with her whip and then casually swinging it
back to catch the tip with the same hand, chatting happily all
the while to Ann, who sat beside her. Perched on the seat
behind, the footman had watched Vanessa's performance
narrowly. No flies on m'lady, he finally said to himself, the
highest accolade in his repertory. The tension eased in his
shoulders.

Ann's first apprehensions were gradually being allayed
also, for she was unaccustomed to being driven by a woman
and had voiced serious doubts about the propriety of Vanessa's
doing so. Ann had also unspoken fears as to Vanessa's
ability.

Vanessa had pooh-poohed every objection, answering with
perfect truth that under her father's supervision she had driven
every sort of carriage since she was twelve years old, and a
better driver than her father would be hard to find on two
continents. Since Mrs. Clarence had concurred in this and
offered no objections to the project, Ann had finally allowed
herself to be persuaded.

Vanessa was somewhat vain about her ability to handle the
reins, but her proposal had little to do with showing off her
skill. After her talk with her aunt and some thought, Vanessa
had decided that something must be done about Ann despite
her aunt's advice to the contrary. Accordingly, she had begun
to complain about the daily round of morning calls and

breakfasts and afternoon salons, going so far as to say that London was becoming stifling. Oh, the balls and dinners and evening parties were pleasant, of course, but she was used to taking more exercise and to breathing more fresh air. Therefore, from now on, she announced, she was going to refuse most daytime invitations.

This move would, of course, necessarily curtail Ann's activities also and, Vanessa hoped, give Ann restful days at home with an occasional drive when the weather was fine for air and diversion.

Vanessa cast a fleeting glance at her companion and suppressed a smile as she noticed that Ann's white-knuckled grip on the seat had relaxed. When she turned her eyes back to the road, she saw that Lord Chance was approaching on horseback, accompanied by another gentleman and two ladies. She was glad to encounter Lord Chance at this moment, for she thought Ann looked better than she had the last time he had seen her and she hoped he would approve. She pulled her horses up and waited for the party to come up to them.

"Peter!" Ann called out happily when she saw her brother.

"Well, well, sister, you are in good looks today. Miss Pymbroke," said Peter, bowing to the girls, noticing the faint flush of color in his sister's cheeks and the brightness of her eyes and turning an approving smile upon Miss Pymbroke. She responded with her impish grin, feeling too proud of his approval to suppress her pleasure in it. "Ann, Miss Pymbroke, allow me to introduce Miss Clayton-Trees and Mr. and Mrs. Braid to you."

While acknowledgments were made, Vanessa silently wondered what on earth Chance was doing with a creature like Miss Clayton-Trees. Was it possible he could be attracted by that washed-out coloring and prim little mouth, now pursed in what was no doubt disapproval at the whip in Vanessa's hand? Oh, she was a passing pretty girl, and clearly the very epitome of elegant respectability, but still . . . The Braids, on the other hand, were a distinctly raffish-looking couple: she in an overelaborate and none too clean habit of mustard yellow, her eyes hard and knowing, her laugh too loud; he a beanpole of a man with a hawk nose and a mouth like a trap. Strange company, indeed, Vanessa thought, in which to find the fastidious Lord Chance.

"A regular lady whipster, eh, Belle?" rasped Mr. Braid to his wife, eyeing Vanessa approvingly. "Drives to an inch, eh?"

"No reason why she shouldn't when she's had more practice. Nothing to say women cannot learn to drive as well as men, is there, Miss Pymbroke?"

"If they have the hands for it," replied Vanessa, smarting under the implication that she had yet to learn to drive. "Do you drive yourself, Mrs. Braid?"

"Oh, anytime this last age," replied Mrs. Braid nonchalantly.

"A real top sawyer, my Belle," boasted Mr. Braid, "back her against anyone."

"Oh, do you race, then, Mrs. Braid?"

"When I can find another woman with the backbone to take me on. Men, of course, refuse to race me. Afraid I'll beat 'em!" She laughed raucously.

"But surely you would not race with men, Mrs. Braid," protested Miss Clayton-Trees in round-eyed horror.

"Would if they'd let me, the silly gudgeons."

"Perhaps Miss Pymbroke will challenge you, Belle. What do you say, Miss Pymbroke?"

"Well, I hardly think—" Vanessa began.

Peter interrupted her. "You cannot be serious, Braid," he snapped.

Ann clutched at Vanessa's arm as though to hold her back and said she was sure Mr. Braid was only funning.

Miss Clayton-Trees' mouth became primmer than ever. "Lord Chance, I believe my mama would like me to return home now, if you please," she said tightly.

"Of course, Miss Clayton-Trees. Ann, perhaps we might ride along with you and Miss Pymbroke if you—"

"Oh, come now, Chance, what's all the to-do? Just a little sport among friends, eh?" cried Mr. Braid in a rallying tone.

"You mustn't press, Braid," said his wife, "only experienced whips care for racing."

"Perhaps you're right," conceded Mr. Braid reluctantly, "though it's not often you see a lady drive so well as Miss Pymbroke."

"Driving's one thing. Racing's another," declared Mrs.

Braid with a smirk. "Don't often find ladies with enough
backbone for racing."

"I should be happy to oblige you, Mrs. Braid," Vanessa
said rashly, goaded beyond endurance by the woman's complacency and conceit.

"Oh, Vanessa," breathed Ann, who, knowing her friend
so well, had feared just this outcome.

"Done!" shouted Mr. Braid. "That's the spirit, Miss
Pymbroke! You're a game 'un, you are for sure. Five guineas
on me wife, Chance. Will you match it?"

"No," returned Peter sharply, staring with obvious disapproval at Vanessa. Vanessa felt the hot color flooding up her
throat and wished desperately she had held her peace and not
allowed herself to be maneuvered into this business. "I will
bid you good day, Ann, Miss Pymbroke." He nodded coldly
to the Braids and led Miss Clayton-Trees away.

"Poor-spirited, if you ask me," commented Mr. Braid.
"Well, ladies, let us get down to it, eh? What's your pleasure?
To Barnet and back, two horses?"

"No, Mr. Braid, not the public roads, if you please,"
replied Vanessa firmly. "Perhaps once around the park in the
early morning before anyone is out. And I will ask you to
give me your word that you will not mention the business to
anyone."

"Famous! Just as you like, Miss Pymbroke, eh, Belle?"

"Your word, Mr. Braid," said Vanessa firmly.

"Certainly, Miss Pymbroke. Our little secret, eh? Now,
when shall it be?"

"Tomorrow morning at six-thirty, if that is agreeable,"
replied Vanessa, thinking that the sooner the thing was finished with, the less chance there would be of word leaking
out about it. "Will that suit you, Mrs. Braid?"

Mrs. Braid had listened to the arrangements silently with
an irritatingly superior smile and now said airily, "Just as
you like, Miss Pymbroke, it's all the same to me. Until
tomorrow, then. Good day to you, Miss Pymbroke, Lady
Ann. Come along, Braid." She trotted off and Mr. Braid
hurriedly tipped his hat and followed her.

Vanessa flicked the reins and they drove slowly off in the
opposite direction. For some time there was silence between
them. Ann could think of nothing to say and could not bring

herself to reproach her friend, who, Ann felt sure, was already reproaching herself enough for both of them.

Vanessa was biting her lip with vexation at herself. How could she have allowed herself to be drawn into such an unsavory affair? She knew Ann would say nothing, but the Lord knew what her aunt would say if she were to hear of it, and Lord Chance would certainly not refrain from voicing his opinion.

She threw up her chin defiantly at this thought. After all, he had no right to censure her. It was not any of his affair, and so she would tell him if he dared to look down that aristocratic nose at her and inform her that he did not approve. "Much I care what he thinks," she muttered, unaware that she had spoken aloud.

"I beg your pardon, dear," said Ann.

"What? Oh, nothing. Are you warm enough? Shall we go home?"

"Oh, no, I am enjoying it ever so much, I do assure you," lied Ann bravely.

But they both knew it was no longer an enjoyable drive for either of them, and presently, with nothing further being said, they returned to Mrs. Clarence's.

The footman jumped down and assisted Ann out, who went ahead into the house. As Vanessa was handed down, the footman whispered, "No fear you can't beat that one handily, m'lady. Seen her drivin' in the park many a time. It's hard hands she has, that one. Drives a pair of blacks and has ruined their mouths for sure. I'll be here in the morning to go with you."

"Thank you, Fred. I will appreciate that."

He gave her the suspicion of a wink and with a grin swung himself into the driving seat of the carriage, took up the reins, and drove off to the stables whistling cheerfully. Vanessa's spirits rose a bit with his encouragement.

She was wakened, as arranged, by her abigail at five-thirty the next morning, forced down a cup of chocolate, dressed, and was down in the quiet dawn by six. Fred, true to his word, was there before her, walking the grays up and down the street. He brought the carriage up, helped her into it, and swung himself up behind.

Outwardly Vanessa presented a picture of calm efficiency,

but her hands were cold inside her York tan gloves and there was a quiver of excitement at the pit of her stomach. In spite of knowing she should not be involved in this escapade, she could not prevent herself from looking forward to the race. She loved to drive, knew she· was good at it, and wanted very much to take the smirking Mrs. Braid down a peg or two.

Her excitement was damped, however, when she arrived at the meeting place to find it swarming with young blades laughing and calling out to one another or to Mr. Braid, who was busily scribbling down their bets in a small notebook as they were called out.

A cold rage swamped Vanessa and she would have turned and driven away had not the young men espied her and come crowding about her carriage.

Mr. Braid put away his notebook and came over to her. "Good morning, Miss Pymbroke. Perfect day for the race, eh?"

"Mr. Braid," said Vanessa coldly, "I had your word that this was to be kept strictly private."

"Oh, well, word always seems to get about somehow, no matter how careful a body is."

"There can be no 'somehow' about this. Only you can have told these people. Also I do not care for wagers being made on the outcome."

"Now, you mustn't bother your pretty little head about such things. The boys just want a bit of fun. Here, Belle, say good morning to Miss Pymbroke. There was you thinking she wouldn't come up to scratch, but I told you she would."

"So you did, Braid. Good morning, Miss Pymbroke. I admit I made sure you would back down."

"I cannot think why you should do so. Well, shall we get on with it at once? I am hungry for my breakfast. Once around the park, yes?"

"Certainly, my dear, certainly," replied Mrs. Braid indulgently, and winked broadly at her audience. She lifted her reins and moved her team into position beside Vanessa.

Mr. Braid raised a large white handkerchief and called to them to make ready. After a tense moment he dropped it and they were off, Mrs. Braid whipping her horses unmercifully into a wild gallop that left Vanessa behind almost at once, to the vociferous satisfaction of those spectators who had backed Mrs. Braid.

Vanessa ignored everything and concentrated on slowly nursing her grays into a steady gallop. By the time they were lost to the sight of their audience, she was close behind Mrs. Braid, who hugged the inside of the road. Vanessa moved out to pull around on the outside when suddenly Mrs. Braid swerved over in front of her, forcing Vanessa to fall back. She then prepared to pass on the inside and again Mrs. Braid pulled in front of her, flogging her horses unsparingly.

Why, Vanessa thought, the woman is not going to allow me to pass her! She does not mean it to be a fair race at all! And in an instant Vanessa understood everything: the insulting remarks about her driving and her courage, the crowd of young men. She had been deliberately gulled into this race and the reason was not hard to find. All those bets being made meant the Braids stood to make a tidy amount from it if Mrs. Braid won, which she clearly had every intention of doing, by whatever means were necessary.

Well, we'll see about that, thought Vanessa grimly. She swung to the outside again, and when Mrs. Braid pulled over to prevent her passing, Vanessa edged even farther over. Mrs. Braid flicked a glance over her shoulder, and when she saw what Vanessa was doing, she grinned and swung out even farther. Too far, in fact, for she misjudged her distance and her offside wheels left the track and slewed the back end of her carriage out across the dew-wet grass for a few yards. She lashed her horses viciously as she tried to control it, and cursed loudly. Vanessa shot past her, and applying only a flick of her whip to her leader caused her grays to leap forward in the burst of speed she asked from them. She stayed on the inside of the road for the rest of the way and Mrs. Braid could not catch her.

Fred, clinging on behind, was finally moved to relieve his feelings and shouted "Hurrah" happily and Vanessa turned to give him a brief grin. Then they were approaching the crowd of men, who roared their approval when they saw her coming, even those who had not backed her.

She slowed her horses as Mr. Braid reluctantly dropped the white handkerchief again, and drove sedately past him without a pause or a glance in his direction and went straight out of the park.

When she reached the house, it was barely seven o'clock, to her astonishment, for it seemed to her she had been away for hours. There were only the servants about and she was able to go straight to her room without encountering anyone.

When she came down to breakfast some time later in a dainty rose-sprigged dimity, she found her aunt and Ann at the table before her.

Ann looked up with anxious eyes. Vanessa kissed her aunt first, then went around the table to kiss Ann. As she bent over her, she whispered, "I won!" Ann pressed her hand and smiled, but the worried look remained in her eyes. She could say nothing on the subject before Mrs. Clarence, however, so she merely inquired how Vanessa had slept. The conversation continued as usual at breakfast with a discussion of the invitations that had arrived, which would be accepted, and what would be worn. Presently Hay came in to announce that Lord Chance was calling and requested an interview with Lady Ann.

Ann threw Vanessa an apprehensive glance and rose at once. She found Peter pacing up and down the drawing room.

"Ah, good morning, my dear. Forgive me for calling so early, but I wanted to be sure to find you in."

"Good morning, Peter. What is it?"

"Well, the thing is—this is deuced hard to— I think it would be best if you returned home, Ann."

"Returned home? Why ever should I do so? I have only been here a short time and had always planned to stay for the Season."

"Then come to me at Carrisbrooke House. Robin is there and I am sure he would be pleased to see more of you, and the Lord knows there is plenty of room, not to speak of a pack of servants with very little to do."

"But I am very comfortable here, and having accepted the invitation to stay, what possible reason could I give for leaving?"

"After yesterday's performance by your friend I should think no reason would be necessary."

"It is *your* friends, I think, who were responsible," Ann retorted defensively.

"Those were no friends of mine. I had invited Miss Clayton-Trees to ride with me—"

"I cannot like Miss Clayton-Trees," she interrupted, "and cannot believe you could be dangling after such a missish-behaving girl."

"I am not 'dangling' after her! That is by the way, however, and has nothing to do with anything. I had met Braid on several occasions, and while he is not a man I would pursue a friendship with, he was accompanied yesterday by his wife, and when he asked if they might ride along with us, I did not like to be rude."

"Yes, I can see that it was difficult for you," said Ann fairly, "but you did introduce them to us, and it is clear to me, if not to you, that they set out deliberately to goad Vanessa into that race as soon as they saw that she was driving."

"That may well be, but she should not have allowed herself to be goaded."

"I should have been goaded if I had been driving," she retorted spiritedly, "all that talk of not having enough back-bone and— Well, you heard her. I would hope that Vanessa is not so poor-spirited she would back down before that creature."

"No, she is too spirited for her own good. And if you are going to stay on here, I wish you will try to dissuade her from going on with it. It will cause a great deal of talk, none of which will do Miss Pymbroke's reputation a whit of good."

Ann looked stricken. "It is too late," she whispered. "They—they raced this morning."

"Good God!"

"I am sure it was best to get the thing over with before word got around about it. And they went very early—at dawn, really—so the park was empty. Oh, please, Peter, stop glowering like that. It is not so dreadful a thing and you are upsetting me."

Peter was instantly contrite. He pulled her into his arms for a hug, kissed her forehead, and said, "There, now. I won't tease you anymore on the subject. But you must try to curb

Miss Pymbroke's impulses before she creates a scandal. I must go now. Do you go to the Mayos' ball tonight?''

"Yes, we do. And you?''

"I will try to look in.'' He patted her shoulder and crossed to the door.

"Peter.''

He turned back. "Yes?''

"She won.''

He stared at her for a moment, then grinned slowly. "Beat Belle Braid, did she? Well, well.'' Then he was gone.

6

For Vanessa the Mayos' ball was proving a sadly dull affair. She had danced exactly twice and sat out all the rest, an activity that had heretofore never come her way. It also seemed to her that wherever she looked she saw heads bent together in confidential conversations as avid eyes sought her out speculatively. Gentlemen who, at her last ball, had clustered clamorously about her, now only bowed briefly upon encountering her and passed on, or refused to meet her eyes at all.

She had little doubt that news of her race with Mrs. Braid were forming the latest *on-dit* of the evening. The hypocrites, she thought disdainfully, there are not above five or six people in this room whose private lives would bear examination. Nevertheless, she wished heartily that she had had better sense than to become involved with the Braids, though she would not give these people the satisfaction of knowing she was even aware of their condemnation. She managed to display a calm, smiling facade as she chatted animatedly with her aunt and Ann, who sat with her, on every subject but what was going on in the room and the reason for it. She had confided the entire story to Ann, including the swarm of young men who had witnessed the race and made wagers upon its outcome, so Ann could be in little doubt as to what was going on now.

From time to time Mrs. Clarence said she did wish the girls would not feel obligated to keep her company, as she liked to see young people enjoying themselves. The girls hastily changed the subject each time.

Vanessa would dearly have loved to leave, but would not allow herself such a cowardly relief, or the whisperers to think that she cared what they thought. Why must people be so busy about other people's business? she thought angrily. I'm sure I shouldn't care two pins if, say, Lady Mayo decided to race Mrs. Braid, though Mrs. Braid *is* a vulgar, ill-bred woman. *Especially* since she is! For, after all, one cannot allow such people as Mrs. Braid to jeer at one and imply that one is less capable of handling a carriage and pair than they.

I suppose, she thought bitterly, Lord Chance would say I should not stoop to acknowledge such speeches as Mrs. Braid's, but after all, he is the one who accepted her into his circle of acquaintances and introduced her to me and to his own sister. She became more indignant as she thought of the injustice of Lord Chance's imagined condemnation of her, which somehow seemed to ease her own guilt as she apportioned a share of the blame onto him.

Nevertheless, she prayed he would not come to the Mayos' ball tonight, for she could not bear for him to see her being subjected to this humiliating punishment, and besides, she could hardly fling his share of the guilt into his face at a ball.

Peter, for his part, had enjoyed an extremely pleasant dinner with three friends and they had all gone along afterward to White's for a game of whist. During the game a foppishly overdressed young gentleman came up to the table to greet one of the gentlemen, who then introduced the young man to the others as Gervase Bynge. Mr. Bynge plunged immediately into the topic that clearly engaged his enthusiasm to the exclusion of all else.

"Did you hear of the race in the park this morning?"

Peter stiffened, while the other three disclaimed any knowledge and asked to be enlightened.

Nothing could have pleased Mr. Bynge more than this fresh audience. He entered into a spirited description of the event, to which Peter listened expressionlessly.

". . . and old Belle sitting there like a cat who's lapped up all the cream. Then, when the beauteous Miss Pymbroke arrived, I feared for a moment she was going to turn right around and leave. But old Braid made some remark about making sure she would back down and Belle agreed and that put the iron in Miss Pymbroke's spine for sure. Well, you couldn't blame her, really. Can't have liked being told they thought her too cowardly to go on with it. Oh, she's a grand girl, Miss Pymbroke, and a picture of loveliness too, with her eyes flashing like that. You could see she was mad as fire at the Braids. I put a guinea on her to win just for her spirit, though I couldn't see how she could beat old Belle.''

"Do you tell me there was wagering going on?" asked Peter icily.

"Well, for the Lord's sake, why else would Belle race? They were all over town yesterday passing the word. Positive mob appeared. Well, I wish you could have seen the expression on Braid's face when Miss Pymbroke came sailing past him with old Belle eating her dust.''

This caused a great outcry of disbelief from all but Peter, who was already aware of the outcome of the race. No doubt, he thought, each of those onlookers had, just as had Mr. Bynge, entertained their friends with the tale, which would by now be all over London. Of all the bird-witted escapades for the girl to have gotten herself mixed up in—and Ann with her.

He suddenly remembered that he had half-promised Ann to look in on the Mayos' ball this evening, and making his excuses to his friends, he left at once. He hurried home, ordered his carriage brought around while he went upstairs to change into formal dress.

The ball having been in progress for some time, his host and hostess were no longer at the door of the ballroom and he was able to slip into the room behind another couple and take stock of the situation. Because of the crowd of dancers he did not see Ann for some time. She was not dancing, that he was sure of, and after vainly searching, he realized that neither was Miss Pymbroke. Was it possible, he wondered, that they had elected not to come, after all, which would certainly have been the wisest course for Miss Pymbroke?

Then the dance ended and the crowd on the floor thinned and he espied them sitting either side of Mrs. Clarence on the far side of the room. As he watched, he could see that all was not well by their too bright and set smiles, by the too nervous fans they plied, and the too studiedly casual glances they cast about them. No one approached them in the interval, and when the music struck up for the next set, no partners came hurrying toward them. He knew then that his worst fears were realized, and that the *ton* were showing their disapproval of Miss Pymbroke's hoydenish escapade. Miss Pymbroke, he thought grimly, deserved what she was getting, but he was filled with a cold fury that anyone would dare treat a Chance in such a way.

He marched indignantly around the edge of the dance floor, ignoring the encouraging smiles aimed at him by young women who would have been glad to be noticed by him, and presented himself to the seated ladies.

"Mrs. Clarence, Miss Pymbroke, your servant," he said, bowing. Then he turned to his sister, "Ann, will you do me the honor?"

It was more of a command than a request, and Ann, obedient to his tone and the hard glint in his eye, rose at once.

"I might have known this affair would become the latest scandal," he said grimly as he led her onto the floor.

"Oh, Peter, it is not her fault! She made that odious Braid person give his word he would not reveal it to anyone, and then when she arrived, she found he had brought along an enormous crowd of young men, all betting on the outcome."

"So I have heard."

"You cannot blame her for that, Peter. If he had kept his word, no one need ever have known of it. Oh, it is infamous, for she believes now that they set out deliberately to tease her into it. Well, you heard them at it yourself."

"And the result is as you see," he replied, "a pretty state of affairs, I must say, for you to be in the middle of. I cannot care for you to be castigated for her folly."

"She is my good friend, Peter, and I was there when they challenged her. Would you have me not stand by her? Besides, I think you must admit none of this would have come about had you not introduced them to her."

Peter was silenced, for in spite of his disapproval he was a fair-minded man. From the age of sixteen he had been used to listening to all sides of disputes and making judgments. It was then that his father had begun Peter's training as heir to several estates and a vast fortune, and all the cares and responsibilities those things entailed. Fortunately, he would inherit more than these material things from his father, who was a responsible, levelheaded gentleman who took his duties seriously and administered his estates, his tenants, his servants, and his family with an evenhanded justice for all and had inculcated the same qualities into his children, especially in Peter.

Now Peter could not help feeling Ann had some right on her side, and began to look at the event from Miss Pymbroke's point of view. He knew little of the Braids, but what he had heard was not much to their credit. However, what he *had* heard had been secondhand and he was not the man to give another the cut direct when the man had done him no injury, especially when the man was accompanied by his wife. However, he had to accept the responsibility for having been instrumental in making it possible for the pair to taunt Miss Pymbroke into this indiscretion by introducing them to her.

When the set ended, Peter led Ann back and stood talking amiably until the music struck up again, and then he requested Vanessa to stand up with him.

"This is kind of you, Lord Chance," she said as he led her onto the floor.

"Kind?"

"Yes, to reestablish my credit. I fear my reputation is sadly tarnished."

"Nonsense, in a few days they will have something new to whisper about and this will be forgotten. However—"

"However, you hope I will not make such a poor showing again."

"Oh, it was my understanding you made a very good showing," he said, his eyes twinkling, amused in spite of everything at the thought of how much out of pocket the Braids must be at this moment. "Mrs. Braid is famous, I hear, for her skill at driving."

"Pooh! I should imagine even an average driver could beat her in a fair race."

"Well, well. Tell me about it."

She told him of Mrs. Braid's ploys to keep her from passing and of her own trick, and Peter laughed aloud delightedly, causing a great deal of astonishment, speculation, and dismay, depending upon the individual character and hopes of the various onlookers.

Peter felt again the pull of her beauty, the glinting silver-gilt curls, the deep-blue eyes, and the perfection of her tiny form. Her hand in his was as small and delicately boned as a child's. It seemed impossible that such a hand could control two horses and outmaneuver Belle Braid.

When their set ended, he took all three ladies down to supper and fetched them lobster patties, jellies, and champagne. When he returned with them to the ballroom, he was gratified to see that quite a number of young men had decided their reputations would not suffer too much if they stood up with the two girls, since Chance seemed to make little of Miss Pymbroke's disgrace, and everyone knew what a stickler he was for the proprieties.

Peter managed to secure another set with Vanessa. He would have liked more, but felt that might cause even more gossip. After returning her to her aunt, therefore, he said good night and went home, his mind dwelling on the exact shade of the blue of her eyes. More like the intense blue of the Mediterranean skies, he decided at last.

Ann, convinced that Giles was not going to make an appearance, began to tire and refused any further invitations to stand up. She had not seen Giles for several days now and wondered dismally if he were dancing attendance upon the entrancing Miss Chamfreys.

7

Indeed, Giles had been seeing more of Miss Chamfreys than would have been good for Ann's peace of mind, had she known of it, but their meetings could not have been, under any circumstances, described as dalliance. It was Camilla's genuine interest in his writing that had breeched the defensive wall Giles usually kept between himself and women, and her connections to the theater that held his interest, for her suggestion that he attempt a drama had fallen on fertile ground.

When Oliver had left for Italy, it had seemed Giles' muse went with him. He had been able to write only one poem dedicated to their friendship, and after that, the emptiness left by Oliver's departure had created a desert in Giles' soul where no poetry could grow.

Oliver had been Giles' mentor from their Oxford days, when Oliver, two years older, had condescended to notice and take under his wing a shy, awkward newcomer. It had seemed to Giles that a god had bent down to shed his golden benediction over him. It was under Oliver's protection that those poems which had recently been published in a slim, gilt-edged, calf-bound volume had accumulated, and it was Oliver himself who had taken them to his own publishers after Giles had come down from Oxford. Oliver had by this time established himself as a playwright and his publishers were happy to oblige him by giving Giles' poems a reading, and even happier after publication when they were received favorably by critics and public.

Oliver, however, was a restless creature whose habit of disappearing from time to time had caused Giles much distress before this. His latest defection to Italy, however, was already of some weeks' duration, much longer than Giles had had to endure before, and there was no one, not even Ann, to whom he could confide his unhappiness.

Camilla's suggestion, therefore, had come at a most providential moment, and her open, interested manner, with no hint of flirtation in it, had overcome his wariness. He had visited her nearly every day, either at her home in the mornings or after a performance in the evenings, to discuss plays and performers and stagecraft. Mrs. Chamfreys had tended initially to be profoundly disturbed by his constant attendance upon her daughter.

"I vow, Mr. Chamfreys," she fumed to her husband, "I believe she encourages these perfectly unsuitable persons to upset me. First a vicar and now a poet, of all absurd things."

Camilla, however, had not been around the theater and theater folk all her life without learning far more of the vagaries of human nature than it was given other young women her age to know. She had realized after a few meetings that Giles' only interest in her was her intimate association with the theater. She had, therefore, brought her mother into their conversations as often as possible, and in no time at all Mrs. Chamfreys' agitation regarding Mr. Dalzell had subsided. She knew as well as Camilla that he posed no threat and in the meantime it could do no harm for such an attractive and sought-after man to *seem* to be dangling after her daughter, a circumstance that roused Lord Threlfall to ever more ardent pursuit. Mrs. Chamfreys was sure he was bound to come up to scratch at any moment.

Then Giles received a payment from his publisher and immediately purchased a rather showy chestnut. The first day he put her through her paces he invited Camilla to accompany him. He would ordinarily have shared such an event with Ann, but Ann had never been able to ride—it was too tiring for her—so it was Camilla, followed at a discreet distance by a mounted footman as chaperon, who rode out with Giles. Camilla was looking extremely smart in a claret habit trimmed with black braid and a small riding hat of black beaver trimmed with gold cordon and tassels with a long black ostrich feather in front. They trotted along talking animatedly, clearly very much in charity with each other and attracting a great deal of attention, for they made an exceedingly handsome couple. A great many eyebrows were raised and a wealth of speculation passed among the other riders and carriage passengers.

One of the former was Miss Clayton-Trees, escorted by an elderly uncle, who nodded and smiled with gracious condescension to both of them as they passed. My word, she thought, is the little actress trying her hand with the illusive Mr. Dalzell? Miss Clayton-Trees always referred to Camilla as the little actress when Camilla was not present to hear her. Now she felt the little thrill of excitement experienced by true gossips when they believe they have stumbled upon an interesting tidbit to pass along with a heavy gloss of surmise. She turned to peer at them over her shoulder and then rode on, her eyes bright with speculation. Poor, dear Lady Ann Chance has kept him dangling for so long he has finally lost interest, she thought happily. How dreadful it must be for her at five and twenty to lose her only suitor. Miss Clayton-Trees looked about eagerly for someone to whom she could impart this delicious *on-dit*. Uncle Brough was no good, for besides being hard of hearing, he was from Yorkshire and cared nothing for London gossip.

It was some moments before she saw anyone with whom she was acquainted, and then she quite pointedly looked the other way, for it was that hoydenish Miss Pymbroke driving along with her fat aunt in an open carriage. Lord Chance may have been obliged to overlook Miss Pymbroke's behavior, since his sister was staying with her, but Miss Clayton-Trees was under no such obligation. She certainly would not acknowledge her.

Uncle Brough, however, knew nothing of these self-righteous sentiments, nor the reason for them. Espying his very old friend, Mrs. Clarence, he at once rode up to the carriage and doffed his hat.

"My dear Mrs. Clarence," he said loudly in the way of the deaf, "how do you do?"

"Goodness me, is it General Brough? Pull up, Dakers. General, how good to see you again! I never thought to find you here."

"Oh, yes, I can hear you perfectly, my dear lady. You must be astonished to meet me here. Oh, allow me to present my niece. Hester"—he turned and found Miss Clayton-Trees hanging back, studiously observing the shrubs beside the road—"here, Hester, don't be shy. Come along and meet Mrs. Clarence and, er—" He looked admiringly at Vanessa.

"Vanessa Pymbroke, General, my niece."

"Yes, yes, my niece. Clayton-Trees' eldest, you know. But who is this pretty creature?"

Mrs. Clarence, grasping the problem at last, raised her voice. "My niece, General. Pymbroke's daughter."

"Ah, Pymbroke, yes, of course. Where is the rascal? Still tearing about the Continent, eh? 'Servant, Miss Pymbroke. Here, Hester, meet Miss Pymbroke."

Miss Clayton-Trees was forced to give the ladies a frozen little nod. Mrs. Clarence looked somewhat taken aback by this treatment, but Vanessa gave Hester a blinding smile.

"Ah, we have met, have we not, Miss Clayton-Trees? That day you were with your friends the Braids."

Miss Clayton-Trees stiffened with affront and the corners of her tight little mouth turned down, but she disdained to refute the statement, or indeed to have any further conversation at all if she could prevent it. She stared again at the shrubs.

"Goodness, child, if I ever saw such a Friday face," cried the general. "Doesn't do to go about looking that way, girl. Sure to chase away all the beaux, eh, Mrs. Clarence."

"Do you make a long stay in London, General?" asked Mrs. Clarence, firmly changing the subject.

"Only another fortnight, madam."

"Then you must dine with me one evening."

"With the greatest of pleasure, my dear."

"And you must come with him, Miss Clayton-Trees. Must she not, Aunt?" asked Vanessa sweetly.

"Certainly. General, you must bring your niece with you, and you will meet also Lady Carrisbrooke's daughter, who is staying with us."

"What? Lady Carrisbrooke is staying with you? My word, it has been many long years since I have laid eyes on her. I shall look forward to it."

"No, no, General. It is not Lady Carrisbrooke. It is her

daughter, Lady Ann. You will be delighted with Lady Ann, I know. She is very like her mother."

"Oh, dear Lady Ann," cooed Miss Clayton-Trees, able to overcome her own prohibition against speaking when this unexpected opportunity arose to vent some of her irritation and relate a piece of gossip at the same time, "is she still with you? I made sure she had returned to the country when I saw Mr. Dalzell out riding with Miss Chamfreys a few minutes ago. One knows how devoted he has always been to dear Lady Ann. Truly, I was never so shocked, for they were speaking together with such, ah, intimacy, and so much animation. So unlike his customary dour expression. He seemed quite smitten, I must say. Men are so fickle, are they not? After all these years of apparent devotion to dear Lady Ann."

"Now, now, Miss Clayton-Trees," replied Vanessa, her eyes glinting with angry sparks that belied her playful tone, "you cannot have it both ways. Mr. Dalzell cannot be called fickle in one breath while with the next you speak of his years of devotion."

Mrs. Clarence put a calming hand on Vanessa's arm. "Well, we must go along or we shall be ever so late. Charming to have seen you again, General. I will send you a note to fix the day for our dinner. Good day to you, Miss Clayton-Trees. Dakers," she ordered her coachman, who immediately set the carriage in motion.

Out of earshot, Vanessa exploded. "Of all the poisonous creatures! How I should like to box her ears."

"My dear child, Miss Clayton-Trees is much too paltry a girl to get into such a passion over."

"But she will spread that story all over London and Ann may come to hear of it."

"But Miss Clayton-Trees will be bound to be proved wrong in the end, of course," replied Mrs. Clarence quietly.

"What if she is not? Maybe there is something in it, after all."

"Nonsense, my dear. If Mr. Dalzell were a marrying sort of man, I make no doubt he would have married Ann anytime these past seven years. There can certainly be no doubt that he cares for her as deeply as do her brothers—unfortunately in the same sort of way. As for his riding with Miss Chamfreys, I make little of that. Ann does not ride, so he could not ask her, and I imagine the animation Miss Clayton-Trees spoke of had more to do with his own concerns than with Miss Chamfreys. He does become quite animated when discussing his own work, I have noticed, and Miss Chamfreys expressed her admiration for his poetry when first they met, if you remember?''

Vanessa tried to take what comfort she could from these words, but was nevertheless uneasy on Ann's behalf.

8

Though Robin did not see them riding together in the park and talking with great intimacy and animation, he was no less uneasy about the rapidly flowering friendship growing between Miss Chamfreys and Giles Dalzell. He had been present on most of those occasions when Giles had paid Camilla morning visits or had come to the green room at the theater after a performance. He knew, for he had overheard or been included in most of their conversations, that Giles was working on a drama and consulted with Camilla and her parents on matters of stagecraft. Nevertheless, he could not be happy to see the rapport that had developed so easily between them. Giles was more compellingly handsome than ever when talking of his writing, and Robin wondered if any woman could help falling in love with such an attractive and interesting man—a man whose book of poetry had just been published to some acclaim.

Robin did not believe for a moment that Giles was in danger of losing his heart to Miss Chamfreys, for it was perfectly clear to him that there was nothing in the least loverlike in Giles' attitude toward her, but he feared for Camilla's susceptibilities. Robin knew he had no claim on her affections, for while he took every opportunity to be with her and had clearly shown his admiration, he had made not the least push to engage her affections, fearing, humbly, that he had very little right to do so at the present. And if this were not enough, Mrs. Chamfreys made it quite clear to him that she held him in little account and would never countenance his suit. Mr. Chamfreys, being a son of the manse himself and much less starchy than his wife, was always most pleasant and welcoming to Robin, but this, in Robin's opinion, had little to say to the matter, since in all domestic decisions Mr. Chamfreys bowed to his wife's dictates.

There was also the problem of Ann's feelings, for, if nothing more, she would be bound to be feeling unhappy at seeing so much less of Giles than she would expect. Robin felt an impulse to go to her at once, but then remembered that he would be seeing her—and Giles as well—tonight at the Dortleys' dinner.

They were both already there when Robin arrived, and at first sight he was reassured. Ann sat laughing up at Giles, who stood before her. She had never been in better looks, Robin thought. Her gown was of palest pink that matched perfectly the faint flush of color in her cheeks.

"Oh, dear Robin," she cried happily as he came up to them, "how good to see you. Giles is telling me of his new mare. She does sound lovely."

" 'Evening, Robin. She's a chestnut, and a real high-stepper, too, I do assure you. I will bring her around tomorrow, Ann, if you would care to see her."

"I should like to, would not you, Robin?"

Robin agreed that he would quite like to have a view of Giles' new mare, and the conversation went on pleasantly. Robin, however, upon a closer and purely subjective view, began to feel that all was not as well with his sister as he had at first thought. The color in her cheeks he now thought to be somewhat hectic and not the flush of health he had first thought it, and the sprightliness of her manner seemed to him so forced that he became less and less confident of her happiness.

In fact, the only solace Robin could take from the present situation was that at least Giles was not with Miss Chamfreys at the moment, and Robin wished that he might offer this comfort to Ann. Giles took Ann in to dinner and was seated on her right, and Robin noticed they spoke a great deal together. From the liveliness of Giles' expression, Robin deduced he was speaking of his latest literary effort. He wondered if it were possible for him to do so without mentioning Miss Chamfreys' almost daily assistance? Robin sighed inwardly, wishing life held fewer complications, and turned belatedly to his own dinner partner.

When the ladies withdrew to the drawing room, Ann settled herself at the end of a sofa near the fire and allowed the aching muscles of her face to release for a moment their lifting of her bright smile as she turned carefully away from the chattering women around her. Her respite was brief, however.

"Will you mind if I sit with you, Lady Ann?"

Ann started and turned, forcing her tired muscles back to duty. "Please do so, Miss, er—" she said with her party smile.

"Thwaite. Lydia Thwaite. My mama told me your name and I was determined to make myself known you. You are Miss Pymbroke's friend, I know, and I do so want to hear of her famous race. Did she truly win over than dreadful Braid person?"

"Yes, but I was not there, so I know nothing more of the matter," replied Ann quellingly.

"Oh. Well, I admire her tremendously," continued Miss Thwaite undaunted. "I wish it had been I who had cut such a dash." Then she added a trifle resentfully, "Though no doubt my mama would have found some way to prevent me, even if I knew how to drive."

Ann's smile relaxed into the real thing, for Miss Thwaite was so clearly not destined to cut a dash, being a round, short, and rather plain girl. "Never mind, my dear," she said kindly, "I doubt the race was a pleasant experience for Miss Pymbroke, and in any case, such adventures are few and far between for most of us mortals."

"I suppose," sighed Miss Thwaite wistfully. Then she brightened. "Mama says Mr. Robin Chance is your brother. I should very much like to be introduced to him."

"Well, so you shall be, when the gentlemen rejoin us."

"He is ever such a handsome young man, very like your older brother, Lord Chance. *He* stood up with me at my come-out, but I was so frightened of him I could not open my mouth. Mr. Robin Chance does not look so—so formidable, I think. Miss Clayton-Trees told my mama and me that he is dangling after Miss Chamfreys. The little actress, Miss Clayton-Trees calls her. I do think that is so romantic. Imagine—an actress! Miss Clayton-Trees says—"

Happily Ann was spared for a time from further *on-dits* from Miss Clayton-Trees by the entrance at that moment of the gentlemen. Robin came straight to her and was immediately introduced to a much-gratified Miss Thwaite, who eyed him with eager curiosity, clearly hoping to espy traces of lovesickness upon his features. Ann had hoped Giles would find her, but saw that he was the center of a group of chattering ladies. She turned away.

"Is this your first Season, Miss Thwaite?" asked Robin kindly.

"Yes, and I do so love the London parties. We have nothing like them in Devon. Oh, we have the assemblies, of course, but they seem drab in comparison. No interesting partners, you know, just the same dull creatures one has known forever. Oh, there is Mr. Dalzell, the poet! So like one's idea of a poet, is he not? Miss Clayton-Trees says she saw him riding in the park today with Miss Chamfreys and it is her opinion we shall be reading an announcement in the *Gazette* of their betrothal at any moment now. It is like a novel, so romantic." She sighed and gazed across the room at Giles, quite unaware that within the space of ten minutes she had linked Miss Chamfreys with two gentlemen and quite ruined the peace of mind of the couple before her.

Giles was at that moment scowling at a bedizened matron who held his arm with one hand while with the other she tapped his chest with her fan to emphasize her words as she spoke to him with great intensity. Had Ann not been so heartsore, she might have laughed at his predicament, for here was all that he disliked in society: overbearing women explaining his poetry to him, flirtatious girls ogling him over their fans, contemptuous gentlemen who condemned him silently for so unmanly an occupation as writing rhymes for women to sigh over.

Why had he not mentioned that he had ridden his new mare today with Camilla Chamfreys? I would have thought nothing of it, but to carefully not mention it seems so deliberate an omission as to make me wonder if there can be any truth in Miss Clayton-Trees' gossip. Oh, why did Miss Thwaite have to tell me? Poor child, I know she did not do so to hurt, for there is no malice in her at all. After all, she has been raised in a society where there is little for her to do *but* gossip, and she does not want to appear behindhand on the latest bits. Miss Clayton-Trees has been very busy. First telling Miss Thwaite of Robin and the actress and then of Giles and—

Oh, Lord, thought Ann, turning stricken eyes to her brother, how selfish I am being. What must he think to be hearing this? Robin was fixedly studying his shoe buckles, and if he was aware of her regard, he chose not to return it. Ann finally managed to say, "I think, Miss Thwaite, with all respect to Miss Clayton-Trees, she is reading far more into what she saw than was actually the case."

"Oh, do you think so?" Miss Thwaite's face fell with disappointment. "It would have been so roman— Oh, good evening, Mrs. Dortley, such an enchanting party," she said as her hostess came up to the group.

"Lydia, dear child, I hope you will consent to sing for us. I am sure we should all like some music. Will you forgive me, dear Lady Ann and Mr. Robin, if I take Miss Thwaite away?"

Ann covered her relief with a gracious smile, and a blushing Miss Thwaite was led to the piano, where she accompanied herself in several songs in a small but silvery-clear voice that was most pleasing. She might never be accounted a beauty, but she looked charming in the light of the candles with her sleek brown hair, clear blue eyes, and fresh complexion, altogether as sweet and wholesome as a nut.

Robin sighed as he watched her, thinking that here was the sort of girl he should have for a wife, a girl who would fit perfectly into a small country rectory. Why had his heart been given so irrevocably to the exotically inappropriate Miss Chamfreys? Was it a trial, a special test of his calling? The ways of the Lord were mysterious indeed.

After several other young women had been persuaded to play or sing to the company and the music came to an end, Ann rose at once to make her departure. She congratulated Miss Thwaite, thanked her hostess, and had nearly come to the door before Giles reached her.

"Going so soon, Ann? I suppose it's the best thing. You look fagged to death. No great wonder, I suppose, with all this chattering. Think I will follow your example. Shall I see you home?"

"Thank you, but that won't be necessary. I have Mrs.

Clarence's carriage waiting.'' She sounded coolly indifferent, but was really swamped by a feeling of revulsion of the whole situation. She simply wanted to be alone.

He looked slightly taken aback, but shrugged. "Just as you like. I will come around tomorrow to show you the mare, shall I?"

"If you like. Good night, Giles." She turned and left him staring after her in puzzlement, then he shrugged again and turned back to make his good-byes.

Ann went to bed with the nugget of Miss Clayton-Trees' gossip lodged uncomfortably in her mind. I am not jealous, she told herself firmly, for I know perfectly well Giles is not pursuing Camilla Chamfreys. It is only that I am so accustomed to being the only woman in his confidence I am spoiled. Am I so small-spirited I cannot bear to share him with anyone? After all, it is not such a wonderful thing if a published poet attracts women, especially if the poet is darkly handsome and aloof.

Not that she ever thought of him so. She still saw him as the scowling, overly thin, withdrawn boy, only grown taller. Did he see her still as a frail little girl, his forever-ailing playmate who, more often than not, was kept in her bed just when he had planned a special expedition over the moors or to the brook? Was that why he had never declared himself, never proposed that they marry? Or was it just that he feared she could not be a good wife, being so sickly? Or simply that he did not love her? Was she truly the fool her father had called her to have turned down young Thornley, the Duke of Cairne's heir? And George Seekes—and Peregrin Verney— and . . .

This is foolishness, she thought, turning on her side and giving her pillow an angry thump, counting over one's former suitors like an old maid. But you are an old maid; whispered a voice within her, five and twenty and on the shelf anytime these past five years, all for the sake of a vow made at the age of twelve that you would never marry anyone but Giles.

She remembered it all vividly. Giles had overheard her mama and an old aunt nattering away over their needlework on that most enjoyable of subjects: the various advantages and disadvantages of possible marriages for the daughter of the house. Giles had only then seemed to become aware that someday she would leave him, and had withdrawn into a fit of the sullens that lasted for days. He glowered at her when they chanced to meet and would not speak to her. When finally she had coaxed him to tell her what was the matter, he had flung his accusation at her and, despite himself, the tears had welled up in his eyes. She had thought her heart would burst with love for him, and had thrown her arms about him, crying passionately that she would never leave him, indeed, would never marry anyone but him and they would be together forever.

She had gone straight to her mama to so inform her of this decision, and very shortly after that Giles had been sent off to school. From that time on she had seen a great deal less of him, for Lady Carrisbrooke made sure he was regularly invited to visit with his school friends or relatives of her own on school vacations so that he was rarely at home. Ann had kept her vow nevertheless and had always been sure he also remembered and would someday make it possible for her to fulfill her pledge. But he had never once since that day referred to it. Was it possible he had forgotten the whole incident, a moment that had shaped her entire life until now? Or had he remembered it from time to time, but with so much shame at his unmanly behavior he had finally managed to bury the memory forever?

Would it have been different if they had never shared a childhood, but met as boy and girl at some London ball? She tried to picture such an event and finally drifted into sleep and a dream of dancing with a gentleman whose face was Giles' sulky, little-boy face, who would not look at her but only scowled and finally flung away her hand and stalked off the floor, leaving her cringing in humiliation and misery before the pitying eyes of the other dancers.

9

In spite of Ann's dull eyes at the breakfast table the next morning—or rather, because of them—Vanessa insisted upon taking her for a drive.

"Dear child, I am loath to be disobliging," said Mrs. Clarence, "but I have already asked Fred to bring the barouche around for me this morning as I have some calls I must make."

"Never mind, darling, we will take the curricle," replied Vanessa blithely.

"Oh, my dear, should you do so?" asked Mrs. Clarence doubtfully.

"Why should I not?"

"Well, it is thought to be rather, ah, fast for a woman to drive such a carriage and Dakers will be driving me."

"Pooh! I make nothing of that. They will think me fast whatever I do. In any case, I shall have Ann, whose credit is very good. You will come, dearest Ann, will you not?" And Ann, who really would have preferred staying at home, felt she could not be so disagreeable as to demur, and went to fetch her bonnet and pelisse.

They set off some time later, muslins and ribands fluttering prettily, bonnet plumes blowing, on a perfect spring day. Declaring that since they were not out to socialize, Vanessa refused to pull up no matter how often they were hailed. She smiled sweetly, raised her whip in acknowledgment, and drove steadily on. Even Peter received this treatment when he saw them, reined in, and lifted his hat. When they sailed past without stopping, he stared after them bemusedly for a moment before shrugging and continuing on.

"Vanessa, dear, that was Peter!" Ann exclaimed with a laugh.

"Did you need to speak to him?"

"No, but I am sure he expected us to stop."

"We are driving for relaxation and refreshment, not for social exchange. Now, you are to lean back and take deep breaths and think of nothing."

"Has there been another, ah, disagreement between you and Peter?"

"My dear, there has never been any disagreement *between* us. You must have such an impression because of things he has said to you about me that were less than agreeable."

Ann protested, blushing, and subsided, wishing she had not spoken of the matter at all. She had thought last night they had seemed to have made up whatever quarrels there had been, for certainly they had seemed to be enjoying each other's company during the dancing and at supper. Perhaps, however, something had occurred of which she was unaware, to bring them to daggers drawing again. Ann sighed, wishing there were fewer thorny temperaments surrounding her.

They had now passed through the section of the drive where most of the carriages and riders thronged to see and be seen, and come to a winding empty stretch where it was almost possible to believe oneself in the country, so far away did the clamor seem.

Ann sighed again, this time with pleasure, and relaxed as Vanessa had told her to do, looking about at the new young green of the foliage and the daffodils waving their bells in the gentle breeze. She looked up to the tender blue above and wished it were possible to find just such a color for a gown. Then she became aware that clouds were piling up on the horizon, rather dark clouds which, even as she watched, came rushing up the blue vault of the sky with menacing rapidity, shouldering and pushing as though racing to be first to reach the opposite horizon.

"Vanessa!"

"Yes, I just noticed. Well, it is too bad, but I think we must turn back or risk a wetting." She slowed her pair and with great competency and economy turned them about, and in a moment they were bowling back the way they had come. A strong gust of wind came up as though to urge them along, and behind them the thunder threatened with warning rumbles. Lightning jinked across the now completely gray-bruised sky and Vanessa touched her leader lightly, causing the pair to step out into a brisk trot. Then there came an enormous crack of thunder and the horses broke stride, tossing their heads about, ears pricked forward in terror, but Vanessa held them firmly and soon had them under control.

Now from behind them came shrieks of terror, and as the girls jerked their heads around to look for their source, a horse came pounding around the curve, eyeballs rolling wildly as though pursued by a devil. A female figure was bent low, clinging to the horse's mane, her habit and hair streaming backward, screaming all the while and begging that someone please help her.

"Good God!" Vanessa exclaimed, turned back to her pair, pulled them to a halt, and handed the reins to Ann. "Just hold these for a moment, dearest," she said, and rose to vault lightly out of the carriage.

"Vanessa, do not—" Ann cried, but it was too late. As the terrified horse thundered past, Vanessa leapt up to grab the halter. The horse galloped on in its headlong rush for several yards before it could stop, dragging Vanessa with it. Then, with a whinny of fear, it reared back on its haunches, front legs pawing the air wildly, raising Vanessa, still clinging, several feet off the ground, while the girl in the saddle shrieked even louder. The horse dropped to its feet only to rear again, while Vanessa, her skirts whipping wildly about in the wind, clung on and talked soothingly to it.

The rain came then in a driving, slanted sheet, and at the same moment Peter came galloping up from the other direction, saw Vanessa dangling in the air on her second ascent, flung himself off his horse with an oath almost before it had stopped, and ran up to the other side of the rearing horse to help pull him down. The horse was no match for their combined efforts and in a moment stood quivering and snorting between them.

"Of all the hen-witted, cork-brained starts I have ever seen! What in the name of God do you think you were doing?" he shouted furiously.

"I should have thought it would be evident to even the meanest intelligence that I was attempting to halt a runaway horse," she managed to gasp out breathlessly.

"You must be mad to have attempted such a stupid thing," he raged, his eyes blazing.

"I had very nearly accomplished it before you came up, sir, and while I thank you for your assistance, I have no doubt I should have managed it alone in another moment," she replied scathingly, stung to anger at last by his tone.

"Or gotten yourself killed in the attempt, I suppose! How you—"

"Excuse me for interrupting," called Ann, "but do you not think the point might be argued out between you at a more propitious time?"

They both turned, startled, to stare at her, having completely forgotten everything in the heat of their exchange. Now they became aware of the drenching rain, the heaving horse, the sobbing girl on its back, and Ann, who had managed to get the curricle hood up and sat sheltered beneath it, still holding the reins as she had been bidden to do.

"Good Lord, Ann, you will catch a chill—" began Peter.

"Much more likely you will, dear, since I am not wet through as you and Vanessa are, not to speak of the poor child on the horse."

With an exclamation Vanessa turned back and persuaded the girl to dismount and helped her across the road into the curricle. She was a very young girl, no more than fifteen, and though clearly undone by her experience, managed to issue a strangled thank-you to Vanessa. Ann handed her a handkerchief and put an arm about her.

"There, there, Miss, er—"

"Wilmott. Caroline Wilmott."

"How do you do. Were you riding out alone, Miss Wilmott?"

"No. My groom—there was this dreadful noise and his horse threw him and ran away, and my horse bolted before I could do anything. He was just lying there. Oh, I am sure the poor man is d-dead!"

"I will go look for him," said Peter brusquely. "If you will just climb up, Miss Pymbroke, and drive on, I will take Miss Wilmott's horse and find the man."

"Very well." Vanessa disdained the hand he held out to assist her and climbed back into the curricle. Taking the reins from Ann, she gave her horses the office to start and drove away without another word, too angry to trust herself to speak further or even to look at him. Ann wisely busied herself with comforting Miss Wilmott.

Peter remounted and, leading Miss Wilmott's horse, rode off to find the groom. The rain eased up and then stopped as the clouds rolled back and a watery sunlight bathed the new-washed scenery. Presently Peter saw a liveried figure hobbling toward him.

"You will be Miss Wilmott's groom, I think," called Peter.

" 'S right, m'lord. Ah, you've caught the brute, I see. I 'ope the mistress is safe?"

"Quite safe, and being driven home. She was worried about you. I have brought her horse for you. Think you can manage it."

The man eyed the ladies' saddle askance, but then grinned and said, "I reckon needs must, m'lord, and I've no mind for walking. It's me knee, you see. Gone bust it 'as, from the fall. Still, I'll try it."

Peter dismounted and helped the man into the saddle. He hooked his good right knee into position and took up the reins.

" 'Ope I gets back before I'm seen. Right figure o' fun I must look on this 'ere rig," he said ruefully. "Thanks for your 'elp, guv, much obliged." He trotted away, jouncing awkwardly in his unaccustomed position.

Peter remounted and followed. He rode straight home, where his valet, clucking with distress, stripped off Peter's soaked garments. When he was rubbed dry and dressed again, he set off at once for Mrs. Clarence's.

His mind was still clinched upon his anger with Vanessa. Each time he pictured her swinging in the air like a bell clapper, so tiny and fragile-looking beside the horse's wildly pawing hooves, an icy chill raised gooseflesh over his entire body, to be followed by a rush of heated rage that she could have exposed herself to such danger. For a time these feelings possessed him to the exclusion of all reason, but then those thoughts began to be tempered by wondering what on earth could have possessed her to attempt such a foolhardy thing? Even a man double her size and weight might have hesitated to throw himself at a bolting, terrified horse. Despite his anger he began to feel admiration for her courage seeping into his consciousness. She was a game 'un, right enough, pluck to the backbone, if somewhat overly impetuous.

He began to feel ashamed to have behaved so to her. To have stood there calling her names and berating her without giving her a chance to even recover her breath, while the rain soaked her to the skin, was churlish behavior, regardless of what his feelings were. He had meant to be coolly solicitous with both girls when he reached Mrs. Clarence's, allowing them to feel his disapproval even while courteously making sure they had taken no harm. Now he saw that he owed Miss Pymbroke an apology.

He found Mrs. Clarence alone before her drawing-room fire, her embroidery frame lying idly in her lap. "Dear Lord Chance! Such an adventure you have all had," she exclaimed as he entered.

"The young ladies arrived back safely, then?"

"Oh, yes, they only delivered the little girl to her home and came straight here."

"Ah, yes, Miss Wilmott. I gather she took no harm from the experience?"

"Only shaken up and quite frightened, Vanessa tells me."

"And my sister and Miss Pymbroke?"

"Why, they seemed well enough. Only somewhat damp." Mrs. Clarence chuckled richly.

"Do you think they will feel like coming down?"

"If you would be good enough to pull the bell rope there beside the mantel, I will send Hay to inquire."

This was done, and Hay returned presently to announce that Lady Ann would be down in a few moments. Peter felt his spirits plummet as he heard this news, for it was clear to him that Miss Pymbroke did not wish to see him.

Mrs. Clarence struggled up, saying that he must excuse her as she must consult with her cook, and left him to wait alone for Ann. When she came in, Peter strode quickly across to her and, taking her hands, peered intently into her face. "Are you all right, my dear?"

She laughed lightly. "Why ever should I not be?"

"I feared the shock and the rain—"

"Good heavens, I am not such a poor creature as that. After all, I had nothing to do but sit there. It is Vanessa who—"

"What?" he interrupted her, his hands tightening their grip on hers. "Is she hurt?"

"No, no. She has taken no harm, I assure you. Peter dear, you are hurting my hands."

"Oh—oh, sorry." He released her and turned away. "I suppose she refused to see me."

"I do not know that, Peter. Though I do believe her abigail insisted that she have a hot bath."

"It was a very foolhardy thing for her to do."

"What? Have a hot bath?" she teased.

"You know very well what I mean," he snapped, feeling his temper reasserting itself. "It was dangerous and unnecessary to throw herself at that horse. Why, her own horses might have bolted with you! She cannot have been thinking of *your* safety when she did such a thing."

"No, I suppose not, but it all happened in such an instant, there was little time to think at all. I suppose she felt the immediate danger to Miss Wilmott deserved more of her attention than any possible future danger to me. Besides, I hope that I am capable of holding a pair. I do drive about the estate when I am at home, you know, and am not entirely ignorant of how to handle the reins."

"That is hardly the point."

"Then what is the point? All is well, Peter, no one came to any harm, and the incident is over. Why all this brangling?"

"Never think for a moment everything is over. By tomorrow the story will be all over town."

"But there is nothing in it to anyone's discredit, surely," Ann protested in bewilderment.

"To be the subject of a series of *on-dits* does not redound to the credit of any gently bred young woman."

"Pompous," she said warningly, her eyes brimming with amusement.

"Nothing of the sort. I cannot like to hear your name coupled with hers on the lips of every drawing-room dandy and park saunterer."

"Pooh! Who will know of it anyway? There was no one about to witness it except ourselves."

"And Miss Wilmott," he reminded her, "and if you imagine she will miss such an opportunity to make herself interesting, you know nothing of young girls. Then there will be her family and their servants, all eager to be the first with such a tale."

Her eyes kindled stormily. "Now you are going from pompous to ridiculous. I am afraid I cannot bring myself to care one whit what anyone may say. I admire Vanessa excessively and would be happy to have my name associated with hers. She does not create these adventures, you know. They happen to her because she has the courage to meet a challenge when it arises. I wish I might think I had such backbone. I must say I found it shocking enough in you that you could speak to her as you did, but to come here now without one word of praise for what she did, only these carping complaints of what people will say, is the outside of enough. I never thought you capable of such behavior, Peter."

He stood speechless in amazement for a moment, as always unprepared for his usually soft-spoken sister to lose her temper. Then he said quietly, "I beg your pardon, my dear. You are right, of course. In fact, I came here really to apologize to her for my words in the park. I suppose her refusal to come down to see me put my back up again. Would you—would you convey my apologies to her for me?"

Her anger melted away instantly. "Oh, darling Peter. I knew you could not have meant what you were saying. But, no, my love, I think you must convey your own apologies to her, you know. She deserves that consideration, I think."

He studied his toe caps in silence for a moment. "Then I will call again this afternoon. Perhaps you would be good enough to inform her of that—and persuade her to see me."

10

After her brother had taken his leave, Ann wrote a long overdue letter to her mother before partaking of a light luncheon with Mrs. Clarence. Vanessa made no appearance during this time and Ann was undecided as to her best course regarding the message from Peter. Should she give it to her now or wait in the hopes that, given time to allow her anger with him to cool, Vanessa would be more receptive?

Feeling restless herself, Ann decided she would go out. She went upstairs to her room to change into a walking dress of fawn cambric and a beehive bonnet of moss straw. She draped an India-silk shawl over her shoulders and handed her parasol to Mabel, her abigail, bidding her to wait downstairs for her. She then went along to Vanessa's room and, after hesitating a moment, tapped and was told to "Come."

She found a sleepy-eyed Vanessa curled up on a chaise before her fire, looking ravishing in a sapphire-blue velvet robe. "My dear, forgive me, I had no idea you were sleeping," exclaimed Ann remorsefully.

"No, no. The hot bath has made me dozey, is all. Why, are you going out again?"

"I thought I would walk along to Pall Mall to purchase some white gloves from Harding and Howells. Can I do any errands for you?"

"Goodness, how energetic! I do believe danger must agree with you."

"I certainly could not agree that I was in any danger, but I must admit sitting at home for the remainder of the day seems tame,'' laughed Ann, pulling on her York tan gloves. ''Well, will you have anything from the stores?''

''If it is not too much trouble, a dozen pairs of silk stockings, if you please. I know I should offer to get up and come with you, but I am too lazy.'' She stretched and yawned to illustrate.

''Will you, ah, be getting up at all this afternoon?''

''Oh, presently, I suppose.''

''Good. I mean—well, I mean good, actually. You see, Peter is coming to call upon you again this afternoon.''

''Oh,'' said Vanessa, visibly stiffening.

''Now, please, my love, do not fly into the boughs. He came this morning to apologize and is going to try again this afternoon. He is truly repentant and I hope you will see him. I cannot be happy when two so dear to me are out of charity with each other.''

Vanessa relented. ''Very well, I will graciously accept his apology for your sake. It is all so stupid anyway. I cannot imagine what can have been in his mind to speak so to me.''

''Have you never seen a mother or a nurse give a child a shaking or even slap it after the child has taken a dangerous tumble? It is fear you see. They become angry that the child has so endangered itself.''

''Hmm,'' was Vanessa's only comment to this.

Ann took her leave, and Vanessa, after staring into the flames of her fire for a few moments, was suddenly galvanized into furious activity. She rang for her maid and began flinging gowns onto the bed. Presently, in a round gown of seafoam-green muslin, her silvery curls tied back *à l'anglaise* with a matching riband, she tripped demurely downstairs to sit with her aunt, where Peter found her when he was shown into the drawing room.

Her greeting to him was cool but not flinty, and he sat down, somewhat dismayed by the presence of Mrs. Clarence. He had pictured himself saying his piece to Vanessa alone. After some ten minutes of stilted conversation he despaired of privacy and proceeded.

''Miss Pymbroke, I believe I owe you an apology,'' he began.

''You 'believe,' sir?'' she said gently.

"I know, I should say," he amended hastily. "I spoke harshly to you this morning, and what I said was uncalled for. I hope you will believe that I regret it very much, and accept my apologies."

There was a short, pregnant silence while Mrs. Clarence turned an eye bright with interest and speculation from one to the other. Then Vanessa smiled and held out her hand. "We will forget the entire matter, Lord Chance."

He rose to take the hand she extended and bent to kiss it. "You are too kind," he murmured.

Mrs. Clarence sighed contentedly. "Since you are up, Lord Chance, please be kind enough to ring for Hay. I think we should all have a glass of wine."

Ann, meanwhile, with Mabel following, had strolled to Pall Mall, made her purchases, and was on her way home again by a route that took her along a footpath beside a pleasantly shady small park.

Suddenly, some thirty yards ahead, a burly, roughly dressed man emerged from the park leading by the hand a small boy who hung back and dug in his heels with every step, protesting tearfully that he did not want to go.

"Shut yer yap or I'll break yer bleedin' arm," growled the man without stopping.

"But I have changed my mind. I do not want to see the pony," the child cried, tugging frantically to free his hand from the great paw that enveloped it. With his free hand the man boxed the child's ear ringingly. The child screamed.

Without hesitating, Ann ran forward. When she came up behind them, she began beating the man over the head with her parasol, crying furiously, "Release that child at once! How *dare* you strike him?"

Taken completely by surprise, the man did drop the child's hand in order to protect his head. The boy ran to Ann and threw his arms about her knees, burying his face in her skirts.

" 'Ere, whotcher think yer doin'?" bellowed the man, backing away.

"I might ask you the same question," Ann replied indignantly.

"I'm takin' 'im 'ome to his mam, is what I'm a-doin'. I suppose I can take me hown child 'ome to his mam if I wants ter."

At this the child pulled his face out of Ann's skirts long enough to shout indignantly, "I am *not* your child!" With his delicately refined features, expensive little nankeen suit, and frilled shirt, even the slowest intelligence could see that this was patently true.

"Ar, I only meant that I was hin charge of the little fellow," the man said with an oily attempt at ingratiation. " 'Is mam asked me to bring 'im to 'er, you see."

"She did not," cried the little boy, "for my mama is with God and His angels in heaven. My papa told me so."

The man growled, "Little devil, yer callin' me a liar?" and lurched forward. The child hid his face in Ann's skirts again and screamed. Ann raised her parasol threateningly and Mabel, who had been watching the proceedings in a paralysis of disbelief, was jerked back to herself at this menace to her mistress and advanced with raised shopping basket, prepared to clout him with it.

The man halted, looked about in a harried sort of way, and at last, evidently deciding the game was not worth the candle, took to his heels with a curse.

Ann dropped to her knees and took the sobbing child in her arms and spoke soothingly to him. Mabel produced a large handkerchief and between them they calmed him down and dried his wet face.

"Now, little man, were you with your nurse in the park there?" asked Ann.

"Yes, and I was rolling my hoop and it went behind some shrubbery and then this man came and asked did I want to see his lovely pony? I did want to, very much, and he took me with him, but we walked and walked and I was tired and didn't want to go with him anymore and he—he hit me."

Ann decided they should go back into the park in search of the nurse, who would no doubt be frantic by this time. However, it was late in the afternoon and the park was nearly deserted, and search as they might, they were unable to find a frantic nurse or anyone who could tell them of such a person.

The boy said, "I want my Bickers," as the tears welled up again and ran down his cheeks.

"We will find her, darling. Now, can you tell me your name?"

"Dalby."

"And your last name?"

"Rivers," he said proudly, "Dalby Pennington Coke Rivers."

"And do you know where you live?"

"On Mount Street."

"Very good, Dalby. Now we have only to go to Mount Street and you will find your Bickers waiting there for you, I make no doubt."

They regained the street and she hailed a passing hackney cab. After only one inquiry, upon reaching Mount Street, they were directed to a large imposing Georgian mansion. Her knock was answered so instantly it was clear the butler had been hovering in the hall, but before she could speak, there was a shattering shriek and a round little woman broke from a cluster of women servants and ran to swoop up the boy in her arms.

"Master Dalby, oh, thank the Lord," she sobbed, pressing him to her bosom.

"Bickers, Bickers," he cried excitedly, struggling from her enveloping hold, "I have had an enormous 'venture," while at the same time all the servants were exclaiming and crying at once. Over this babel of noise Ann managed to inquire of the butler if Mr. Rivers were at home.

"No, m'lady, and a blessing it is, too, to save him all the worry and upset we've had this past hour since Mrs. Bickerton returned without the young master."

"Then I won't wait. Here is my card. Perhaps Mr. Rivers will like to call and hear the details of what has occurred."

"You may be sure he will, m'lady," replied the man fervently.

While Ann was dressing for dinner that evening, a footman came to say that a Mr. Rivers was calling and begged for a few moments of her time. She sent word that she would be down directly and finished dressing.

When she entered the drawing room some moments later, a handsome, giant of a man turned eagerly toward her, his mouth opening to speak, and froze in amazement, gaping at her. Whatever he had expected, clearly Ann was not it. Tall and delicately slender in a gown of *jonquille* muslin, she was a vision to cause any man to stare.

"Mr. Rivers," she said, coming toward him with a welcoming smile.

"*You* are Lady Ann Chance?" he asked in disbelief.

"I am, sir."

"But—but—you cannot have routed that great bully alone!"

She laughed and blushed at the look in his eyes. "It was the surprise, I think; he was not expecting it, and then I had Mabel to back me up."

"Lady Ann, forgive my manners. I am Andrew Rivers," he said, bowing, "but you have put me at such a nonplus my wits have flown. I suppose I had pictured a great, strapping sort of woman, not—not—" He stopped helplessly.

"How is Dalby?" she said, firmly changing the subject.

"Very well, though in a highly excitable state. His sister is terribly envious of his 'venture. Being the eldest, she feels it should have happened to her. I realize it is very rag-mannered of me to force myself upon you at this hour, but I was so anxious to express my gratitude to you—and to hear the story. Will you mind very much recounting it to me? I received, as you may well imagine, a somewhat garbled version."

She invited him to have a seat and, seating herself opposite him, told him all she knew.

"Dear God," he breathed when she had finished, "what a tiger for courage you are, to be sure. I am too much in your debt, dear Lady Ann, ever to express it properly, but at least I can thank you from the heart."

She was much embarrassed and welcomed the entrance of Mrs. Clarence and Vanessa. Ann introduced them, and Mr. Rivers apologized all over again for calling at such an inconvenient time, but said he felt sure they could understand how pressing was his need to come at once to thank Lady Ann. Both ladies looked mystified by this speech and turned inquiring eyes upon Ann, who flushed uncomfortably and looked away.

"Good Lord," Mr. Rivers exclaimed, "is it possible she has told you nothing of what she has done this afternoon?"

They turned with interested surprise to Ann, but she remained mute. When Mr. Rivers saw that she would not speak, he told the story himself, causing them to stare at Ann in astonishment.

"Well, I vow, Ann, if you are not the sliest thing in nature," cried Vanessa. "Imagine not telling us a word of this!"

After both ladies had exclaimed and made a great deal of Ann and required to be told the story all over again, Mrs. Clarence invited Mr. Rivers to stay and take dinner with them. He said that unfortunately that would not be possible.

"Then you will have to give us another evening, sir," decided Mrs. Clarence emphatically. "Was your mother a Miss Gloucester before she was married?"

"Why, yes, she was."

"Ah, then I knew her when we were girls. You must promise me to dine one night soon. I will send you a note."

When he had taken his leave, the three ladies went into the dining room and the subject of the abduction was reexplored until Ann begged them to speak of something else.

"Then let us speak of this handsome Mr. Rivers," said Vanessa. "Who *is* he and why have we never seen him before?"

"He is widowed, I know," volunteered Ann, "for the boy said his mother was dead."

"Yes, so she is," said Mrs. Clarence, "some three years now, if I remember correctly. As I said, I knew his mother, but when she married, we lost touch. Though they keep a house in town, they are very much country people. Derbyshire, I believe. A great deal of money, a very old family, the Rivers, and very proud. Always refused titles and honors, I have heard."

"Good heavens, what a fount of information you are," laughed Ann.

"Oh, I keep myself informed on such things," replied Mrs. Clarence complacently. "Mr. Rivers comes to London only very rarely. Poor man, how difficult it must be for him with two small children to care for. I shall invite him for tomorrow week and you must both keep the evening free."

Peter and Robin called the following afternoon, both in a state of some perturbation, but were told Lady Ann was from home. Peter asked for Mrs. Clarence. Hay went away and presently came to ask them to please wait in the drawing room and Mrs. Clarence would be with them directly.

When she came in, they both turned to greet her rather perfunctorily before Peter asked tersely, "My sister, Mrs. Clarence, where is she?"

"Why, she has gone with Vanessa to Lady Drumm's breakfast."

"But surely she— I mean, should she not be in her bed?"

"In her bed?"

"After her ordeal of yesterday, we made sure she would be ill today. We have only just learned of the matter and came around at once."

"Where did you hear of it?" asked Mrs. Clarence curiously.

"One of the footmen had it from a maid next door, whose sister works for Mr. Rivers in Mount Street. He came to me with the story not half an hour ago."

"Fascinating," commented Mrs. Clarence. "I am always astonished to find what great gossips servants are. Tell me, what did he say had happened?"

"That this dreadful man in a mask snatched Rivers' child from his nurse's arms, leapt onto a horse, and galloped off. Then Ann heard the boy's screams and chased after them, dragged the brute from his horse, beat him over the head with her parasol until he was unconscious, then returned the child to his home," recounted Peter, something like awe in his voice.

Mrs. Clarence's great girth was quivering with convulsive laughter by the end of this lurid recital.

Peter and Robin exchanged bewildered glances and Robin said, somewhat reproachfully, "Forgive me, Mrs. Clarence, if I speak too plainly, but I find little amusement in the story. We cannot feel that such an experience could be other than harmful to Ann's health."

"Oh dear, oh dear," chortled Mrs. Clarence, fishing a handkerchief from her reticule and mopping her streaming eyes, "what vivid imaginations they do have. It makes up for their hard lives, I suppose. But tell me, gentlemen, does that sound like something Ann, or indeed any woman, would be capable of: running fast enough to catch up with a galloping horse, dragging a man from the saddle, and beating him unconscious with her parasol? Why, the parasol would break long before he became unconscious, and what on earth would the man be doing all this time?"

"Do you imply that this is all some tarrididdle made up by servants?" demanded Peter.

"No, no, not *all*. There is a core of truth beneath all those embellishments. Now, do sit down and you shall hear the truth of the matter."

After she had told them what had really occurred, they were somewhat reassured, though still concerned for her health.

"Believe me, she came to no harm at all," said Mrs. Clarence. "In fact, she seems quite set up by it. I think it was good for her to have proved that she is not so delicate as she is always being assured she is. But you may depend upon it, I will clap her in her bed in a trice should I notice any signs of a decline."

With this Peter and Robin had to be content and took their leave without the opportunity of seeing Ann for themselves, since Lady Drumm's breakfasts were notorious for lasting well into the early evening.

11

Giles came bursting into the breakfast room the next morning ahead of an outraged Hay, who was attempting to announce him properly. The ladies of the Clarence household were dawdling over the remains of their meal while making up a list for a dinner party for the general and Mr. Rivers. Giles, his heavy brows drawn together in a scowl of worry, went straight up to Ann.

"What is this story I have just heard of you dragging some man from a horse and beating him?" he demanded peremptorily.

"What?" Ann was round-eyed with astonishment while Mrs. Clarence began to laugh.

"I had it from my valet this morning. I must say it is not the sort of thing I like to hear first thing upon awakening."

"Well, naturally, I am devastated to have upset your morning, Giles," returned Ann tartly. "You will of course wish to greet Mrs. Clarence and Miss Pymbroke?"

"Oh, beg pardon. Good morning, Mrs. Clarence, Miss Pymbroke. Now please tell me, Ann—"

"Good morning, Mr. Dalzell. Will you not take some breakfast? Hay, bring a cup and plate for Mr. Dalzell," ordered Mrs. Clarence smoothly. "Now sit down, Mr. Dalzell, and do not put yourself in such a pucker. As you can see, Ann is perfectly well."

"Yes, but—" he began impatiently.

"Oh, Giles, it was really the most minor sort of incident, blown all out of proportion." Ann proceeded to detail the affair for him, making light of it all. "And you shall meet Mr. Rivers, for he is coming here to dinner and you will be sent a card. Now let us not speak of it anymore. Did you bring your new mare to show me?"

"I rode her over. But really, Ann, I cannot like—"

"Then why do we not have the carriage brought around for Ann and me and we can all go to the park?" Vanessa suggested.

"I don't know. Are you sure it would not be too much for Ann after all she has been through?" said Giles, unable to let go of the fear he had experienced when he had first heard his valet's tale.

"My dear Mr. Dalzell, I think you would be better advised to worry about any cutpurses or highwaymen you might encounter, for with two such heroines on your hands the Lord knows what they might not do to them," said Mrs. Clarence dryly. "Now, please take some of that ham, it is very good, and we will get on with our list before you take them away for a drive. Where were we—your brothers, Ann, and the general and Mr. Rivers, and—"

"Miss Clayton-Trees, remember," said Vanessa.

"Oh, dear, I suppose we must, though I cannot like her. The Drumms, of course, and the Dortleys—"

"The Riddleys?" suggested Vanessa.

"Very well, but *not* the three mousy daughters," agreed Mrs. Clarence.

"And Miss Chamfreys," said Ann. Mrs. Clarence put her name down without hesitation. Vanessa flicked a glance at Giles, but he seemed engrossed by a plate of coddled eggs and ham and paid no attention to them. Mrs. Clarence counted and declared the list to come out exactly even as to sex and "It is sixteen people, which I consider just right. I cannot like large dinner parties where there can be no general conversation. We shall have to have another, of course, and then there is your ball in a fortnight, Vanessa."

"Dear Aunt, I wish you would not feel obligated to do all this entertaining for me. I do not care to put you to so much trouble," Vanessa protested.

"No trouble for me, my dear," replied Mrs. Clarence comfortably. "I leave everything but the invitations to the servants. Besides, I won't have Pymbroke thinking I am such a squeeze crab I would do nothing for you."

While Giles finished his breakfast, the two girls went upstairs to change their dresses, and presently, after the chestnut mare had been admired, the party set off.

Robin, meanwhile, had gone to call upon Miss Chamfreys, and was much relieved to find her without any company at all other than an elderly and imposing female introduced to him as the Duchess of Afton. Since this lady claimed all of Mrs. Chamfreys' attention, Robin was able to draw Camilla away toward the other end of the room.

"This is surely an unexpected delight for me, Miss Chamfreys. I have not been able to speak to you alone this age."

"Yes, it pleases me also," she said frankly.

"It does?" He looked taken aback.

"Ah, now I have shocked you," she laughed, "but I must tell you, sir, I never dissemble. It is a fault in me, Mama says. Do you find it so?" She raised her great dark eyes to look squarely into his.

"No, though I suppose it is not just the usual thing in a young woman."

"Do you find it repulsive?"

"Nothing that you could do could be so to me," he assured her fervently.

"Now you sound like a seasoned London *galant*, Mr. Chance."

"Yes, I suppose you are used to such speeches, though I must tell you I am no dissembler either," he said, a slight stiffness edging his words.

She looked at him straightly for a moment. "Forgive me. I do not know why I said that."

He softened at once. "I suppose beautiful young women must learn to brush such speeches aside almost without thought. It must even grow boring for you."

"No, no, Mr. Chance, never boring," she protested, her eyes dancing. "How much more boring never to hear them. For instance, I never hear them from Mr. Dalzell, and while it is flattering, of course, to be consulted by London's newest rage, it can be boring never to talk of anything but plays."

He felt a sinking sensation at this disclosure. "You would

naturally prefer him to make pretty speeches to you," he said flatly.

"Good heavens, no! I would never expect him to do so. I only used him as an example of how boring it is to be treated impersonally."

"Never mind," he said consolingly, smiling with relief, "I am sure Lord Threlfall never treats you so."

She shuddered delicately and he laughed aloud, causing Mrs. Chamfreys and the duchess to pause and turn inquisitively toward them. The duchess's eyes were bright with interest, but Mrs. Chamfreys showed suspicion and disapproval. Fortunately, neither of the young people was aware of being the objects of their regard.

"Mr. Chance, while we are speaking of Mr. Dalzell, I hope you will not think me impertinent if I ask you if your sister is—has hopes— Oh, dear, I cannot go on, for I find I *am* impertinent."

"I beg you to continue, Miss Chamfreys."

"It is only that I—I thought she exhibited a—a *tendre* for him and I hoped very much that it was not so," she ended in a breathless rush.

"You do not like him?"

"Oh, I like him very much, but I fear he— I do not think he will every marry," she finished lamely, wishing she had not brought the matter up at all, but wanting desperately to warn him, if such a warning could be of help to him or anyone dear to him. From the expression of bewilderment on his face she very much feared he did not take her meaning.

He looked at her gravely, "I hope, for my sister's sake, that you are wrong. I believe she has always expected to marry him; in fact, we have all expected her to do so."

"Please forget I spoke of it. I should not have done so. Let us speak of something else. Do you go to the Dewinters' masque tonight?"

"I had not thought to go, but if you are going—"

"Well, I am," she said dimpling, "and I shall wear a green domino."

Mrs. Chamfreys, taking advantage of the duchess's pause for breath, called her daughter to her side, but Robin didn't mind. The darling girl had made sure he would find her tonight! She must care something for him.

He spent the rest of the day in a euphoric haze. The only practical thing he did was to consult Peter about borrowing a mask and domino since he himself had never owned such items.

"What? Do you tell me you are going to the Dewinters'? I had no idea vicars attended such affairs," teased Peter.

"There is no prohibition against it, providing one behaves with propriety," returned Robin with an anxious seriousness.

"Come, I am bamming you, you idiot. It will do you all the good in the world. Just the sort of thing you need. I presume the beauteous Miss Chamfreys will be attending?"

"Er—yes, I believe she will be there. Do you go yourself?"

"No, little brother, I am engaged to dine with Avon, so you are welcome to my domino. I will tell Cord to hunt it out and bring it along to your room."

At eleven Robin set off and arrived at the Dewinters' town house, where the lights of thousands of candles blazed forth upon the chaos of the driveway crammed with carriages inching up to the entrance to debouch their passengers. Robin asked to be set down at the gate, much too impatient for such a slow process, and walked up the rest of the way. Once in the ballroom, he registered the crush of people only vaguely as a swirling mass, made up mostly of black dominoes with, here and there, a scattering of white or red ones or guests in just evening clothes without dominoes. He sought only green. At last he saw her! She stood a little apart from an older couple, unmasked, who were not her parents. Perhaps she was being chaperoned by another couple tonight. Her back was to him and her hood was up. He pushed his way through the crowd and came up behind her.

"Thank heaven you told me the color of your domino or I should never have found you in this squeeze," he murmured with a breathless little laugh of excitement.

The figure jerked in surprise and there was a few seconds' pause. He said urgently, "It is Robin Chance. Forgive me if I startled you." The green domino belled as the figure swung around, the hood shadowing the face so effectively he could not see her expression at all. Then she gave a shrill giggle and threw back her hood. Pale-blue eyes stared boldly up at him for a moment before she dropped them in a pretense of modesty. "La, sir, what a start you gave me. I vow, my heart jumped a foot."

He stood wordlessly, too shocked to know what to say. Then, mumbling incoherent apologies, he backed away while Miss Clayton-Trees and her parents stared after him. When the crowd had closed around him, he took out his handkerchief and mopped his brow, then retreated to the wall. Good Lord, what a horrible mistake! That awful giggle and those greedily inquisitive eyes. He must be more circumspect and study any female in a green domino carefully before he approached. At the moment, search as he might, he could see no other. He kept a wary eye on the location of the woman he had approached before so that if another appeared he would know which was which. It was quite thirty minutes before he saw another green figure in the room. She was with a woman masked in a black domino, so he could not be sure if this were Camilla and Mrs. Chamfreys. He edged cautiously around the room, passing the first green domino, still standing with the older couple, talking animatedly to them, tossing her head about with an affectation of liveliness.

He watched the newcomer from a distance for some moments, then edged closer and closer through the swirling couples until he could see quite clearly the gleaming dark eyes, and then she saw him and smiled and there was no longer any doubt in his mind. He came up to her, eyed intently by Mrs. Chamfreys as he took Camilla's hand and bent to kiss it lingeringly. The rules of the masquerade did not require him to introduce himself, a fact he was grateful for in Mrs. Chamfrey's eagle-eyed presence.

"I hope I am in good time to request the honor of leading you out for the first dance, goddess?"

"Very good time, sir, for I have only just arrived."

"And this charmer? Is it possible that you also have a dance left free for me?" He turned to Mrs. Chamfreys in an attempt at dissimulation. She evidently had not recognized him, for she smiled ravishingly and extended her hand, which he bent to kiss.

She was clearly gratified by this, but protested she would not dance tonight since she had come only to chaperon her charge.

"What? You cannot be so cruel," he protested, "and I

doubt the other gentlemen here tonight will allow you to be so.''

She laughed and said, ''There, now, the music begins. Go along and have your dance, but be sure to deliver my charge back to me the moment it is finished.''

He made a sweeping bow and held out his arm to Camilla. Mrs. Chamfreys looked about, saw a sofa behind her, and sat down. Charming man, she thought. Ah, if only I were younger . . .

Miss Clayton-Trees, despite her performance of liveliness, which she hoped would attract dancing partners, had not missed the entrance of another green domino. She had also marked Robin Chance and seen him approach the new arrival and, finally, lead her onto the dance floor. Burning with both jealousy and curiosity, she turned her attention to the other lady, obviously a chaperone, who was now seated. Taking her mother's arm, Miss Clayton-Trees began to make her way nearer to the sofa.

On the floor Robin and Camilla danced in a trance of pleasure, too happy to need to speak for a time, also rather shy with each other due to the depth of their feelings.

Finally he said, ''You cannot know how much I have looked forward to this moment all day.''

She glanced up, her eyes dark and sparkling through the slits of her mask. ''And I also,'' she said with simplicity. His hand tightened on hers and they finished the dance in silence. By this time they were at the far end of the room, completely hidden from her mother by the other dancers.

''I must take you back now,'' he said with a sigh.

''I think if we just stand here quietly until the music commences we could manage one more dance without causing too much upset. That is, if you will contrive to apologize with the same charm you exhibited before to my mama.''

''Oh, my dear, if you are sure, it would give me such happiness. I cannot ever remember enjoying anything so much as these last, far too few moments.''

''Pretty speeches, sir,'' she teased.

''Oh, endlessly, if you will allow it. You are like a goddess in green tonight, you know, and my wits have fled.'' He raised her hand to his mouth and kissed her fingers, all the while continuing to murmur pretty speeches into her ear to both their hearts' content. When the music started up again, they drifted in a dream back onto the floor.

Miss Clayton-Trees meanwhile had been studying the figure seated on the sofa, and suddenly, with a little leap of the heart, she identified the woman. Mrs. Chamfreys! Then the woman in the other green domino was, of course, Camilla Chamfreys! Almost unable to breath in her excitement, Miss Clayton-Trees excused herself to her parents and approached Mrs. Chamfreys.

"Good evening," she said.

Mrs. Chamfreys jumped a little and turned. "Why— Camilla?" she said uncertainly.

"No, no," giggled Miss Clayton-Trees, "just another lady in green. You are the second person tonight who has mistaken me for Miss Chamfreys."

"How did you know my daughter was in green? And how could anyone else have known?" asked Mrs. Chamfreys sharply.

"A delicious coincidence, is it not, that I should have worn green also? And then, you know, when Mr. Robin Chance came straight up to me and thought— Well, how I laughed at the expression on his face when he saw I was not Miss Chamfreys." She trilled merrily to illustrate how amused she had been.

Mrs. Chamfreys was not in the least amused and began to look about with great agitation. The first dance had ended and the second just begun. She had not put too much importance on Camilla's disobeying her edict to return at once. After all, this was a masquerade party and one must allow a degree of laxity in the usual strictures. But now . . . Oh, she would have a great many choice words to say to her daughter when she returned.

Miss Clayton-Trees, judging correctly that her words had done their work, excused herself prettily and returned to her parents, her dissatisfaction at her lack of dancing partners so far this evening soothed by the bit of mischief she had just perpetrated.

Mrs. Chamfreys fanned herself vigorously as she searched the floor for a sight of her daughter and gradually her anger cooled and she began to think more clearly. Camilla was not at all a biddable sort of girl and this matter must be thought out carefully if she was not to be given cause to dig in her heels over young Mr. Chance. By the time the second dance had ended Mrs. Chamfreys had decided on her course of action, and when Robin led Camilla up to her, she managed a wan smile despite the small crease of pain between her brows.

"You were very naughty, sir, but I suppose I must forgive you," she said in a die-away voice.

"Mama, is something wrong?"

"Shh—nothing, my love. Perhaps you will sit with me for a moment."

"Thank you, goddess, for standing up with me. I will return to claim another, if you will allow me," said Robin, bowing to both ladies and withdrawing.

"Now, Mama, what is wrong?" demanded Camilla when he was out of earshot.

"Only one of my heads, love, for a moment there I felt quite nauseous with the pain. But it will go away, please do not fret."

"But we must go at once."

"Nonsense, I would not dream of spoiling your evening by dragging you away so soon."

"Please do not be absurd, Mama. Come along," she ordered, "I am taking you home at once. Now, do not protest anymore. As if I could enjoy myself while you are suffering." She pulled her mother to her feet and led her out of the ballroom.

When Robin, who had gone for a glass of champagne, returned, he searched fruitlessly for them, his disbelief growing by the moment. She could not—would not—leave without . . . Then he remembered her mother's face. The woman had clearly been ill and he knew at once, and with enormous relief, that Camilla had taken her mother home. So kind-hearted a girl would not be able to enjoy herself while her mother was ailing.

He took his own leave, still too happy to even be disappointed by this abrupt ending to a glorious evening. Tomorrow he would call and invite her to ride with him.

12

By the evening of Mrs. Clarence's dinner party, Robin had called, on four successive mornings, upon Camilla only to be told by the butler that she was not at home. There had been no point in attempting to see her after a performance at the theater, for she was not playing this past week and would not be in the green room with her parents. He was at first puzzled, and then sick at heart. What on earth could have happened to cause her to behave in this way? She had said she was no dissembler and had admitted openly how much she had looked forward to the masque. They had been so close and she had been so sweetly accepting of his "pretty speeches." It had been no idle flirtation to fill the moment. No, he would never believe that! And yet, the very next day, and each time he had called since, she had denied him. Why, in God's name?

Pride prevented him from calling again. It seemed clear that she had either changed her mind or been persuaded by her mother that she must not encourage him since an alliance between them would never be countenanced. Pride did not keep him from suffering, however, for he knew he genuinely loved her.

It was in a miserable frame of mind, therefore, that he dressed to go to Mrs. Clarence's dinner party. He would have liked to cry off, but felt it would be inexcusably inconsiderate to do so at the last moment. Peter was in such good spirits himself he failed to notice how unusually quiet his brother was as they set off together.

93

Peter had encountered Miss Pymbroke, since he had made his apology, at a rout, two balls, a musicale, and a dinner party, and she had been open and friendly in manner, had certainly given him as much time as she had any of the other gentlemen who flocked about her, and had been equally as charming to him. At this thought his brows drew together and quite suddenly this did not give him so much satisfaction as it had previously. His complacency vanished. He did not care to be treated by the ravishing Miss Pymbroke with exactly the same charm as she extended to everyone else.

He was gratified when they arrived to note that most of the company had already assembled and that none of the young men who were usually about her was present. In fact, besides Giles Dalzell and a very tall gentleman he did not recognize, he and Robin were the only young, unattached men present. He saw Vanessa at once, sitting upon a sofa across the room with Lady Drumm. She looked up and smiled, and he grinned back, his spirits rising at once.

Ann came to meet them and lead them to Mrs. Clarence. While they were greeting her, Ann went to bring the tall gentleman forward.

"Peter, Robin, allow me to present Mr. Andrew Rivers to you," she said.

"Ah, Mr. Rivers!" said Peter with a bow. "I had forgotten Ann promised we would meet you tonight. How is your son?"

"Very well, thanks to your sister, sir," Andrew replied, bowing to both brothers and smiling down from his great height upon Ann with so much warmth that she blushed and becamed flustered. Murmuring something about seeing to Mrs. Dortley, she hurried away.

Peter took time to survey the room while Robin engaged Mr. Rivers in conversation, and was not a little dismayed to meet the eyes of Miss Clayton-Trees, who nodded and smiled. What on earth was she doing here? he wondered. He nodded and turned back to Mr. Rivers. Eight men and only seven women, he mused. I wonder who is still to come? Then the general came up and Mrs. Clarence introduced the brothers to him in a deliberately loud voice.

"Ah ha!" he shouted genially. "Delighted to make your acquaintance. Knew your mother well. How is she keeping?"

Miss Clayton-Trees watched the encounter and waited for her uncle to call her to his side. When he did not, she gritted her teeth in irritation. Silly old fool, she thought, two bright spots of angry red suffusing her cheeks. She willed Lord Chance to come to her, her eyes drilling holes into his back. In a few moments, however, she saw him bow and walk away, leaving her uncle to his brother, and make his way across the room to Miss Pymbroke without so much as a glance in her direction. She felt a cold rage settle like a stone in her chest. She had not wanted to come here at all tonight, and would dearly have loved to refuse the invitation, or better, send a note at the last moment that she had the headache and could not come, when it would be too late for Mrs. Clarence to adjust her seating arrangements. However, her mama had persuaded her that since Lord Chance was to be there for sure, it would not do for her to miss the opportunity to be in his company. Mrs. Clayton-Trees confessed that a match between them had been her object since the day of her daughter's birth and that she had asked Lady Chance to be her godmother in the hopes of furthering this ambition.

"Though I must say, beyond a silver porringer, she has done little to fulfill my expectations. I must have written her eight or nine letters hinting that she instruct her son to call upon us when he came to town. Well, he has finally done so, and has invited you to ride, and it is up to you to make sure he becomes interested. I can do no more. If you have not learned how to throw out lures by this time, I cannot teach you."

Miss Clayton-Trees would have been only too happy to comply, but since that ride she had had little opportunity to practice her wiles, for he had not called again, and though they had met several times since at various parties and balls, he had done little more than greet her pleasantly. "Well, you can hardly expect me to chase him about the room," she had complained to her mother after enduring yet another lecture on how to be more forthcoming, even flirtatious. Ah, she thought, here comes the brother. Handsome, but only the younger brother, after all, and in orders. Not at all suitable.

Robin had excused himself to the general in order to greet the other guests. In spite of the fog of misery that seemed to hover about his head, he went from guest to guest, greeting them pleasantly. He bowed before Miss Clayton-Trees politely and she gave him a coquettish smile when he introduced himself.

"But we have met before, sir. I believe you have forgotten me."

"I am very sorry," he replied gravely. "Please forgive me. Where—"

"Why, at the masque, sir. I believe you mistook me for someone else," she smiled archly, "but then I was so besieged by partners I lost sight of you."

His whole being recoiled. Of course, those pale, inquisitive eyes, he thought. What can she be doing here? Surely Ann could not have such an unlikely friend. Perhaps it is some connection of Mrs. Clarence's. "Are you a relative of Mrs. Clarence's?" he inquired.

"No, I am not," she said disdainfully. "I am the general's niece."

"Ah, yes, of course. A very fine old gentleman." Then he seemed to stiffen, staring over her shoulder at the door.

"Do you enjoy riding, Mr. Chance? I do so like riding in the early mornings, do not you?" she hinted in an attempt to recapture his attention.

Robin did not hear her. Camilla Chamfreys had just been shown in by Hay, and only by a slight check in her steps as she advanced to Mrs. Clarence did she acknowledge her awareness of his presence. He wondered why it had not occurred to him that she might be here? And how was he to behave? Should he pretend that nothing was amiss? That all was as it had been? But how could he do so when nothing *was* the same? She must know that nothing could have prevented him making a declaration after their glorious evening. Except that she *had* prevented it very effectively, and his *amour-propre* was severely damaged. He looked away as quickly as she did herself, and did not look at her again, but he was aware of Giles going forward eagerly to greet her, then leading her to Ann, where the three now stood in animated conversation. He wondered how it was going to be possible for him to get through this evening with so much unhappiness burdening him.

He was put severely to the test when dinner was announced and Mrs. Clarence assigned him to take Miss Chamfreys in.

Until that moment they had not, except for the brief instant as she had entered the room, acknowledged each other's presence. Now he forced himself to go to her, bow, and extend his arm. She sketched a brief curtsy, eyes lowered, and laid her hand lightly upon his arm and allowed herself to be led into the dining room. She did not look at him or speak, and it was clear to him that she was deeply offended with him, or was at least pretending to be. He could not imagine what cause she thought she had, but he was equally offended by her attitude, since he knew right to be on his side. He felt that she should have at least attempted some excuse or explanation for her conduct this past week. If she had felt he had gone too far at the masque with his lovemaking, she should have discouraged him then, rather than simply to cut him out of her life so coldly and finally. It occurred to him fleetingly that he had been taught and truly believed that one should turn the other cheek, but he was too young and too hurt to break the silence between them. He stared stonily down at his plate.

Since Mrs. Clarence had thought herself to be doing a service to each of them by making them dinner partners, she was somewhat dismayed to notice that they kept firmly turned away from each other at the table and spoke only to the person seated on their other sides. Now, what is afoot here? she wondered. A small lover's quarrel? Ah, well, she sighed with a secret smile, how delightful it will be for them to make it up.

The only other person at the table who noticed that something was amiss between Miss Chamfreys and Mr. Chance was Miss Clayton-Trees. She had noticed the way Giles Dalzell had rushed to greet Miss Chamfreys, which perhaps Mr. Chance resented. On the other hand, he had not spoken to her intimately, but taken her directly to Lady Ann, so either he was a hardened flirt or there was nothing between him and Miss Chamfreys, after all. Miss Clayton-Trees scented something intriguing going on and she studied Camilla and Robin covertly while she chattered with Mr. Riddley on her left and then with Mr. Dortley on her right, all the while, on a deeper level of her mind, she nursed the rancor she felt against her hostess for not having seated her next to Lord Chance, even if Lady Drumm did take precedence over herself and required that Lord Chance take her into the dining room. But naturally, Mrs. Clarence was looking to the main chance and had seated her own niece on his left, where rightfully she should have seated Miss Clayton-Trees, in that lady's opinion, for she certainly had precedence over Vanessa Pymbroke! Of course, Mrs. Clarence would do everything in her power to throw her niece in Chance's way. Really, the woman's pretensions knew no bounds, nor, clearly, the niece's, for only see how she was simpering at him now in what Miss Clayton-Trees considered a vulgarly obvious manner.

Vanessa had just turned with some relief from a rather trying conversation with the general, which consisted for the most part of some rather heavy-handed compliments delivered in an embarrassingly loud voice. Peter grinned in sympathy.

"Taxing, I am sure," he said in a low voice, "but a relief for me to have only the old gentleman to compete with for your attention for a change."

"Ah, but gentlemen thrive on competition, I have always understood."

"Oh, I think that is a story put about by writers of romance to encourage women to think jealousy spurs the lover to declare himself," he said in some amusement.

"How little you must think of women to suppose they are so weak-minded they can easily be influenced by such things."

"No, no, I assure you, Miss Pymbroke, that I would never be so mistaken as to think you could be easily influenced. You have amply demonstrated your strength. For your own safety and my peace of mind, I could wish you *were* more easily influenced."

"Naturally I am sorry to have been the cause of any anxiety to you, my lord. Believe me, it was never in my mind to do so."

"I am not sure I find that a very comforting thought," he said ruefully.

"Sir?" she queried in puzzlement.

"I would like to think that lurking somewhere in your mind was some thought of me and what I might think."

"If there had been such a thought, sir, I am sure it would have been your disapproval that would have come to my mind." She laughed.

"Oh, I do hope, my dear Miss Pymbroke, that you will not think—" he began in laughing protest when he was interrupted by the loud voice of the general over Miss Pymbroke's shoulder.

"A glass of wine with you, sir," the old man brayed, motioning to the servant to fill up their glasses. Peter good-naturedly raised his filled glass and drank to the general, and after that, his *tête-à-tête* with Miss Pymbroke came to an end. Peter could cheerfully have throttled the man. He looked up to meet the sympathetic regard of his sister directly across the table.

Ann had found her own work cut out for her, for she was seated between Giles and Mr. Rivers, and Giles was being somewhat difficult. He complained bitterly of Lady Drumm on his right, who catechized him on his ideas and work habits and, in passing, gave him the benefit of her critique of his poetry, which clearly did not impress her. He turned away from her rudely and just as rudely interrupted Ann's conversations with Mr. Rivers.

"The woman is a monster of ignorance," he muttered in Ann's ear now.

Patiently she begged Mr. Rivers' pardon yet again and turned to ask Giles to be patient. "It is nearly over and you will soon be left with the port and the gentlemen for a time."

"Not nearly long enough," he growled, turning away as Lady Drumm loudly demanded that he explain to her the meaning of his sixth canto.

"He cannot bear talking about his work with people who do not really understand it," Ann said apologetically as she turned back to Mr. Rivers.

"Lady Ann, I beg you will not distress yourself," he replied with imperturbable good humor. "I wonder that he can be persuaded to go into society at all. It is clear he depends upon you. I wonder what might have become of him had he been seated without you beside him?"

"I—I do not know. He dines out quite frequently. I can only suppose he copes somehow," she said, her hand on the table nervously turning a fork over and over.

He put his hand over hers lightly "It does not matter. Try not to let it upset you. Think of it as the artistic temperament, which cannot help chaffing at people like Lady Drumm."

She looked up at him gratefully for this understanding and

for the comfort of his warm hand over her own. Though it comforted her, she withdrew her own shyly.

"I was wondering if I could persuade you to come for a drive with me one day, Lady Ann?"

"I should enjoy that very much."

"Would tomorrow, at ten, be too soon for you?"

"Tomorrow at ten would suit me perfectly."

Across the table Camilla, listening with a slight glazing of the eyes to Lord Drumm's discourse on Parliamentary procedure, wondered if the evening would ever come to an end. She had known, of course, that to accept Mrs. Clarence's invitation to dinner entailed the danger of encountering Lady Ann's brothers, so why had she come? She had fully expected, indeed anticipated with almost unbearable breathlessness, Robin's call on the morning following the Dewinters' masque. He had not called. She managed to persuade herself that some previous engagement had kept him away and that he would come the next day. He had not come then, nor on any of the days to follow, though she had refused all morning engagements for several days in order to receive him. At last she was forced to acknowledge that he was not coming. After all that had happened between them, all that she had allowed him to know of her feelings, he had not called. How could she have been so mistaken in a man? He had seemed so open, so appealingly honest and free of the artifices that she abhorred in most of the men who pursued her. She had finally decided that it had been no more than an evening's flirtation to him. He did not care for her, after all.

She sat at the dinner table, swamped by cold misery, trying to appear interested in all Lord Drumm had to say, for when he had to turn his attention away from her, she could only stare at her plate and push the foot about, intensely aware of Robin's presence on her right, and wonder if it would be possible to get through the wretched evening without bursting into tears. How could she have subjected herself to such an ordeal? But she knew very well why she had done so: she had felt quite desperately that she must see him again, that perhaps he would say something to exonerate himself, or do something at least to prove to her that he was only a hardened flirt.

Well, she had her answer. No doubt when she had been

forced to leave the ball so precipitously he had decided she was a waste of time and gone on to some other conquest. Why he should feel it necessary to treat her so coldly now, she could not imagine.

When the ladies withdrew, she went at once to her hostess. "Mrs. Clarence, I hope you will forgive me. I have the most dreadful headache. I really must go home."

"Why, my dear, I am so sorry. I noticed you were very quiet at dinner. Come along and we'll get your cloak. You must have your abigail make you a tisane."

Miss Clayton-Trees watched Camilla's departure with complacency, not in the least dismayed to note her unhappiness the whole evening, nor to accept that the responsibility for it must almost of a certainty be due to the few words she had dropped in Mrs. Chamfreys' ear at the masquerade ball. Indeed, Miss Clayton-Trees felt close to righteousness for having effected a rift in the unsuitable relationship that had been developing between the little actress and the vicar. Unsuitable for both of them, she thought smugly. It was also to dear Lady Ann's advantage to have Miss Chamfreys out of the way, for now Mr. Dalzell would not be distracted by her. And in line with that, it is really time someone dropped a word in that young man's ear.

Accordingly, when the gentlemen rejoined the ladies in the drawing room, Miss Clayton-Trees did not hesitate to approach Giles. "Mr. Dalzell, I have been wanting to tell you this age how great an admirer I am of your poetry."

"Too kind," he murmured warily.

"Oh, yes, Mama and I read it aloud and I have some bits off by heart. It is particularly moving when you mourn the love that cannot be requited. I must say I wonder at the genius of your imagination, for surely the whole world knows your love has been returned by a *lady*, whom I will not mention, not six yards from where we stand. Why, we have been expecting an announcement in the *Gazette* anytime this past five years."

Giles stared at her with growing horror as she spoke, and it seemed to him the very blood in his veins turned to ice so that he felt frozen and fragile, as though he might splinter into bits if she said another word. He turned abruptly on his heel and walked stiffly out of the room and out of the house.

He strode off up the street, his mind a chaos of words and images, mostly of Ann. Dear God, could that dreadful girl be right? Ah, no, no, it was impossible. Ann was his sister and, besides Oliver, the only person he had any affection for, but—but not in that way!

Her image floated before him, not as she was now, but as she always appeared to him, the thin, pale twelve-year-old girl, eyes ablaze with passionate loyalty, declaring she would never marry anyone but him and they would be together forever. Her words had been an almost miraculous balm at the time, and for many months after, when he had been sent off to school by Lady Carrisbrooke and had suffered torments from loneliness and the sheer beastliness of his school fellows and teachers. He had lived for her letters and for the few times they were reunited after that, until he had reached Oxford and met Oliver. The actual words had faded away, but the assurance that she truly cared for him as did no one else in the world remained with him always.

Was it possible that she was in love with him, had been all this time, was waiting for him to declare himself? Oh, God, surely not—please not, he prayed incoherently. The Lord, however, vouchsafed no comfort, for the more Giles prayed that it might not be so, the more he became convinced that it was.

At dawn, deathly pale but firmly resolved on his course, he returned to his rooms to change his clothes. He set off by carriage an hour later.

13

Peter arrived upon Mrs. Clarence's doorstep shortly after ten the following morning, hoping Miss Pymbroke would not have gone out before he could persuade her to come for a ride with him in the park. He felt that the more he knew of her, the more he understood his sister's fondness for Miss Pymbroke. He was beginning to look forward to knowing her very much better.

He was shown into Mrs. Clarence's drawing room by Hay and requested to wait. In a few moments Mrs. Clarence came in to greet him. "My dear Lord Chance," she wheezed as she advanced upon him like a ship with a good following wind, "how very pleasant this is."

"My pleasure entirely. I hope I am not too early?"

"Dear me, no, not at all. We finished our breakfast long ago, but I must tell you that if you have called for your sister, she has gone driving with Mr. Rivers."

"Good heavens, and I thought I was early. I hope Miss Pymbroke is not also out already?"

"No, she is not," said Miss Pymbroke from the doorway. Peter swung about and his heart turned over. Vanessa wore a blue muslin gown the exact shade of her eyes. She came up to give him her hand. "Lord Chance, good morning. Please sit down. Aunt, shall I ring for refreshments?"

"Please do not bother for me, Miss Pymbroke. Actually, I came to see if you would like to ride this morning."

"I should like that very much. I'll just go change," she said briskly, and hurried from the room. She returned presently in a smart fawn habit and a dashing, white-plumed bonnet.

Trailed discreetly by Fred, they set off for the park and came almost at once face-to-face with Miss Clayton-Trees. She bestowed a frosty little nod upon them. Peter raised his hat, and she passed on.

"I fear you have quite sunk yourself beyond reproach in Miss Clayton-Trees' eyes," said Vanessa lightly.

"How is that?"

"By riding with such a brazen creature as myself. You will have your work cut out for you to win her forgiveness."

"I do not think one's friends will require that."

"Ah, then all will be well between you and Miss Clayton-Trees?"

"I cannot say. We are not exactly friends, nor are we well-enough acquainted for me to predict her actions. She is a goddaughter of my mother's, who asked me to call upon her. I have met her but twice."

"No doubt future meetings will strengthen your friendship. She is a pretty girl."

"Hmmm."

"Perhaps a shade too proper—"

"I cannot think why we are discussing Miss Clayton-Trees," interrupted Peter crossly.

"Oh, I beg your pardon. What subject shall we speak of?"

"You," he said. "Tell me where you learned to drive so well."

"From my father. He is the best whipster I know, I assure you, and a most severe teacher. He could reduce me to tears with a look when I first began, but I was quite young then, of course."

"Surely it was an unusual thing to teach you at a young age?"

"Well, I think he would have preferred a son, really. I used to wish desperately that it was all a dreadful mistake and I would wake up one morning a boy."

"Good God!" exclaimed Peter, turning a shocked gaze upon her.

She laughed. "Yes, I know what you are thinking. I would have made a very poor showing as a boy with my lack of inches."

"For many reasons beyond that," he said fervently, thinking of the fine-boned beauty of her figure and the delicate features of her face. "Not only a poor showing, but a great waste."

She felt herself blushing and turned her face away. "What a lot of people are out today," she said with an effort at lightness.

"Oh—are there?" He looked about as though he had not noticed before.

This remark nearly succeeded in undermining her poise completely and she felt so breathless she could not have spoken even if she could have thought of anything to say.

Peter too was silent, content to study her. The silver-gilt curls escaping from her bonnet glinted in the sunlight and the color bloomed so becomingly on her cheek that he longed to reach out and touch it.

Vanessa scolded herself silently for being so idiotish, reminding herself that she had managed to behave with perfect aplomb before the lavish compliments of the Austrian prince and Monsieur, the French king's brother. She turned her eyes back to him with an effort.

"How is your brother?"

"He is well. I did not see him today. I suppose he has gone to visit Miss Chamfreys."

"Ah ha! I thought he was much struck by her when they met the day he arrived."

"I hope not too much."

"Oh? Why should you do so?"

"My brother is a vicar, Miss Pymbroke, and very dedicated. I doubt there could be any future in an attachment to an actress."

"Do you know, I do not believe she is one, really. She does not seem to care about it above half."

"You may be right, but I think her mother has ambitions for her, and marriage to a vicar is not one of them."

"I hardly think Miss Chamfreys could be swayed by her mother's ambitions for her if she did not care to be."

"Ah, but perhaps she will care to be. She is a very sophisticated young woman, who has always lived very much in society. I doubt she would care for life in a small village where the major entertainment is the Sunday church service."

"Such things do not matter where the feelings are engaged. Besides, there is nothing to say your brother will remain in a small village all his life."

"Touché. I should know better than to cross swords with you, Miss Pymbroke. But let us not quarrel about so remote an event. After all, they have only just met and Robin will be here only a month."

She immediately changed the subject, grateful to him for recalling her, for she knew she had a too hasty tongue and might have said something to put her in his bad graces again. They spoke on inconsequential matters for a time before Peter was hailed. It was Mr. Bynge.

"Oh, good day to you, Mr., er, Bynge," said Peter reluctantly.

"Lord Chance, what a pleasure to meet you again," said Mr. Bynge, though he barely glanced at Peter. He had eyes only for Vanessa.

"Yes. Well, Miss Pymbroke, allow me to present Mr. Gervase Bynge to you," Peter said none too graciously.

" 'Servant, Miss Pymbroke," said Mr. Bynge, removing his hat and making a sweeping bow as best he could while seated upon a horse.

"How do you do, Mr. Bynge," Vanessa acknowledged the introduction with a smile.

"I saw you race, Miss Pymbroke, and I must tell you it was splendidly done!" exclaimed Mr. Bynge enthusiastically.

Vanessa flushed in embarrassment and said, "Thank you," in a stifled voice, wishing the ground would open and swallow her—or better still, Mr. Bynge.

"Oh, it was famous! Never seen anyone beat old Belle. I wonder, Miss Pymbroke, if you would care to come driving with me one day in my high-perch phaeton. I would be happy to teach you to drive it."

Vanessa pulled herself together. "Thank you, Mr. Bynge. I will be happy to come out with you one day. I should tell you, however, that my father taught me to drive a high-perch."

"I might have known. Still, I would be honored and I have some bang-up cattle, I assure you."

"Too kind," she murmured, wishing he would go away.

"Well Bynge, we will bid you good day now," said Peter decisively, gathering up his reins.

Mr. Bynge grinned good-naturedly and raised his hat. "Perhaps I might be allowed to call upon you tomorrow, Miss Pymbroke?"

"Certainly, Mr. Bynge," she said as they moved off, not realizing the devastating effect of the smile she bestowed upon him in her relief to be getting away without any further reference to the infamous race.

"A new admirer for you, Miss Pymbroke. Silly young jackanapes."

"Because he is an admirer?" she inquired innocently.

"You know very well I did not mean that."

"If it is his youth you object to, I feel sure he cannot be above a year or so younger than you."

"Chronologically, perhaps, but I hope I was never so foolish."

"I feel quite sure you were not," she replied solemnly.

He saw that she was amused, and wondered rather dismally if he were only a figure of fun to her, a pompous, boring creature to be polite to for Ann's sake.

He set himself to prove to her that he was not in the least pompous, and when he returned her to her aunt's house, it would have been hard to say which of them was the more pleased to find themselves so much in charity with each other.

A week later, however, he was feeling less than complacent about the situation. He sat in his study at Carrisbrooke House attempting to respond to his mother's latest letter demanding information on the state of Ann's health, on the progress of Robin's holiday in London, and on when she might expect her eldest son to return home for a visit to a mother who lived in daily expectation and hope.

Peter was having some difficulty in concentrating on his letter. His mind reverted continuously to the problem of why, since the felicity of their ride together a week ago, he was finding Miss Pymbroke so mysteriously elusive. He had called three times in the past week. The first two times he had found her out, and had perforce to contain his dismay and make the agreeable to his sister and Mrs. Clarence. He had not liked to ask where or with whom Miss Pymbroke was, but it fretted him intolerably. The third visit, yesterday, he had called with the intention of inviting her and his sister to accompany him

to the theater tonight to view the Chamfreys' interpretation of
As You Like It, only to discover Miss Pymbroke and Mrs.
Clarence were already engaged for just this entertainment by
Mr. Bynge. He had then declared that Ann must accompany
him, hiding his disappointment as best he might. Ann could
not be persuaded, however, saying she was looking forward
very much to a quiet evening alone to read Miss Austen's
new novel.

He was now able to assure his mother in his letter, somewhat evasively but truthfully, that Ann seemed in good health
and was being sensible about getting adequate rest to measure
against London's round of gaieties.

He was less truthful about Robin, since his uneasiness
about his younger brother was as yet too vague to bother his
mother with. Robin seemed always to be about the house
these past few days, and there was something guarded and
unhappy in his manner. When Peter had twitted him about
distressing Miss Chamfreys by shunning her company for so
long, Robin had looked at him gravely for a long moment
before replying that he made no doubt Miss Chamfreys had
all the company any young woman could require, and that he
was quite sure she was too busy to notice whether he appeared or not. He had then returned his gaze rather pointedly
to the tome of sermons he was reading and Peter had not
thought it politic to pursue the subject further. Whatever
Robin's feelings for Miss Chamfreys and whatever had happened between them was clearly none of his business.

It had not prevented his concern, however, and he had
thought a visit to the theater to view the young woman
against her own background, with perhaps a few words with
her afterward under the guise of congratulating her upon her
performance, might give him some indication of what sort of
young woman she really was. With this in mind he had
engaged a box for the evening and gone to invite Miss
Pymbroke and Ann to accompany him, only to hear the
unwelcome news that Miss Pymbroke was already promised
to Mr. Bynge for the evening.

Blast the young popinjay! Peter threw down his pen and
rose to pace the room agitatedly. What on earth could she
possibly see in that pup to persuade her to spend an evening
in his company? After a time he managed to return to and

finish his letter to his mother, using a great deal of London gossip and many solicitous inquiries as to her health and that of his father to disguise the fact that he had left unanswered her question about his visit. He had no inclination to leave London just now. He then decided that he would after all attend the theater this evening, but he would cancel his box, for he certainly did not feel like occupying it alone and there was no one else he wanted to share it with. He would take a ticket for the pit, where he was sure to find many friends and where he could get a good view of the boxes.

Vanessa, while she might look upon Mr. Bynge's pursuit of her with less seriousness than he liked, was not immune to his admiration. No woman, of any age, is immune to it, regardless of the aspect of the admirer, and Mr. Bynge, while not the sort of man for whom Vanessa could feel any positive attraction, was still a handsome, well-conducted young gentleman. She had found no reason not to welcome him to her aunt's drawing room, nor to refuse his invitation to the theater. She had been sorry to have missed Peter's two previous calls, and disappointed to be unable to accept his invitation for this evening, for she would have much preferred his company to Mr. Bynge's. On the other hand, she could not prevent herself from a secret gratification to have had Lord Chance find her busy and sought-after.

Mr. Bynge was now bowing her and Mrs. Clarence into his box with obvious pride to be seen in the company of such a beautiful girl, and being assiduous in attending to their every comfort. He was making himself very agreeable to Mrs. Clarence, which gave Vanessa time before the curtain rose to look about at her neighbors and nod to several young gentlemen in the pit who eagerly sought her attention. Then her wandering eye was caught by a familiar figure in the far back of the pit next to a pillar; he was not seeking her eye, but instead seemed to be studying his clasped hands intently. It was Robin Chance, she knew without any doubt at all. Now, why was he sitting there, so alone and quiet amid the shouting, jostling men all about him? He was, naturally, here to see Miss Chamfreys, but the brown study of his mood did not betoken any happiness in it for him.

The play commenced before Vanessa could speculate too much upon the problem, and she was soon caught up in the pyrotechnic performances of the Chamfreys as the lovers, Rosalind and Orlando.

During the first interval she paced the corridor with Mr. Bynge, Mrs. Clarence having declined to move. "I am enjoying this enormously, Mr. Bynge," Vanessa exclaimed enthusiastically. "I do not often attend the theater, you know. I dislike sitting still for so long. I have always enjoyed most those things which call for participation. Now, if I could act, I would enjoy the theater more, I am sure. Do you see what I mean?"

"Of course, Miss Pymbroke, and may I say that is what makes you so outstanding among women. One senses that spirit, eager to be up and doing. It is so different from anything I have ever encountered in the fair sex before."

Vanessa, rather overcome by this enthusiastic encomium, murmured something inconsequential and turned away to acknowledge an acquaintance. When they had continued on their way, Vanessa tried to think of a subject to discuss that would not call forth compliments.

"Do you belong to White's, Mr. Bynge?"

"Oh, certainly."

"I should like very much to go there."

He looked scandalized. "But that is not possible, Miss Pymbroke!"

"What? That I should want to go?" she said innocently.

"No, that you *could* go! Women are not allowed in White's," he added with not a little smugness.

"How very uncivil. I am sure there could be no harm in it."

"But—but it would be most improper!" Mr. Bynge spluttered.

"Do you tell me they conduct themselves there so shamefully?"

"We are all gentlemen there, Miss Pymbroke, and conduct ourselves accordingly," he replied stiffly.

"Ah. Then why should ladies not be admitted?"

Mr. Bynge's brow creased with thought, but could only repeat doggedly that "It would be most improper."

Vanessa sighed and thought it was a pity that such a nice young man should be so singularly humorless. She relented, however. "I am sorry to have teased you so, Mr. Bynge. It was only that I was thinking how much I would enjoy a truly interesting game of cards. It is not the same when one plays only with women. Well, it is too bad, but I suppose you cannot take me there. Ah, I believe it is time for us to return to our seats.''

As she resumed her seat and arranged her gown, she looked about and found herself looking directly into the eyes of Lord Chance, who was also in the pit, though, unlike his brother, he was near the stage and in conversation with several gentlemen. He stared at her intently for some time, then visibly started as though only then realizing what he was doing. He bowed. She smiled and nodded. He turned back to his cronies.

How odd, she thought, to see Lord Chance in that noisy mob. Surely he had taken a box before he invited us, so why is he not sitting there in comfort? She regretted she was not at this moment sitting there with him, but was selfishly glad to see him in the pit, for she knew very well she would not have enjoyed seeing him in a box with any other guests. Miss Clayton-Trees, for example.

She was so caught up in her musings that the second act had progressed some minutes before she became aware of it. She turned her attention resolutely to the stage. Mrs. Chamfreys, she noted, displayed excellently well-shaped limbs in the tights and short surcoat of her disguise as a young man, and looked not a day over eighteen, while her husband was, at first glance, perhaps a shade too old for Orlando, though one forgot it after a time. He was a truly brilliant actor. Miss Chamfreys was to take the part of Hymen and had not yet appeared on the stage.

Vanessa, along with no doubt any number of women in the audience, rather envied Mrs. Chamfreys her opportunity to wear such a costume. At least those women did who viewed their own legs with some complacency, as Vanessa did. During the second interval she continued to muse upon the subject and it was while thus engaged that the daring idea was born of assuming the dress of a gentleman in order to penetrate the sacred precincts of White's. She almost laughed aloud at the thought of such a lark. She could not go alone, naturally, but must be taken there as a guest of a member. She slanted a speculative glance at Mr. Bynge.

From the back of the pit Robin gazed intently at Camilla when she finally appeared in the last scene. She was so beautiful, so elegant, and if she merely recited her lines, at least she did so in a clear, concise voice. His heart ached with love and at the same time he castigated himself for his weakness. He knew very well he should not have come here tonight, should not have given in to his need to at least look upon her once more. He had wrestled mightily with his wiser self, which told him sternly and in no uncertain terms the folly of his infatuation, but to no avail. I am indeed a weak vessel, he told himself sadly, and since this is now proven, there is but one thing left for me to do: I must take myself out of temptation's way.

His new parish was not above fifteen miles from this theater, but he felt it might as well be on the other side of the moon, so far was its milieu from this. Once there, moreover, he could immerse himself in the life of a small country village and forget London—and, in time, Miss Chamfreys.

As soon as the curtain came down, Robin left the theater and returned to Carrisbrooke House. There he ordered Strother to wake him at dawn, packed his case in readiness, and wrote a short note to Peter explaining that his impatience to take up his duties had overcome him to such an extent that he no longer could enjoy London and was therefore resolved to leave at once. He then retired to bed to toss sleeplessly for hours, unable to blot out his memories of Miss Chamfreys and of every word she had ever spoken to him.

14

Peter had found it difficult to follow the play, so compelling was Miss Pymbroke's presence in the box above him. But when at last Miss Chamfreys appeared, he forced himself to concentrate more fully on the stage. She was certainly quite beautiful, and spoke clearly, and sang her little song charmingly. Since there was little required of her in the way of acting, he was unable to make any judgment concerning her talent.

When the curtain came down, he glanced back at the box and saw that Mr. Bynge's party were on their feet, preparing to leave. Vanessa turned back at the last moment and smiled at him before she disappeared from view, which gladdened his heart to a remarkable degree. He went with a light step to seek out Miss Chamfreys backstage.

He found her seated between her parents, receiving visitors, and when he had at last made his way to the front of the crowd, she looked up and her eyes went wide with shock. Then she visibly pulled herself together and made a flustered introduction to her parents. Mrs. Chamfreys forgot all about Lord Threlfall, who was professing, once again, his ardent admiration while his eyes slid hungrily over Camilla.

"My lord, this is a great honor," Mrs. Chamfreys exclaimed, extending her hand. "Did you enjoy the performance?"

"Exceedingly, Madam. I congratulate you and your husband."

"Ah, too kind, sir. I fear our little girl was not shown to best advantage tonight."

"She was charming, and in that role she was all that was required," he replied smoothly.

"Of course it is, dear Lord Chance, how clever of you to have realized that. Please do not think we are in despair that darling Camilla does not wish to emulate her parents. She has other and unique talents which fit her for a very different sort of life than we have had. She—"

Here Camilla broke in hastily and rather rudely with a murmured "Excuse me, Mama," and taking Peter's arm, drew him away from her mother's embarrassing prattle and out of the crush of people waiting to speak to the Chamfreys. Mrs. Chamfreys did not so much as blink at this blatant disregard of the rules she had set for her daughter's behavior in the green room. After all, thought Mrs. Chamfreys, some leeway must be made for the heir of the Earl of Carrisbrooke. Only Lord Threlfall looked intensely displeased and turned an affronted eye upon Mrs. Chamfreys, who blandly ignored it.

"You are alone tonight, my lord?" Camilla asked when they had found a quiet corner.

"Alas, yes. I had thought to accompany my sister and Miss Pymbroke, but they were engaged. At least Miss Pymbroke was. As a matter of fact, she and her aunt were here tonight."

"And Lady Ann? She is well, I trust?"

"Yes, she only wanted a quiet evening at home."

"And—and—"

"My brother is not with me, Miss Chamfreys," he said teasingly.

She did not speak and her eyes slid away from his, but not before he saw her unhappiness in them. Well, well, he thought in some surprise, for while it was not difficult to accept that Robin had formed a *tendre* for Miss Chamfreys, however unsuitable, it was less easy to imagine the fashionable Miss Chamfreys returning his regard. Not that his brother was not more than worthy of it, being far beyond her in birth and breeding, and being also a kind and lovable creature. But he was sure there were men of more substance, and perhaps title as well, whom he would have thought she would be more apt to encourage. And yet, unless he was very much mistaken, there was some interest there. Or was it, after all, only the

nique of a pretty girl unused to beaux who did not seek her
company every day?

"I imagine my brother is preparing himself for his new
duties, Miss Chamfreys," he said comfortingly. "He is very
serious about his calling, you know."

"Yes, I know," she said faintly, not raising her eyes.

Oh, Lord, thought Peter ruefully, now what have I done?
Poked my nose into the middle of a lovers' quarrel, it looks
like. Attempting to make amends, he said, "I will tell him he
must concentrate on pleasure while he is in London. I will
call upon you tomorrow, if you will allow me, and make sure
he accompanies me."

Mrs. Chamfreys watched them covertly, breathless with
happiness. The Countess of Carrisbrooke, she thought testingly.
She felt the gooseflesh rise on her arms in thrilled anticipation.

Peter was handed his brother's note the following morning
at the breakfast table. He frowned over it in perplexity. Now
what the devil is Robin up to? he wondered.

"When did my brother leave, Strother?"

"At first light, m'lord. I woke him myself, at his request,
and saw to it he had a hot breakfast to set out on."

"Very good of you, Strother."

"He looked something peaky, if I may say so, m'lord."

"Too much dissipation, no doubt. Very well, thank you,
Strother."

Strother bowed and left. Peter read the note again. Impatient to take up his duties, indeed! he snorted his disbelief. A
deal of pious stuff and nonsense involving self-sacrifice more
like.

Peter fumed for some moments, for he was fond of his
brother and had wanted him to enjoy himself in London. Now
it seemed Robin had only stored up unhappiness for himself
by becoming too fond of Miss Chamfreys and then running
away before the disease became fatal. Peter could only pray it
was not already too late, having met Miss Chamfreys himself
and being very much aware of her charms. He could not
really blame Robin for succumbing to them, but for all that,
Peter saw little future in hoping for Robin's happiness in that
direction despite the unexpected side of her nature revealed to
him the night before.

This thought reminded him that he had asked to be allowed to pay a morning call upon her today in Robin's company. She would be expecting them and he, at least, must attend, if only to explain why Robin could not. He sighed, but rose to do his duty.

The day being fine, he elected to walk and was strolling leisurely along Bond Street when he saw Miss Pymbroke emerge from a shop ahead of him in company with her maid. Quickening his step, he came up with her and noticed in some surprise that the shop was that of a wigmaker.

"Good morning, Miss Pymbroke," he said.

Vanessa started, turned, and then blushed rosily. "Oh, ah, good morning, Lord Chance," she said, thrusting the box she carried into the hands of her maid. "You may wait in the carriage, Ellen. You are about very early, sir."

"And you are before me, madam. I hope you do not plan to cover such beautiful hair with a wig."

"Oh, well, a commission for an aunt—" she equivocated, hoping she would not be forced to tell an outright lie.

"Can I be of service?"

"Oh, no, though I thank you. But I am all finished now."

"Perhaps you would allow me to escort you back to Mrs. Clarence's?"

"Too kind, but you see I have my aunt's carriage. Perhaps I could be of service to you. Would you care to be dropped someplace?"

"Thank you, but as I am so near, I will continue on foot. I am on my way to visit the Chamfreys, who live only in the next square."

"The Chamfreys—oh, how nice," she exclaimed brightly. "Please take them my regards. I will bid you good day then."

She turned to her carriage at the curb and he accompanied her to assist her into it. She thanked him, smiled, and was driven away. She looked about with a great affectation of interest in the shops and passersby, but she actually saw nothing. She was too busy with her thoughts for that. Was it possible both brothers were now dangling after Miss Chamfreys? she wondered dismally. Both had attended, separately, Miss Chamfreys' performance the evening before. It was possible they were there only to see the parents perform, she thought, but then brushed this aside as unlikely. If that were so, then surely they would have spoken of it together and joined company to attend. They had not, and from what she could see at the time it seemed fairly certain they were each unaware of the other's presence. Of course, Lord Chance had seemed to spend almost as much time looking at her as he had looking at the stage, until Miss Chamfreys' late appearance, when he *had* seemed to be engrossed with her. Perhaps it was only then that he had been stricken with a need to further his acquaintance with her and here he was hurrying off first thing in the morning to pay a call upon her, no doubt hoping to arrive before his brother.

Men were so unimaginative, she sniffed contemptuously, they only notice a woman when they see other men find her attractive. But besides being attractive, Miss Chamfreys had the exotic glamour of the stage to offer, though by all accounts she had little interest in such a career for herself. Still . . .

Vanessa thought rather wistfully for a moment of Miss Chamfreys' beauty, then shook herself mentally. Papa would tell her sternly that she was being gooseish and losing her objectivity. She could almost hear him reminding her that while she was a very well-looking girl, good looks were nothing to congratulate oneself upon, being something one was born with, not something one accomplished for oneself. Vanessa agreed with this often-stated opinion of her father's, but felt rather disheartened than strengthened by the reflection, for she could hardly claim to have accomplished anything for herself yet. On the other hand, neither had Miss Chamfreys, unless one were inclined to count her brief strolls across the stage as a lady in the train of some nobleman. However, as Papa would say, this was all havering, since the question was not what Miss Chamfreys had accomplished, but what Miss Pymbroke had—or had not, as it happened. It was somewhat difficult, in any case, to know just what a woman could accomplish, beyond making a respectable marriage and producing an heir for her husband. When queried on this point, Papa had replied—rather vaguely it now seemed, though at the time it had appeared a grand response—that she was to be true to herself and all else would follow.

Vanessa's father, being the only parent she had, was all in

all to her, far above all other men in her estimation for wisdom and humor and wit. This was the first time she had been apart from him in her life, and while she was enjoying her London stay, she missed him sorely.

Despite the outraged protests of relatives and friends, he had taken her, at her mother's death when Vanessa was four, to the Continent with him and had been her constant companion and mentor ever since. He had taught her to ride and drive, to shoot and fish, to gamble and play cards. He had also given her her lessons, taught her how to comport herself and, when the time came, how to dance. If he had engaged in romantic liaisons during those years, it had been done with such extreme discretion that word of it had never reached Vanessa's ears. When she had told Peter her father had sent her to England in order to pursue an affair, she had only been attempting to shock him, to punch holes in his stuffy propriety.

She wondered if her papa would have approved of her behavior on that evening? She wished he were here now to talk it all over with. She desperately wanted to talk over with someone the problem of Lord Chance dangling after Miss Chamfreys, for she found it more displeasing than she would have thought possible only a week ago.

Not that I really care, she thought, throwing up her chin defiantly. I'm sure I wish him luck if that is where his fancy lies, though I cannot admire a man who treads on his brother's toes.

Peter, blithely unaware of the opprobrium being cast upon him by Miss Pymbroke, went happily on his way, thinking tomorrow would not be too soon to pay his respects to the Clarence household again. He found the Chamfreys' reception rooms already quite full of guests, all eager to pay homage to London's most famous acting couple. When he was announced, Mrs. Chamfreys came hurrying forward, her lovely face wreathed in smiles to welcome him.

"My lord, this is an honor you do us. Camilla said you might come, but I made sure you would be far too busy for us."

"Not at all, madam. I would not have missed it. However, my brother has decided to leave London and does not accompany me."

"Oh, how sad," replied Mrs. Chamfreys with automatic

politeness, though she had forgotten all about his brother. "Come, sir, allow me to present you to some of our friends."

She took his arm and led him about the room from group to group, talking charmingly all the while. After a time she excused herself, saying she would just step upstairs and fetch her daughter.

Camilla came hurrying into the room in a few moments, her glance raking the company eagerly. When she saw Peter, she came forward at once. "Lord Chance, how do you do? I am so glad you could come." Her eyes strayed about again.

"My brother did not come with me, Miss Chamfreys," he said quickly, sensing that she was looking for him.

Her eyes flew back to him. "Oh! Mama said only that you were here and I assumed—"

"He decided, quite suddenly apparently, that his new parish could not get along without him another day and left first thing this morning."

The eager light had now died completely from her beautiful dark eyes. She suddenly looked like a child in her disappointment and Peter was stunned by the realization that this sophisticated creature had fallen in love with the new young vicar of Medford Yatter. Really, he thought, it is too bad of Robin to dangle after the girl, engage her affections, and then disappear abruptly without even taking leave of her.

"Camilla, what must Lord Chance think of you," cried Mrs. Chamfreys, breaking into their silent confrontation abruptly, "standing there with that schoolgirl pout and not offering him any refreshments."

Camilla pulled herself together, smiled, and managed quite creditably to act the part of hostess. Peter longed to take his leave at once, feeling this presence was leading Mrs. Chamfreys into looking upon him as a suitor for her daughter. But however false his position, he felt it was kinder to stay a seemly length of time or cause Miss Chamfreys further distress, for her mother would be sure to scold her for chasing him away with her unhappy face.

So they both spoke with as much animation as possible for Mrs. Chamfreys' sake, and Peter told Camilla of Robin's new parish and how near it was to London. He suggested that in a few weeks, when Robin had had time to settle, he, Peter, would be happy to drive her there to visit.

She smiled rather wanly. "That is very kind of you, but I doubt your brother will have any further use for his London acquaintance. He must have found us sadly frivolous and lacking in interest to cut short his stay so suddenly. I would not dream of intruding upon him."

Peter assured her heartily that he, for one, had every intention of doing so, and he felt sure his sister would demand to be taken there, so he hoped Miss Chamfreys could be persuaded to change her mind and make one of the party. She did not give him any reason to be sanguine in this hope. Her mouth firmed into a straight line and a stubborn light replaced the hurt in her eyes.

He took his leave shortly after that and upon reaching home set down at once to write a letter to Robin demanding to know why he had felt it necessary to go haring off in that discourteous manner, without so much as taking farewell of any of his friends, in particular Miss Chamfreys, who, Peter assured him, was made very unhappy by his action.

That should bring him back to London with all speed, thought Peter with great satisfaction as he folded and sealed his letter, for though he had initially looked upon Miss Chamfreys with a somewhat jaundiced eye, he now found that he liked her very much indeed and would not be displeased to call her sister. What his parents might think of the match was another matter entirely, but he was sure they could not help being charmed by her as he was himself, once they had made her acquaintance. Of course, it was early days to be thinking of such things. The young people had known each other too short a time for any talk of marriage, but he decided that he would help them if he could. The problem, of course, would be Robin, who had clearly decided he must renounce his feelings for Miss Chamfreys, since he no doubt felt he could not offer such a girl a less-than-brilliant marriage to a country vicar.

But as Miss Pymbroke had reminded him, there was no reason to think that Robin would always remain a country vicar. After all, he was connected to some of the oldest and finest families in England, people of power and influence, and would not be a pauper either. All of this should go a long way toward appeasing Mrs. Chamfreys' ambitions.

15

Anyone in the vicinity of Mrs. Clarence's front door two mornings later might have had their curiosity piqued by the extreme care with which a well-dressed young gentleman in a well-cut coat, white muslin stock, gray nankeen breeches, and gleaming Hessian boots, slipped out and pulled the door closed softly behind him. This accomplished, the young man straightened, cocked his tall beaver hat at a jauntier angle on his brown curls, and strode off briskly down the street.

Fortunately no one was about, so Vanessa was able to effect her escape without observance. She had taken advantage of the fact that her aunt and Ann were both out of the house this morning. Claiming stacks of letters that must be answered, Vanessa had arranged to be left behind, dismissed her abigail, and set about transforming herself into a young gentleman. First the clothes she had acquired by claiming the needs of a fictitious young nephew. Then the brown wig she had purchased the day she had met Peter on his way to visit the Chamfreys. She had then clapped on her beaver hat and surveyed herself in the glass. A very elegant-looking young man, she had decided, though somewhat wanting in inches and a shade more youthful than she had hoped. Still, she thought she would have no difficulties. She had made sure the French window in the back drawing room was unlocked to facilitate her return, and she slipped out of the house when all the servants were in the back quarters.

Now as she marched down the street with long and what

she hoped were manly-looking strides, she looked boldly about, confident that her disguise was complete. She was heading in the direction of White's, hoping to encounter Mr. Bynge. She was aware of a number of curious, not to say interested, stares from young ladies she passed, and hoped it was because she was a handsome young man rather than a queer-looking one. Presently she saw Mr. Bynge sauntering along the pavement with an acquaintance. When they came abreast, she took off her hat and bowed. "Mr. Bynge."

Mr. Bynge, taken by surprise, halted and gaped for a moment before acknowledging the greeting. "Er, ah, sir?"

"You don't know me, of course. Allow me to introduce myself. Anstruther Portland. We last met when I was two, my mama says. But when she wrote your mama—they've kept up a correspondence for years, bosom bows, you know— anyway, when she wrote that I was coming up to London, your mama said I was to be sure to look you up."

"Oh, did she? Well, good, very good. I am, of course, delighted to meet you again. But might I ask how you, er, recognized me? I imagine I may have changed not a little since our first meeting, even if you managed to retain any clear memory of the event."

Vanessa managed a deep laugh. "Ah, very amusing, sir, you are a wit. Well, as a matter of fact, you were pointed out to me in the park one day, but as you were riding with a young lady at the time, I did not feel it quite the moment to force myself upon your attention. Very attractive gel, if you don't mind my saying so."

Mr. Bynge could not prevent a satisfied smirk at this comment. "Ah, yes, that would have been Miss Pymbroke. Most beautiful girl in London this Season."

Vanessa was forced to turn away to hide the blush she felt warming her face. She foresaw that one of her problems would be to deter any talk of women. Good heavens, what might she not hear? She had an idea men spoke quite freely among themselves about women. Not nice women, of course, that would have been ill-bred, but she had no wish to enter into any discussions about the other sort either.

She hastily pointed out a great raking bay being ridden down the street at that moment and began to discuss, quite knowledgeably, its good points. They went on to speak of horses in general, and from that to cockfights, which Mr. Bynge assured Mr. Portland he would be happy to take him to. This allowed Vanessa to bring up gambling and card playing, which led quite naturally to Mr. Bynge offering to take Mr. Portland to White's any evening he would care to go. They set the engagement for two night's hence and arranged to meet at nine o'clock in front of the club. Vanessa then made a very courteous farewell and set off back down the street. She hailed a hackney cab and instructed him to drive her home, though she got down two streets away from Mrs. Clarence's.

She slipped around the side of the house, found the unlocked French window, and slipped quietly in behind the drape—and froze! There were people in the room!

". . . to receive you here, Miss Clayton-Trees, but the drawing-room fire was smoking dreadfully and we had to get the sweep in to clean it."

"Think nothing of it, dear Mrs. Clarence. This is so much more cozy. How is dear Lady Ann—and your niece?"

"They are both very well. Will you take some refreshment?"

"No, no, I must not stay. So many calls to make, you know. I merely wanted to thank you for the delightful party. Such an amusing evening. Mr. Robin Chance and the little actress not exchanging so much as a word all evening, did you notice? So mysterious, when they had been getting along so famously not a week before at Mrs. Dewinter's masque."

"Miss Clayton-Trees, I really do not think—" Mrs. Clarence began repressively, but Miss Clayton-Trees rushed on unheeding.

"So amusing, really. You see, Miss Chamfreys and I were both wearing green dominoes and Mr. Chance clearly had been informed in advance by Miss Chamfreys of the colour of hers, for he came straight up to me and said—"

"I know you will forgive me, Miss Clayton-Trees, but I always lie down for a time after a morning excursion. It is my heart, you see. It begins to pound most unpleasantly."

"Oh, do forgive me, Mrs. Clarence. Of course, I will go at once. Please convey my regards to dear Lady Ann—and your niece, of course, and do—"

Still chattering, she was shown firmly out of the room by a determined Mrs. Clarence, and Vanessa let out a long breath.

"Poisonous creature," she muttered, tiptoeing to the door and peering carefully around it. She heard the front door close and the ponderous tread of her aunt mounting the stairs. When, faintly, she heard her aunt's bedroom door open and close, she slipped out of the room and ran lightly down the hall, up the stairs two at a time, and regained her room without encountering anyone.

She quickly stripped off her disguise and hid it away. While she struggled with the fastenings of her gown, she began to think over what she had heard Miss Clayton-Trees saying. She wished her aunt had not been quite so nice in refusing to listen to gossip, for it would have been interesting to learn more of the story about the Dewinters' ball. It was clear that Camilla had told Robin beforehand that she would be wearing a green domino and that Robin had approached Miss Clayton-Trees, unfortunately also in green, thinking that it was Miss Chamfreys. It was also clear that he had at last found the right domino and they had enjoyed each other's company. Then what had happened?

Now that she thought about the dinner party, she did recall noticing at one point that they seemed very quiet together, but when Camilla had left immediately after dinner, saying she had the headache, Vanessa had put it down to that. Now it seemed there was more to it than that. She briefly pondered the idea of attempting to get the whole story from Miss Clayton-Trees, who, Vanessa would be willing to wager, knew more about it than anyone but the couple themselves. She discarded the idea, for Miss Clayton-Trees was always at great pains to show her dislike of Vanessa Pymbroke and she could not think of any way of breaking down her resistance without using a great deal of hypocritical sweet-talk, which went too much against the grain for her to contemplate. Almost anyone else could, with no trouble at all, get the story out of her.

Like Anstruther Portland, for instance! Yes, indeed, Mr. Portland was just the article, for he could flatter and cajole as hypocritically as he liked—and practice his disguise at the same time. Miss Clayton-Trees rode every morning and Mr. Portland would contrive to meet her on the bridle path tomorrow morning. Vanessa jigged around the room in an impromptu little dance of excitement.

The next morning she rose very early, dressed in her costume, and tiptoed to the door. She inched it open and peered around—straight into the eyes of Ellen, one hand holding a jug of hot water, the other extended toward the doorknob. Ellen's eyes widened in shock at the sight of a gentleman in Miss Vanessa's bedroom and opened her mouth to scream.

"Ellen," hissed Vanessa, "don't scream. Do you not recognize me?" Ellen seemed incapable of response, so Vanessa pulled her gently into the room. "Ellen, it is only me in men's clothing. Please stop gaping that way. Here, I will take that jug before you drop it."

"What—why—is it really you, miss?"

"Of course it is."

"But what are you doing in them clothes?"

"Well, it is just—just a little joke I am going to play on someone."

"But it's not decent to go out like that. Showing your legs and all," protested a scandalized Ellen.

"No one will know who I am. Even you did not until I told you."

"I shall have to speak to the mistress—"

"Oh, Ellen, please do not. I promise you I will tell her myself—later. It is just that I have this small wager with someone that I can pass myself off as a gentleman—just as a joke, you see. No harm will come of it."

"Well, I'm sure I don't know, miss."

"Please, Ellen, please promise you will not say anything to my aunt. I will be back very soon and no one but you and my aunt will ever know anything about it. Please promise me."

"Very well, miss, but I don't like it one bit, and that's for sure."

Vanessa kissed her cheek and quickly slipped out of the room before Ellen could protest any further. She waited on the landing until she saw the front hall was clear, then ran down and out of the house. She made straight for a nearby stable to hire a horse, for of course she could not ride her own or one of her aunt's, lest they be recognized.

Soon she was cantering along, grateful to her father for having taught her to ride astride as well as sidesaddle, and to the early hour, which precluded the park from being over-

crowded. It took her longer than she had thought to find Miss
Clayton-Trees, and she had nearly reached the conclusion that
the woman had chosen today of all days not to ride, when she
espied her trotting along sedately, accompanied by a groom
who rode some way behind.

Vanessa rode boldly up to her and removed her hat for a
sweeping bow. "Good morning. A beautiful day for a ride, is
it not?"

Miss Clayton-Trees returned this pleasantry with a cold
stare, one eyebrow raised to register her surprise at this
presumption, and then rode on. Vanessa fell in beside her.

"Please forgive me, but I could not resist. To ride alone on
such a day is so boring, especially when there is such attractive company at hand. Allow me to introduce myself, since
there is no friend about to do it for me. Anstruther Portland
at your service."

Miss Clayton-Trees slid a glance at the gentleman, found
him presentable, and allowed a small relaxation of her rigid
posture. "You are very bold, sir."

"Ah, I have found one must be bold in this world when the
reason is compelling enough, or one would get nowhere.
Now, I saw you and, being an impulsive sort, decided I must
know you. After all, your man is there to protect you, should
I behave with any impropriety."

"You have already done so, sir, by approaching me at
all," she replied with a coy inflection that showed she was
not too displeased.

"And no harm has come of it. Indeed, only good, for now
we have both enlarged the circle of our acquaintance and we
each have someone to converse with as we ride, which is so
much nicer than riding alone, do you not agree?"

"Well, it might be so," she allowed.

"I would be truly honored to know your name." She gave
it to him and Vanessa exclaimed, "Why, can it be so? I
believe we have a mutual acquaintance in Mr. Robin Chance,
for he told me of a dinner party he had attended and mentioned your name."

"Oh, did he?" She bridled with pleasure. "Now, why
should he have done that, I wonder?"

"Why, I do not think we need be at a loss for the answer
to that, Miss Clayton-Trees," Vanessa replied gallantly, bend-

g upon her such an admiring look as to cause Miss Clayton-
Trees to drop her eyes to hide her happiness with the
ompliment.

Deftly Vanessa led her on to speak of Robin, Lord Peter,
Lady Ann, and heard herself castigated as a hoydenish flirt
nd Miss Chamfreys designated ''the little actress'' whose
parents hoped to marry her to a title but who was not indis-
osed to dalliance if the opportunity arose. When Vanessa
poked shocked and pretended some disbelief, Miss Clayton-
Trees went on with relish to tell the story of the masquerade
all as far as it obtained to Robin and Camilla, not omitting
er own part in the affair, which she described with self-
ighteousness.

Carefully disguising her disgust, Vanessa congratulated Miss
Clayton-Trees upon her cleverness in recognizing Mrs.
Chamfreys and her wisdom in dropping a word in that lady's
ar regarding the deception that was being practiced upon her
y her daughter, and finally, her own happiness that Robin
hance had been saved from such an inappropriate liaison.

As soon as possible after she had the entire story, she
managed to make a graceful escape and made her way with
ll speed back to her aunt's house, her mind seething with
idignation at all she had learned.

There was little doubt in her mind that due to Miss Clayton-
Trees' interference, Mrs. Chamfreys had taken matters into
er own hands. What action she had taken, Vanessa could not
now, but its effectiveness was evident.

Oh, that dreadful creature, she fumed, remembering Miss
Clayton-Trees' self-congratulatory recital of her actions.
Vanessa, being an impulsive girl, was sorely tempted to go at
nce and reveal her duplicity to Camilla Chamfreys. But the
ifficulty of raising such a subject, so far from being any
usiness of Vanessa's, caused her to think again, and she
ealized it was impossible unless Camilla confided to her that
 problem existed. It might very well be that Camilla had no
roblem, that she herself had, for reasons of her own, de-
ided to spurn Robin's suit. Oh, dear, it was all so difficult.

16

Ann lay comfortably ensconsed on a chaise before a cheerfully burning fire in her bedroom, the rain spattering occasionally against the windowpane emphasizing her coziness. It was the first rain in several weeks of fine spring weather and a good day to stay at home and recoup one's strength. This past week had been filled with social events and had included several drives with Mr. Rivers. He had also turned up at two evening parties she had attended and made the evening more pleasant for her with his calm attentiveness. He had confessed to her that he had not gone into society since the death of his wife, being for the most part at his country estate for his children's sake.

"And have you missed society?" she had asked.

"Not in the least," had been his prompt reply. "I was never much given to parties and entertainments, except in my own home."

"But you seem to be going about a great deal now, Mr Rivers."

"That is because I am enjoying the company I find these days," he had replied, smiling so meaningfully that she had reddened and felt uncomfortable, at the same time she felt gratified. Still, she must be very careful not to encourage him in the future, for it would never do to allow him to form an attachment. She felt sure his present feeling was mainly one of gratitude to her for her service to his son, and while she enjoyed his company and the way he had of always seeming to know when she needed to sit down or have a cup of lemonade and producing the chair or the drink without the least fuss, she had no intention of allowing herself to become too accustomed to it.

A tap at the door interrupted these musings and Ellen entered to announce that Mr. Dalzell had called and asked if he might see her privately. He had been shown into the back drawing room.

Ann rose eagerly and went to smooth her hair before the glass before hurrying to meet him. "Giles," she cried with a glad smile as she entered the room, "how I shall scold you! Where have you been since the night of our dinner party? No one has seen you about at all."

"I have been to Chance Court," he said, taking the hands she held out to him.

"Oh?" Her smile changed to a somewhat puzzled look. She saw that his face was tense, the skin looking taut and stretched over the bones, and he was pale, extremely pale. "Why, Giles—what is it? Has something happened? Mama?"

"She is well. Nothing has happened."

"Then why do you look so? And why—"

"I went to see your father."

"To see Papa?" She was even more bewildered, for Giles and her papa had never been known to agree on anything, and of late exchanged only the briefest acknowledgments of each other's presence when they met.

"Please, Ann, come and sit down. I must speak to you." He led her to a sofa and sat down with her, then almost immediately rose again, paced to the fireplace, and ran his hand distractedly through his dark hair.

"Giles, you are frightening me," Ann said at last, her eyes wide with apprehension, for though she was accustomed to his strange starts and moods, she had never seen him like this, wound up to the shattering point, eyes glittering strangely in his white face and not quite meeting her own. He seemed intense and closed off in some way, so that she could not understand him as she could most of the time.

He turned abruptly at her words and came to sit beside her again. "Forgive me, I am all nerves, as you shall understand in a moment. I went to see your father, Ann, to—to ask his permission to address you."

Ann felt for a moment that she had just sustained a sharp

blow to the solar plexus. Her mouth opened and closed several times in a ridiculous way while she attempted to draw in a breath. Finally she managed to gasp, "My—my papa—what did he—"

"Well, he consented, of course, or I should not be here. He was not very happy about it, nor was your mother, as I am sure will come as no very great surprise to you. But he said they had resigned themselves to the inevitability of the match some time ago." He halted, staring into space while he raked his hand again through his hair as though in amazement at this last statement.

She was in too much agitation herself to ponder this, but because she knew him and his every expression so well, she noted it unconsciously. After a moment he seemed to become aware of her again and said stiffly, "So I came to you at once to ask if you would—would marry me."

The world did not spin; she did not feel faint, turn pale, or burst into tears of happiness. After all the years of dreams of just this moment, she felt curiously detached from what was happening. She said slowly, "I would you had spoken of your feelings for me, Giles, before you spoke of marriage."

"My feelings? But you know those by now, surely!"

"I know that we have always been friends, my dear, but not—" She stopped, unable to utter the words, "but not whether you love me as I would have my husband love me." She looked away so he could not see her eyes, which she was afraid might exhibit a humiliatingly abject pleading.

"I must say I never expected this missish, romantical behavior from you, Ann," he snapped in exasperation. "I would have thought—"

"What? That I would leap at the chance? It is rather late in my life for any such girlish leaping," she replied with some asperity at his tone.

"I suppose you mean by that that I have waited overlong," he said, going white again, recalled to his duty. "If you can forgive me for that, I hope you will consider my proposal and know that I will try to take care of you always."

She felt a lump rise in her throat, but swallowed it resolutely. "After all this time, I wonder what can have brought you to this now," she said softly, "for I must tell you that I cannot feel it is giving you any joy."

"You know I am not good at all this romantical farrididdle women expect, Ann, and this is, after all, a momentous step for me. I never thought to—"

"To marry?" she finished for him. "Or to marry me?"

"There is no other woman in the world I would even consider," he burst out, then pulled himself up short, turned slightly away, and began again. "Come now, Ann, what is all this about? I have come to ask for your hand in marriage, an event that has evidently been expected anytime this past age by everyone, even your parents, and when I finally realize how derelict I have been, you put me through all this—this nonsense. I vow, I expect any moment some speech from you about how aware you are of the honor I have done you, but it is so sudden, et cetera, just as though we had not played together since we were still practically in leading strings. You, who know me better than anyone in the world, must know how difficult this sort of thing is for me."

"Yes—yes, I do know, which makes me wonder just *why* you are doing it now." She had turned her face away, her head drooping on her slender neck, her voice strangled, barely audible to him.

His heart smote him. How the devil had it come about that he, of all people, was making her so unhappy? He went up to her and, with a finger beneath her chin, tilted her face up to his own. "I think you forget that you have already promised to marry me—many years ago," he said gently.

She smiled tremulously. "You—you remember that?"

"Could I forget my first proposal?" He laughed.

"I did *not* propose," she protested, smiling.

"But you swore to marry no other. However, I would not hold you to a promise made when you were no more than twelve and trying to comfort an unhappy boy. If there is someone else . . ."

"No, but—"

"Then have done with all this havering and give me an answer. If you do not care for it, why, only say so, it will make no difference between us, as you must know. You will still be my dearest friend. Now, what is it to be?"

"It will be yes, Giles."

He pulled her to her feet and for one instant she thought he was going to take her into his arms, but he only planted a chaste kiss on her brow and patted her shoulder bracingly. "There, then, that is settled. You must think when you want it to be; I know there will be your bride clothes to purchase and all sorts of fuss that women make over these affairs. I will, of course, send an announcement to the *Gazette*."

"No—no, do not do so yet, Giles. Let it be only between ourselves for now. I will speak to Peter and Robin, of course."

He agreed to this and very shortly after made his departure. As he strode off up the street, he admitted to himself it was more like his escape. He had done it! He had committed himself. There was now no turning back. He felt a wave of black depression rising with the thought, threatening to engulf him, but with an effort he managed to throw it off. He knew that to submit to it was the worst thing he could do for himself.

Miss Clayton-Trees' disclosures had come as a shattering revelation to him. It had never occurred to him that Ann could have such feelings for him. He had always treasured their friendship, so steady, so warm, but unemotional. He had taken for granted that she loved him as he loved her, but only as a brother and sister with a closer bond than most.

Miss Clayton-Trees' manner—amused, casual—had done more to convince him of the truth of her words than anything else could have done. After he had become convinced, there seemed only one course open to him as an honorable man. He could not allow Ann to suffer. If she expected this of him, then of course he must give it to her. He had therefore set off at once for Chance Court and requested her father's permission to address her. This required that he overcome a natural revulsion against marriage in general, against marriage to Ann in particular, as being almost unnatural, and against having to ask anything of Lord Carrisbrooke, who had never bothered to conceal his scorn for a boy who preferred reading, dreaming, and the company of a girl to the usual manly pursuits. Fortunately, upon his arrival, he found Lord Carrisbrooke away for several days and was received by my lady.

"Dearest Giles, this is a happy surprise," she had greeted him warmly, holding out her arms to embrace him. She then looked him over critically. "You are looking somewhat pulled, my boy. Perhaps you will be well advised to make a long visit and get some proper rest.''

Within a quarter of an hour she had had the whole story from him and advised him to let her speak to her husband first. ''For I will not conceal from you that he will not be happy about this. Nor, for that matter, am I. Not, my dear, for any fault in you. I think you know I have always been fond of you. No, it is for Ann's sake. You are aware that she has always been delicate—her heart, you know—and though I did hope for a time that she would grow out of it, she never has really been strong. I do not think, you know, that marriage for her could be quite what it is for most women, if you take my meaning.''

He had taken her meaning very well, and had not been dismayed—rather the reverse, in fact, for it seemed to him that if Ann wanted to marry it was just as well that she wanted to marry him, a man who would not expect, or even want, heirs.

Lady Carrisbrooke had continued. ''Of course, I have always known of her feelings for you. That, too, I thought she would grow out of, but as we both know, she has not. Well, well, I suppose if she must have you, she must, for I would have her know all the happiness possible. Carrisbrooke will disapprove, but I suppose I know by now how to talk him around.''

So it was that when Giles came to speak to Lord Carrisbrooke, a grudging consent was given and Giles set forth for London at once to face the equally disquieting task of making his proposal in form to Ann. He had no very clear idea of how he was going to set about this, but was grimly determined to carry it through, for he could not bear the thought of his dear Ann suffering in any way, nor could he bear for her to endure any longer the humiliation of having it known that she had been expecting a proposal from him for years. It shocked him to realize that he was so selfish that he had never realized what seemingly was perfectly clear to everyone else.

Well, now it was accomplished. He had proposed and been accepted. He plodded on blindly, unaware of the rain soaking through his coat and dripping from the brim of his tall beaver hat.

As for Ann, she sat on in the back drawing room, staring into space, attempting to sort out her feelings. She felt curiously drained, certainly not experiencing any of the elation she would have expected to feel at this moment. She was now formally betrothed to Giles Dalzell. She repeated this over and over to herself, but it produced nothing, although she realized after a time that her face was wet with tears that welled up without any conscious volition on her part and streamed down her cheeks unheeded. She found her handkerchief and wiped them away but still they came. She could not stop them. Tears of happiness, she told herself, and why not? Had she not been given, at long last, her dearest wish?

I must stop this foolishness and be practical, she thought. I must write to Mama at once and send a note around to Peter and Robin asking them to call so that I can tell them the news. She rose and penned a short note to them, mopping her face to keep from blotching the paper.

She rang for Hay and asked him to see that her note was taken around at once to Carrisbrooke House. He accepted the missive and his instructions without so much as a flicker of the eyelid to betray his awareness of her condition. When the door closed behind him, she sat down to the desk again and drew a sheet of paper to her and dipped her pen, but beyond the opening greeting to her Dearest Mama, the page remained blank. After ten minutes she put it aside for a time when her thoughts had settled and hurried up to her room, praying she would meet no one on the way, and bathed her eyes again and again in cold water. By the time a servant came to announce Lord Chance she had regained control of herself and was able to go to him with a semblance of calm.

"Your note caught me just as I was leaving the house," he said, coming across the room to take her hands, "so I came at once. I hope nothing is amiss?"

"No, no. It is only that I—I have news that I wanted you to be the first to hear. Giles has proposed—and I have accepted him."

"Giles has— Good Lord, I mean, you have taken me by surprise, sister," Peter floundered, between shock and dismay. "What of Papa? Has he consented to this?"

"Giles went first to Chance Court for Papa's permission to address me."

"Very proper, but not, I would have thought, Giles' usual style."

"And what is that, if you please?" she snapped somewhat defensively.

"Now, do not fly up into the boughs. I meant only that I would have thought he was too much a romanticist to heed such niceties."

"Well, it seems you are wrong. In fact," she smiled ruefully, "he is the very opposite of the image he presents to the world. Not in the least romantic."

"My dear, I know you—I mean, are you sure this is the right thing?" Peter had begun to say he knew it was what she had always hoped for, but realized in time it would hardly be kind to let her know he had been aware of her feelings for Giles. She would not appreciate anything that smacked of pity.

"Ye-es," she said slowly; then, aware that she sounded less than convinced, she forced a smile and said, "Yes, of course, or I should not have accepted him."

"Then, I will be the first to wish you happy, dearest Ann," he said at once, pulling her into his arms and hugging her warmly.

"Thank you—oh!" She pulled away. "But where is Robin?"

"Oh, the silly juggins went haring off to his new parish. Left me a note about the call of duty—silly nonsense, if you ask me. I think it was the result of some little lovers' quarrel between himself and Miss Chamfreys. You will have to write him your news. Or better still, why do we not drive down to visit him? It is a short journey. We could get there in no more than an hour and a half, have a visit, and drive back the same day, if it does not tire you too much. We could make up a party for the excursion if you like. Take along Giles and Miss Chamfreys and Miss Pymbroke."

"Oh, yes, Peter, that would be nice. I should like it of all things."

"Do the ladies here know your news yet?"

"No, only you. I asked Giles if we could keep it just between ourselves, except for my family, of course. I suppose he will write to his father of it, but it will take weeks for him to get the letter. But I think now I must tell Mrs. Clarence and Vanessa. After all, it has happened while I am their guest and in their house. Yes, I will tell them. Giles will not mind, I know.''

"Shall we make our excursion the day after tomorrow if the weather clears?''

"If it is agreeable to everyone. I will ask Vanessa and Giles. Shall I write a note to Miss Chamfreys?''

"That will probably be the best thing. Her mother is more likely to allow it if you request it.'' He thought such a request coming from him would only encourage Mrs. Chamfreys' ambitions concerning himself.

He took his leave of Ann and went away, trying to take a positive view of her betrothal. He had nothing against Dalzell, though they had never been close as boys or as grown-up men, and Lord Carrisbrooke had consented and, most important of all, Ann wanted him. Beyond that, though Giles could not be accounted a wealthy man, he certainly had enough to give Ann all the comforts she was accustomed to, and was not known to be a gambler, a drinker, or a womanizer. Still, Peter could not pretend the match brought him any great happiness.

Mrs. Clarence's reaction was not dissimilar when she was told the news, for try as she might, she could not picture any lasting pleasure in it for either of them. Giles, she had decided upon their first meeting, was not a man who cared for women in general, with the exception of Ann Chance. Even there, he had never betrayed any signs of a man in love in Mrs. Clarence's presence, and while this was not a necessary ingredient for a good marriage, in Ann's case, Mrs. Clarence felt it most definitely was. Ann, she felt, was of a romantic and passionate nature, and love in marriage was necessary to her. The proposal might convince her for a time that he did indeed love her, but she would come to see that it was not the sort of love she had thought it and be very unhappy. However, Mrs. Clarence made all the suitable responses and kept her own counsel. She never believed in interfering.

Vanessa had no such reservations. If her dear Ann was happy, so was she. She bubbled over with an ebullience that covered up the fact that neither of the other two women were quite able to match her excitement.

17

The party that finally set forth for Medford Yatter two days later to visit Robin was much smaller than had originally been planned, since Miss Chamfreys had very politely but firmly declined the invitation, and Giles had declared that, having just returned from the country, he had no desire to go again, and besides, he was too far behind in his play to be able to contemplate such an expedition.

The weather held fine and Vanessa and Ann were driven off in Mrs. Clarence's barouche, with Peter riding beside the carriage. The girls talked together from time to time, with long spaces of comfortable silence between them. Ann was content to enjoy the country air and the spring countryside around them, while Vanessa was much preoccupied with the enterprise she had planned for the evening when Anstruther Portland was to make his appearance at White's with Mr. Bynge.

Peter had written to Robin to expect them and he came out at once to greet them when the carriage turned into the drive. He told himself that he was not disappointed when he saw that Camilla was not one of the party, for he had known all along that she would not come, but nevertheless the sunny day dulled and turned gray for him. He covered his unhappiness with a great bustling of greeting and inquiries about the drive, ushering them all inside busily, calling for refreshments to be brought, and insisting upon showing them over the house, a solidly built mansion of some twelve or so rooms.

"I rather rattle around in it now, and I have had little time to make any improvements in the furnishings. Mama threatens to come and decorate it properly," he smiled, "and no doubt it could use her help. The curtains and carpets are sadly threadbare, but you must take me as you find me."

They all trooped around, upstairs and down, before settling in the drawing room, where they were served wine and cakes and Ann told Robin of her engagement. He received the news with every sign of happiness, but when the two girls had been taken upstairs by his housekeeper to wash their hands and smooth their hair, he expressed himself more openly to his brother.

"I am surprised that Papa consented, for I am sure he has always been dead set against the match."

"I expect Mama talked him around. After all, Ann is five and twenty and has never accepted any of her other suitors, and Mama would always try to give Ann what she wants."

"Then I expect we must look upon it in that way also, though he is not exactly what I— Still, he is a good man and he cares for her."

When the women came down again, they all set off to see the church, an extremely old Norman structure, with, inside, several effigies of long-dead lords and their ladies lying serenely atop their sarcophagi, and afterward to explore the village, so small that after a very short walk they found themselves walking along the road lined with hedgerows white with may blossoms, and bluebells swaying in the light breeze in the fields beyond.

Vanessa fell behind with Robin on purpose and said quite casually, "I know you must be disappointed that Miss Chamfreys could not accompany us today, Robin."

He said, after a long moment of silence, "Why, no, I cannot say that I expected her to come, so I was not disappointed when she did not."

"I am sure she would have come if she could. Perhaps her mother prevented it. She keeps Camilla on a very tight rein, you know." He did not reply to this, and after another long silence, she peeked up at him from beneath the brim of her bonnet and saw that his face was set and unhappy. She said, "If you would care to write to her, I could undertake to deliver a letter to her privately."

"No, though I thank you for the kind thought. It is not her mother who prevents her from seeing me. Miss Chamfreys herself has refused. I called upon her four mornings in a row before I left London and was denied, though I was quite sure she was at home. That seems very definite to me."

"Was this after the Dewinters' party?"

He looked at her in surprise. "Why, yes. Though, how could you know?"

"Only that someone mentioned seeing you at the ball," she said hastily. "Tell me, are there any assemblies in the neighborhood?"

"Well, there is one in Stokerton, but I doubt I will have any time for dancing, nor much inclination."

Ann and Peter had turned back and Ann came to take Robin's arm for the return walk. Peter and Vanessa fell behind when Peter stopped to pick a small bouquet of violets, which he presented to Vanessa with a bow. "They should be in an ivory holder, I suppose, but perhaps you will forgive the omission."

"I think they look delightful in their own green leaves. A lovely gift, and I thank you, sir."

"Only the first, I hope. Now, tell me, what had my brother to say for himself?"

"Very little, but enough to show he is very unhappy. It seems he called a number of times upon Camilla before he left London and was not received."

"He should not have given up so easily. I would take my oath Miss Chamfreys cares for him more than a little. But perhaps a spell down here will help him to see the light and he will go back to press his suit. Enough of that. I really wanted to ask you if you are going to Almack's tonight, and if so, will you save two dances for me?"

"Well—I would, of course, but we do not go."

"What, the first night of the Season? Do not tell me you have not had vouchers?"

"Oh, yes, of course, but Ann did not feel she would be equal to it after today's excursion and I thought I would prefer to go with her," she finished lamely, wishing heartily that she had not arranged to meet Mr. Bynge tonight.

He grimaced with dismay. "And here I promised Lady Castlereagh that I would be there, for I was sure you and Ann would go. The devil's in it but I must go or she will never forgive me. I shall without a doubt be inexpressibly bored now.''

She twirled her little bouquet of violets and felt too flustered to know what to reply to this. At the same time she was glad to know that there was no possibility of coming face-to-face with him at White's tonight.

Ann was so weary when they reached London again that she declared she was going straight to her bed and would ask for a light dinner on a tray in her room. Vanessa and Mrs. Clarence dined together, and Vanessa, pleading sleepiness from so much country air, went up to her room at half-past eight.

She changed into her male attire and presently, when she heard Mrs. Clarence's bedroom door close, slipped out of the house by the French window in the back drawing room, leaving it unlatched for her return, and made all haste by hackney cab to White's. She found Mr. Bynge on the pavement outside conversing with a friend.

"Ah, there you are, Mr. Portland. Thought you had changed your mind.''

"No, no, only a dinner with my aunt that held me up a bit. Sorry to have kept you waiting.''

"Not to worry, it was but a few moments. Now, come along in. I hope you are prepared for some deep play. These fellows take their cards seriously. What is your pleasure, piquet, whist, faro, deep basset, dicing?''

Vanessa was too interested in gazing about to reply and Mr. Bynge smiled in indulgent amusement. He was a good-natured young man and glad to provide an evening's entertainment to this grass-green lad from the country. They wandered from room to room and Mr. Portland was introduced to all Mr. Bynge's acquaintances and acquitted himself without embarrassing his host. They finally entered a room where a gentleman was just leaving a card table where three other men still sat.

"Here, Bynge, just the chap we need. Have a few rubbers of whist with us,'' one man called out.

"Oh, no, you know full well it has never been my game. Allow me to introduce my friend, Mr. Portland. Mr. Portland, Lord Gale, Mr. Rembling, and Mr. Thatch. Perhaps you would care to play whist with these gentlemen, Mr. Portland?''

Vanessa, bowing right and left to acknowledge the introductions, agreed that it would be her pleasure, and seated herself in the vacant chair. Mr. Bynge, feeling that he had done his duty for the time and could now amuse himself, left the room as the stakes were announced and the deal began. For himself the rattle of the dice in the cup called to him, and he found his way unerringly to the game. The holder of the bank offered to throw Mr. Bynge for it; Mr. Bynge won the throw and settled himself to a very agreeable winning streak. At least an hour must have passed thus pleasantly before a servant came hurrying in to whisper in his ear. Mr. Bynge rose in shock, shoved the bank at his nearest neighbor, saying, ''Here, Wantaugh, take charge, something urgent has come up,'' and hurried from the room to a chorus of protest, his mind filled with horror at the message he had received: ''Your guest, sir, has just been challenged to a duel. I think you had better come at once.''

He rushed into the card room to find an angry, red-faced Mr. Thatch being entreated by the other two players to be calm, while Mr. Portland, his face drained to a green-white color, stood rigidly beside the table.

''By God, I'll be damned if I retract it! He has accused me of cheating and I will have satisfaction,'' shouted Mr. Thatch, brushing aside his friends' soothing hands.

''What in God's name has happened?'' cried a horrified Mr. Bynge.

''Your friend has accused me of cheating, sir,'' shouted Mr. Thatch.

''No, sir, I did not,'' said Vanessa through stiff lips. ''I said you could not have two aces when each of the rest of us was holding one.''

''Really, Thatch, he is right, you know. There are only four in the deck,'' said Lord Gale. ''How *did* you come by the fifth ace?''

''Are you accusing me now? If so, I shall be happy to call you out also,'' blustered Mr. Thatch.

''No, no, my dear fellow. You must not be so hasty-tempered. I only asked, just as the lad did. Perhaps the pack had five aces in it by mistake,'' replied Lord Gale pacifically.

"Then why did we not notice it in the previous hands?" queried Mr. Rembling hesitantly.

"I'll be damned if I'll stand about any longer to be insulted. Mr. Portland, name your second."

Gervase Bynge promptly stepped to Vanessa's side. "Naturally I stand with my friend, but I cannot believe you are serious about this, Thatch. Why, this is a scarce-grown boy and—"

"Then he should not be playing with men and making accusations. Of course, if he would care to retract it—" replied Mr. Thatch in a hard voice.

"I made no accusation, sir, but I will not retract my question. You could not have been dealt two aces, so where did it come from?" Vanessa's voice could not help betraying the fact that she was trembling all over, but she stood firm, her head up, not taking her eyes from the man's face.

"Very well, if you will have it so. Will you second me, Mr. Rembling?"

"No, sir, I will not. It is against the law, for one thing; the boy's too young, for another; and last, you have not answered the question to my satisfaction."

"Lord Gale?" Mr. Thatch turned to him challengingly.

"I must decline also," declared Lord Gale simply.

"Very well. Now I know my friends. I will provide my second and the pistols and meet you at six in the morning at Burney's Field, Mr. Portland. You know it?"

"I will find it," she said shortly. "Gentlemen"—she bowed to the other two—"a pleasure to make your acquaintance. Good night." She turned on her heel and left the room, Mr. Bynge following. They left the club in silence and were some way down the street before Mr. Bynge spoke.

"This is insanity," he burst out. "You cannot go through with it. Why, the man is said to be a crack shot."

"I am reputed to be a fair shot myself," replied Vanessa.

"But—but, you are only a boy. I cannot allow it. I would never forgive myself if— I feel responsible! I should never have left you with them. How could I ever explain it to your parents? No, no, it must stop. I will go to him, reason with him—"

"If reason were possible, I would not now be meeting him. The man clearly cheated. We all knew it. He knows we know it. If he backs down now, it would be as good as an admission and the whole town will know of it.''

"But you will be killed for sure. Oh, God, how could I have been so stupid as to take you there in the first place? What shall I do? God in heaven, what shall I *do*?''

Vanessa's conscience gave a violent twinge, for the man was so genuinely distressed, for her as well as for himself, and she was solely responsible for the predicament in which he found himself. Neither of them, of course, had envisioned anything so unlikely as a duel resulting from an innocent visit to White's, and had she not been so unfortunate as to play cards with a cheat, all would have been well and the evening would have been just the lark she had meant it to be. Now, she was responsible for dragging him into a most unsavory, as well as unlawful, duel, and he would be held to account if anything should happen to her.

"Mr. Bynge, I will never forget that you came forward for me back there, but of course I have no intention of allowing you to go on with it. There is no need for you to become involved at all. I am going to bid you good night now and I want you to put the entire business out of your mind.''

"Then you will not meet him?''

"Well, I think I must do so, but I will not allow you to accompany me.''

"And a pretty creature you must think me to suppose that I will just quietly do as you bid and go home to a good night's sleep," he said indignantly.

They argued the point for a few minutes, but Mr. Bynge held firm to his resolution and Vanessa had to give in finally. She decided that the least she owed the man for his steadfastness and friendship was honesty.

"Mr. Bynge, I am very much afraid the situation is even worse than you suppose it to be. You see, I am not really Anstruther Portland.''

"Not—''

"No," she said, squaring her shoulders for courage. "I am Vanessa Pymbroke.''

His eyes nearly started from his head as he took in the import of her words. At last he croaked in a harsh whisper, "You cannot be serious. This is some silly joke, is it not?''

"No, Mr. Bynge, it is not. I am very sorry to have played

such a trick on you. Very sorry indeed, but you must believe that I never dreamed my little masquerade would end up so disastrously.''

''Then—then that is it. There is no question now. I will simply go to him and explain—''

''No! I could not allow you to do that. Think what would happen. Thatch would be very angry and would spread the story to cover up his own cheating. Everyone would be sure to think you knew all along who I was. You would be asked to resign the club and be ostracized by all your friends.''

''Oh, Lord,'' moaned Mr. Bynge, recognizing the truth of this statement. He suddenly saw a picture in his mind of his father's face, should this escapade come to his ears, and the elder Bynge being a man of uncertain temper and stern moral rectitude, the picture was not a pleasant one.

''So, you see, the business must go forward. If the worst should happen and my identity is discovered, you will surely be believed when you claim you did not know, for no one would believe you would have allowed a female to participate in a duel, had you been aware of my true identity.''

This seemed irrefutable logic to Mr. Bynge in his present state of panic and befuddlement. ''Then—then we must—''

''Yes. We must.''

''Very well. I will call for you at five-thirty.''

''No—no,'' she said hastily, ''that will not be necessary. I will make my own way there and meet you at a quarter of the hour.''

Though he was determined to call for her, she prevailed at last and the arrangements were made. Vanessa espied a hackney cab and hailed it. ''Good night, then, Mr. Bynge. Do not be too distressed. I really am a very good shot, you know. My papa saw to that. And I am not afraid to meet him. I have a feeling his reputation as a crack shot may be just as imaginary as his prowess at cards. It is all done by cheating.''

Despite these brave words and a jaunty wave of the hand as she was driven away, she was a very frightened girl. This time she had got herself into a real corner, a life-and-death situation with nothing larkish about it. What her father would say if— Oh, Lord, she thought, I must write him a letter tonight, and one to poor Aunt Clarence— What am I to say to them? Then, quite clearly, the face of Lord Chance came into her mind, angry as it was that day when she stopped the horse. He had forgiven her that escapade, but this one he would never forgive. Her shoulders slumped with unhappiness and weariness.

When she was a square away from her aunt's house, she asked to be put down. As she paid the driver, she asked if he would be willing to come to this same spot to pick her up at five-thirty in the morning. He frowned. She offered to pay him double for the early hour and he finally agreed. She ran around the house, slipped inside and back up to her own room. Once inside, she fell across the bed just as she was and, incredibly, dozed off, muscles too long held tense jerking her into consciousness from time to time, though she never came fully awake.

She woke slowly, chilled and stiff, to find her candle guttering out. She rose groggily to get and light another, seeing herself, with a shock of disbelief, in the glass. She had not even removed her wig, much less her clothes. They were slightly rumpled and she wondered if Thatch would guess that she had slept in them, or sneer at her for wearing the same coat and trousers she had worn the day before.

Good Lord, she thought, what possible difference can it make what he thinks? She found her little pocket watch and saw that it was half-past four. No point in thinking of clothes now. She had her letters to write. She made them as lighthearted as she could, not mentioning Mr. Bynge's name, and leaving them with her love and gratitude for all they had done for her.

She sealed them up and left them on her blotter, blew out the candle, and went to sit at the window until it was time to leave. She hoped the cabman would not fail her. She hoped her courage would not fail her. She wished desperately for the comfort of a strong masculine shoulder to cry on.

18

Mr. Bynge watched the carriage bearing Miss Pymbroke out of sight with great foreboding. He finally turned away, feeling helpless and ineffectual, thrust his hands deep into his pockets, and wandered off down the street. He walked aimlessly, blindly, his mind turning the problem over and over, presenting him with dialogue that might have saved the situation had he been quick-witted enough to think of it at the appropriate moment: placatory phrases that might have cooled Thatch's ire, arguments that might have rallied Rembling or Gale to take a firmer stand, refutations of Miss Pymbroke's own logical-seeming reasons on why she must go through with it. As he thought more on her reasoning, it became apparent to him that it all had to do with saving himself from embarrassment and censure.

Good God, he thought wildly, am I to allow her to die in order to save me from embarrassment? No! He must do something, speak to someone and take advice. But who could he turn to? There were no gentlemen in the Clarence household, and though for one wild moment he contemplated going to Mrs. Clarence, he abandoned the idea after trying to imagine what the consequences might be of rousing her from her bed at this hour with such news. Why, the woman might have hysterics, might have a seizure, and what Miss Pymbroke would think of him for betraying her didn't bear thinking of. Of the people close to her, there remained only Lady Ann, but her health was so poor he could not dream of troubling her, and besides, what could Lady Ann say to persuade Miss

Pymbroke to change her mind that he had not already said.

He wandered on, sinking further and further into despondency, all his thinking always circling back upon itself frustratingly, for he could think of no solution. A door opened up the street ahead of him, throwing a patch of light across the sidewalk that caused him to raise his eyes from the cobblestones at his feet. He saw a man in evening dress come out the door and realized he was approaching Almack's. A porter hurried ahead of the gentleman to summon up his carriage, and as the man awaited it, he turned in Mr. Bynge's direction. It was Lord Chance. Without even a pause for thought Mr. Bynge called out to him as he began to run forward. Many reasons flashing instantaneously through impelled him: his respect for Lord Chance as a man of decision and principle; Lord Chance's relationship to Lady Ann, who was Miss Pymbroke's best friend; and his knowledge, hitherto resented, that Lord Chance had a personal interest in Miss Pymbroke.

He panted up to Peter and gasped, "I must speak to you privately, sir, on a matter of great urgency!"

Peter studied the pale face, the entreating eyes, and said, "Very well, here is my carriage. In you go. We will be quite private."

They climbed in and were driven off. Several pregnant moments passed in silence as Peter waited attentively and Mr. Bynge sought a way to begin his tale.

"The matter of urgency, Mr. Bynge?" prompted Peter gently.

"Yes—yes, well, it is all so difficult—and so—so nightmarish, I can hardly hope you will even believe me."

"Calm yourself, Mr. Bynge, and just start at the beginning."

"Ah, oh, the beginning—well, that would be a few days ago when I was standing with Horsham in front of White's and this—this young man came up to me and—" He proceeded to outline the meeting and arrangements made as a result in such great detail that Peter had some difficulty containing his impatience. Mr. Bynge glanced nervously at him from time to time, aware of the restiveness his narrative style was engendering, but plowing on determinedly, intent on exposing his entire innocence before he reached the horrifying climax of his tale. When he reached that point, he paused to gather courage.

Peter, supposing that he had heard all of it, said, "Well, well, Mr. Bynge, this is indeed a sad tale, but I cannot quite see what it is that you require of me."

"Wait, sir, there is worse to come. We left the club and I attempted to dissuade her from going through with—"

"One moment! You said her?"

"Yes, you see he—she—finally confessed to me that it was only a disguise and he—she—was really a girl."

"A girl! Good God!" Peter laughed in spite of himself at this unlikely development.

"Yes," remarked Mr. Bynge bitterly, "it makes an amusing story, and someday I too may be able to laugh at it. I certainly hope so, for that will mean the story had not a tragic ending."

Peter sobered up at once. "Forgive me, sir, you are right. Of course you are upset, but I think we can sort this out easily enough. Even Thatch cannot be so cheese-brained as to insist on carrying out a duel with a girl. Why, he would be a laughingstock. You must simply go to him and explain."

"That is exactly what I said," replied Mr. Bynge dejectedly. He then proceeded to relate all Vanessa's arguments against such an exposition. "Naturally I realized later why she was so insistent upon going ahead with it and determined I could not allow her to do it only to save my reputation, but I have been walking for hours and could not think of any way to stop it."

"Well, I must say the girl has backbone. Who is she?"

Mr. Bynge swallowed convulsively. "It is—Miss Pymbroke."

"*What?*" Peter swung around to Mr. Bynge, his eyes blazing so fiercely that Mr. Bynge winced away, afraid for a moment Lord Chance meant to strike him.

"I made sure you would not like to learn this, sir, which is why I hesitated so long before mentioning her name," explained Mr. Bynge defensively.

Peter turned away and sat glaring silently straight before him, nor did he utter another word until the carriage halted before his own door. Then he turned a set, hard face to Mr. Bynge and said, "You need not worry any further, Mr.

Bynge. I will undertake the matter from this point and you may rest assured there will be no duel and no scandal. I must thank you for bringing the matter to me. I will naturally let you know the outcome in the morning. My driver will take you home now. Good night, sir.''

''But—'' called Mr. Bynge, but it was too late. Peter had disappeared behind his front door already. Mr. Bynge leaned forward to give the driver his direction and sighed, relaxing back against the comfortable red velvet squabs. He was a very nice young man without any vices at all, but intelligence and decisiveness were not his strong points. However, he was able to recognize and appreciate those qualities in others and he had not the least doubt that Lord Chance could be trusted to manage the situation satisfactorily.

Peter went straight to his room and to his valet's astonished disapproval ordered another, less formal suit of clothes to be laid out. When he was dressed again, he left the house and set out on foot. He did not know Mr. Thatch, nor did he know where Lord Gale resided, but he was acquainted with Mr. Rembling and had once been to his house for a dinner party, so he made his way there, though the hour had now advanced to half-past three in the morning. His insistent application of the door knocker finally produced Mr. Rembling himself in a dressing gown.

''Good Lord, Chance! Sorry to have kept you waiting. The servants have all gone to bed.''

''It is I who must apologize, sir, for dragging you from your bed.''

''No, no, dear fellow. I was not asleep. Come along into the library. I have an excellent brandy. You look as though you could do with one, and I am sure I could.'' He led the way down the hall and into a small but well-appointed room, where a fire burned briskly in the grate. ''Actually, as you can see, I was sitting here, couldn't sleep for some reason.'' He poured the drinks and sat down opposite Peter. ''Now, Chance, what is wrong? Your face looks like thunder, you know.''

''I believe you were present this evening at an abortive whist game at White's?''

''Heavens! Has word of that leaked out already?''

"I hope not. Mr. Bynge came to me with the story. Please tell me what you thought of what happened."

"Well, it was clear as clear Thatch was cheating. No other explanation. None of us quite liked to come right out and say so, of course. Difficult situation—a man one has played cards with any number of times and so forth, though I did let him know that I was not satisfied. He would not call me out, though, when he had that green lad there to answer the purpose. I see now the man is a coward as well as a cheat. I shall cut him dead when next we meet."

"Could not you or Lord Gale have taken him aside and reasoned with him?"

"We tried, but he would have none of it. Fact is, he had been caught flat out and the only thing he could do was challenge the boy or admit he had cheated, and he wasn't about to do that. I thought I would draw him off when I refusd to stand his second because he would not explain, but he wasn't having any of that. I have spent too much time at Manton's for him not to be aware of my ability with a pistol. I thought of offering to fight the boy's duel in his place, but I could not bring myself to do it, somehow. He has a mighty proud look about him for all he is so young."

"This is an ugly story, sir," said Peter sternly, wondering at it that three grown men could stand by and allow this to happen to a mere "lad."

"Yes, I have been damned worried about it, I can tell you, and ashamed. I could not sleep for fretting, as a matter of fact, which is why you find me still awake. I had just decided to wait up and go along to Burney's Field at six to try persuasion on Thatch at least once more."

Peter relented somewhat at this confession. "I really came to you to see if you could give me Thatch's direction."

"You are going to see him now?"

"I am."

"Then I will go with you," declared Mr. Rembling eagerly, jumping to his feet and heading for the door. "Just give me a moment to fetch my coat."

He was back very quickly and they set off at once. "It is not far. He has rooms at Pitkins Terrace Houses," said Mr. Rembling.

When they arrived, it took a considerable amount of thumping on the door before it flew open to reveal an irate Mr. Thatch in dingy bed gown. "What the devil do you mean by making all this racket?" he snarled, his face distorted by rage at being haled out of sleep. "Here, is that you, Rembling? What is the meaning of this, eh?"

"Thatch, here is Lord Peter Chance, who would like a word with you."

"Then let him come around tomorrow at a decent hour," snapped Mr. Thatch, swinging the door forward to slam it in their faces. Peter, however, stepped forward and caught the door on his shoulder, opening it wide and stepping into the hall.

"I will speak to you now, Mr. Thatch. And I must say I cannot care for your manners."

"Nor I yours," Mr. Thatch retorted, "forcing your way into a gentleman's house in the middle of the night like a common bully-boy. What do you mean by it?"

"I mean to have a word with you, sir, and now. Will you have it here or shall we step into your rooms?"

"Be damned to that. I'm in no mood to entertain guests at this hour. Say your piece and be done with it."

"Very well," replied Peter crisply, "you were caught cheating at cards this evening in—"

"Here! How dare you come—"

"—in company with Mr. Rembling, Lord Gale, and a young man, Mr. Portland," continued Peter imperturbably.

"I should like to know what business it is of yours," demanded Mr. Thatch truculently.

"I am making it my business. Mr. Portland is a friend of mine and I have no intention of allowing him to take part in a duel. Now, there are several alternatives, only one of which will be of any benefit to you. That is that you drop this whole business at once, without a word of it to anyone outside those of us who already know. I will undertake that none of us will ever speak of it. The matter will simply be over as of now."

"And if I do not?"

"Ah, now we come to the unpleasant alternatives. I had hoped we would not need to explore them, but if you insist, I will be happy to oblige you. One is that I go to the authorities, who will effectively stop you or imprison you. In which case, I would make sure you never set foot in White's again and would have trouble finding a welcome in any decent drawing room in London. Another is that I allow you to go on with it and then settle with you myself.'' Peter's eyes bored into Thatch's with deadly intent and his voice became flat and iron-hard. "And I assure you, Mr. Thatch, that you would not live for more than a moment after our encounter.''

"And if by some perverse chance he should miss, I will be standing by to rectify the matter,'' added Mr. Rembling with relish.

Mr. Thatch slowly blanched and his eyes took on a hunted expression. "You—you are making a great deal too much out of this affair,'' he said, licking his lips. "I was not— I would not have really hurt the lad, only wanted to teach him a lesson, give him a good fright, teach him he could not go about accusing his elders and betters of—''

"Elder I will grant you,'' Peter said, interrupting the man's rambling speech impatiently. "Now, come to the point. What is your choice? I haven't all night to stand about.''

"Well, you can hardly blame me. I did not invite you here,'' cried Mr. Thatch peevishly.

"Your decision, please,'' demanded Peter inexorably.

"Well, if the lad cares to retract his—''

"He retracts nothing,'' snapped Peter. "Your answer, at once!''

"Oh, very well, very well. I will drop the matter, of course. It is of no importance, in any case, only a country lad with the straw still in his hair. Beneath my dignity even to have noticed him.''

Peter stared at him contemptuously for a long, very rude moment before turning on his heel and going out the door without another word, Mr. Rembling following.

In the street Mr. Rembling chuckled softly. "Well done, my lord. You called his bluff right and proper. Knew it all the time, the man is a coward and a Captain Sharp.''

"Naturally, we will not speak of this to anyone else, though I will of course confide the outcome to Mr. Bynge, and Lord Gale has a right to know, should he ask you about it.''

"Naturally. It will be only between ourselves. Glad I came with you. Wouldn't have missed that scene for worlds.''

They shook hands and parted at Mr. Rembling's door and

Peter walked home again, where he was greeted by a reproachful look from his weary valet as he let himself into the
front door with his own key.

"What the devil do you think you are doing?" demanded
Peter.

"I am waiting for you, m'lord," the man replied with
massive dignity.

"Stupid fellow. You should have gone to your bed hours
ago."

"And who would help you undress, m'lord?"

"I hope I would be able to get out of my clothes without
help at my age."

"Yes, and throw your coat down in a heap so that it would
take hours to get out the wrinkles."

"Well, never mind. I do not intend to undress, in any case.
I will be going out again presently. Since you are up, you can
make yourself useful and fetch me some breakfast and send
word to the stables for my carriage to be brought around."

The man bowed, signifying his disapproval by his silence,
and withdrew.

Peter deliberately set out late, timing his arrival for some
twenty minutes past the appointed hour. He felt a grim satisfaction with the idea of the extended anxiety this would cause
Miss Pymbroke. He had had to put an immediate cap on the
anger that had exploded inside him when Mr. Bynge had
pronounced her name, realizing it would hamper the clear
thinking he needed to deal with the problem. He had managed to keep his anger successfully bottled throughout the
extraordinary hours that had followed. Now, however, as he
drove himself along toward Burney's Field in the pale-gray
dawn, it began, slowly at first, to seep out as he contemplated
the fact that but for the fortunate coincidence that had brought
Mr. Bynge to Almack's just as he himself was leaving, Miss
Pymbroke would without doubt be lying dead by now. The
more he thought upon the rashness of her behavior, the more
his anger boiled, until by the time he reached the appointed
place he was in such a towering rage that he could barely
contain it. If she had been in the carriage with him at that
moment, he could not have prevented himself from striking
her.

19

Vanessa shivered in the damp, wreathing fog, not only from cold, but from tension and fear, though less than most young women of her time would have felt, for she truly had great confidence in her marksmanship. Apart from this, it was as impossible for her to imagine her own death as an outcome of this escapade as it was to imagine the pain a bullet would make in her flesh. Neither was thinkable. Her chief worry was that this confounded trembling might spoil her aim.

She had arrived early, dismissed the surly hackney driver, and paced quickly up and down, peering intently through the ghostly outlines of the fog-shrouded trees for a glimpse of an approaching carriage. She wished Mr. Bynge would come soon. She took out her pocket watch and saw that it wanted only five minutes before the appointed hour was upon her and thought it odd that neither Bynge nor Thatch had yet appeared. Perhaps Thatch thought to draw out the suspense for her by coming late, but what could Mr. Bynge be doing? Surely he could not have overslept?

She began to swing her arms about vigorously to warm herself and relieve her tightened muscles. She had only her coat to keep her warm, for it had not occurred to her that she would have need of a gentleman's cloak. Her watch now informed her it was five minutes past the hour. Really, this was outrageous. After another long five minutes had passed, she began to wonder if Mr. Thatch was coming at all. What was the proper time to wait in such situations? Then she thought it was not possible for Mr. Thatch to avoid this meeting. He would never allow his friends to learn he had been too cowardly to meet a mere boy. Despite her resolution not to be intimidated by being kept waiting, her stretched nerves had nearly reached the limit of their endurance and her body shook so that she could barely stand and her breathing became more and more erratic. The deadly quiet was nerve-racking and the fog, lifting slightly to shred upon the trees, seemed to be liquefying, causing her clothing to feel heavy with a penetrating dampness.

Then she became aware of the thud of hooves and a creaking of carriage wheels, the sound increasing by the second. To Vanessa, however, each second seemed agonizingly long, as though time had inexplicably slowed down, creating an unbearable suspense. When the carriage finally loomed through the fog, she nearly shrieked aloud, for it seemed to be bearing directly down upon her. It pulled up only yards away, the horses throwing up their heads and snorting. Her heart pounded jarringly and her eyes were wide with fear. The driver leapt down with a swirl of his cloak as she stood paralyzed. Then he turned to her and she gasped in disbelief and put out a shaking hand as though to hold him off. It was Chance, his expression stony, with a patch of angry color high on each cheekbone. He stared at her coldly for what seemed an eternity before grinding out through his teeth, "Get—into—the—carriage."

"Wh-wh-what are you—"

"*Get in!*"

She came forward reluctantly and climbed up, without any offer of assistance from him. When she was seated, he sprang up beside her, flicked the reins, turned the carriage, and drove off.

He did not speak or glance in her direction, and she stared miserably down ar her hands, tightly clenched together in her lap. A hundred questions buzzed in her head, but she was too frightened by his manner to ask them. What was he doing here? Where had he heard? Oh, Mr. Bynge, of course. Mr. Bynge had lost his nerve and confided the story to Chance. Oh, how could he have betrayed her? And to Chance, of all people in the world? Oh, God, she thought wildly, I would far prefer to have met Thatch every day for a week than have

Chance hear of this. She felt her throat tighten and tears well
up at the thought of what he must be thinking of her now, of
the contempt in his eyes and voice when he had spoken those
few words to her, as though he had had to force them out, so
great was his disgust with her. She thought of the picture she
must have presented, her brown wig straggling with the
damp, her rumpled coat and trousers, the limp, grubby
neckcloth, and a sob shook her before she could stop it.

He did not even look around at the sound and she realized
she was so sunk beneath reproach that he would never speak
to her again, and with that realization came the knowledge
that she loved him—loved him, it seemed, with desperation
as the pain she was feeling at her discovery became unbearable,
for there was no hope in it for her. She stared miserably at
her hands and felt the hot tears burning the skin of her fingers
as they fell. She stole a covert glance sideways. His profile
seemed carved of stone, his eyes never moving from the
roadway before him.

Suddenly she felt ashamed to be crying before him, for it
would only make him more contemptuous of her. After all,
she had got herself into the situation without help from
anyone, and should have more backbone than to sit sniveling
because her own foolishness had lost him to her forever. She
should have thought of these possible consequences before
going ahead with what she saw now was a harebrained scheme,
should have at least paused to think what he would have
thought of such a lark. She straightened her shoulders and
forced her head up, commanding herself to stop crying. Pride
held her up stiffly through the rest of the drive, through
streets only barely coming to early-morning life as a few
servants hurried about on errands, hardly glancing up at the
two gentlemen in the carriage.

When he pulled up before her aunt's house, she climbed
down without a word. She knew she should at least say thank
you, but she could not trust herself to speak a word or even to
meet his eyes. He clearly felt the same, for she was aware
that he had not turned his head, but continued to stare ahead
with granite-hard impassivity. She walked stiffly through the
gates and around the side of the house, grateful to be out of
his sight at last.

Once safely in her room, she ripped the wig from her head

and threw it and the hat across the room, fell upon her bed, and burying her face in her pillow to muffle her sobs, gave vent to all the pent-up misery and tension of the past hours.

She was so intent upon her grief that she was unaware that Ellen, hot-water jug in hand, had entered the room. Ellen stared at the disheveled figure racked with sobs, turned quietly, and left the room. In the hall she paused to ponder the situation. In them men's clothes again, she thought, and only just come in! A young girl out all night, unchaperoned, and now crying her eyes out. God only knew what trouble she'd got herself into. Well, there's nothing for it but to get the mistress. Ellen marched firmly down the hall to Mrs. Clarence's bedroom, entered, and went to shake her mistress gently awake.

"What? Oh, Ellen, have I overslept?"

"No, madam, it is not quite seven. It's Miss Vanessa. I think you'd best go to her."

Mrs. Clarence sat up abruptly. "Is she ill?"

"No, ma'am. She's crying—and—and she's been out somewhere—"

"Good Lord, hand me my robe quickly."

"And, madam, she's—she's wearing men's clothes."

Mrs. Clarence halted, staring at the maid in astonishment for a second before hurrying out of the room. She opened Vanessa's door and stood panting as she took in the coat and trousers, the wig and beaver hat on the floor, the heaving shoulders and the sobs. Then she crossed the room and put her hand on her niece's shoulder.

"Vanessa, dearest child, what has happened?"

The sobs checked abruptly. After a moment Vanessa raised herself on her elbows and asked in a choked voice, "Do you have a handkerchief, Aunt?"

Mrs. Clarence took one from the pocket of her robe and silently handed it over. Vanessa wiped her eyes and blew her nose before turning over to face her aunt and sitting up.

"I have made a fool of myself, Aunt Clarence, and I am crying in humiliation," she said, her normal husky voice thickened by her crying. She looked straight at her aunt, disdaining pity.

"Well, if you were wearing those clothes, I should imagine you *were* foolish, for you are not at all the well-dressed gentleman,'' replied Mrs. Clarence critically.

Vanessa managed a shaky little laugh. "Oh, I was quite smart, really; it is only that I fell asleep in them and they became rumpled.''

"You could use a change of neckcloth also.''

Vanessa suddenly threw her arms about her aunt and kissed her fervently. "How my uncle must have adored you,'' she cried. Then, because her aunt had not fussed or scolded or been outraged, it was quite easy to tell her the entire story: the deception of Mr. Bynge, the disastrous whist game, the terrifying wait in the cold dawn, and the inglorious conclusion. All of it but the fact that she now knew she loved Peter Chance and had lost him at the same moment of her discovery.

"I do not have a clue to what—what Lord Chance did to draw Mr. Thatch off, for he was so angry he would not s-speak to me.'' She caught back a sob as she admitted this.

Mrs. Clarence eyed her shrewdly, reading everything Vanessa hoped to hide in the tone of her voice. She held her own counsel on the subject, however, and only replied, "Well, my love, perhaps you were unwise, but not with malice, and nothing dire has come of it, after all. You must take comfort from that and not dwell on the experience any more than you can help. Now, I am going to tell Ellen to make you a bath while you get out of those damp clothes before you take a chill. I think a good soak in a hot bath will be very effective against a chill, and make you feel more cheerful, besides. Then you will come down and have a good breakfast. You must be starving.'' She patted Vanessa's shoulder and went away, and quite suddenly Vanessa realized that she was indeed very hungry. She jumped up and began stripping off the costume she wore, and when Ellen came with two maids to fill the tub, she told her to burn the clothes.

"What? I should never do anything so wasteful as that, miss,'' cried Ellen in shocked tones. She held the coat up and examined it for a moment. "Just wants cleaning up and it should do very well for my young brother, if that's all right with you, miss.''

Vanessa assured her she might do anything she liked with the clothes so long as she removed them from the room at once. She stepped into the hot bath and sank into the water with a sigh.

The exquisite young lady who entered the breakfast room sometime later bore no resemblance at all to the red-eyed, bedraggled creature Mrs. Clarence had found on being awakened so abruptly earlier. She looked up and smiled her approval at the transformation.

Vanessa had had time to think over her feelings and had come to the conclusion that what could not be changed must be borne. She had dismissed as cowardly her impulse to go back to her father, or even to cancel her social obligations and remain skulking in the house. No doubt she would have to face a certain amount of unhappiness from the knowledge that she had lost any regard Lord Chance may have developed for her, but the pain would lessen with time. She believed women went into declines over lost love only in novels. In real life, women were much stronger than that. At least she knew herself to be, and also that her temperament would not allow her to pine and sigh for long, or perhaps her pride would not allow it. At any rate she must pretend that nothing momentous had happened to her and go on with her life.

She therefore set herself down at the table and ate baked eggs with appetite, and when Ann entered, Vanessa smiled up at her and declared that she felt an urgent need of a new bonnet, indeed of several new bonnets, and proposed a shopping expedition if Ann should feel equal to it. Ann being agreeable, they set forth some time later. After bonnets were chosen, they found kid dancing slippers irresistible, then fans and gloves, and any number of other things so dear to feminine hearts. They were just approaching the entrance of Hatchard's Book Store when they came face-to-face with Mr. Bynge.

He halted, turned bright red, and stuttered out a confused greeting. Ann smiled upon him kindly, supposing his discomposure due to the intensity of his feelings for Vanessa. Vanessa greeted him with all the calm at her command and asked him how he did.

"V-very well, Miss Pymbroke. I have just seen your brother, Lady Ann. Wonderful fellow. Equal to any situation," he said, sliding a nervous, meaningful glance at Vanessa.

Ann agreed that her brother was very capable and tactfully

said that she would go along inside as she was eager to inquire if the new novel by Miss Austen had arrived.

Vanessa did not waste a moment of this unexpected but fortunate meeting. "How could you have betrayed me to Lord Chance, Mr. Bynge? I would never have thought it of you."

He looked stricken at this attack, but replied, "I simply could not allow you to—you must see that I could not—it was impossible! Then when I happened to meet Chance, I just— Well, if you had had a male relative, I would have turned to him, but since you had not, Chance seemed the nearest thing—being Lady Ann's brother and her staying with you. Please try to understand my position, Miss Pymbroke. I—I could not bear for anything to happen to you because I was too stupid to prevent it."

"Very well, Mr. Bynge. We will say no more about it. What did Lord Chance do?" She tried not to reveal her very real curiosity about this.

Mr. Bynge, happy to be off the subject of his betrayal, eagerly told her everything that had been told him by Lord Chance earlier. "I do wish he had taken me with him to visit Thatch. I should very much have liked to witness his backing down, but Chance left me so abruptly I had not even the opportunity to ask him what he intended to do. Of course, one does tend to believe him when he states so definitely that he will take care of everything. Very capable fellow. I hadn't a doubt that he would very quickly rout the man. Did he not come to tell you there was no need to go to Burney's Field?"

"No, he did not," said Vanessa shortly.

"Oh! I would have thought— Do you mean you actually went there?"

"I did. Yes, Mr. Bynge, I went there. What time did you meet up with Lord Chance?"

"Well, it must have been well on toward two in the morning. I really do not understand it. I made sure he would go from Thatch to you to prevent your leaving the house. Or at least, I suppose he would not rouse the household at that hour, but he had surely enough time in hand to wait until you came out and then he could send you back."

Vanessa thought so too. She quickly added up the time it would take for the interview with Rembling, the confrontation with Thatch, even the time he would have needed to change from the formal attire required at Almack's to the plain dark clothes he had worn when he arrived at Burney's Field, and came to the inescapable conclusion that he had deliberately allowed her to go there. Not only that, but he had made sure she had an uncomfortable wait besides. Oh, the wretch! Her eyes glinted with anger at his cruelty. Of all the loathsome revenges to take. She hated him! To torture her in such a way and then to behave with such extreme disagreeableness on the ride back, as though she were too contemptible to speak to! Her fingers itched with the need to deliver a ringing slap to his cheek, and had he appeared at that moment, she was sure nothing could have prevented her from doing so.

She saw that Mr. Bynge was eyeing her uneasily and she swallowed, forced a smile, and said sweetly, "Well, never mind, Mr. Bynge, perhaps he had other things to attend to first that we know nothing of. At least nothing dreadful has happened and we are well out of it. I hope you will forgive me for putting you through such an ordeal. You behaved so splendidly, you know, and I shall never forget that."

Mr. Bynge flushed with pleasure. "Dear Miss Pymbroke, I must tell you that though I was a great deal overset at the time, I never ceased admiring your courage. I would never have dreamed that a delicate woman could behave with so much—"

"Could we not speak of it again, Mr. Bynge?"

"Anything you wish, Miss Pymbroke, it will give me entire happiness to fulfill. May I request that you save a dance for me tonight at the Cookes' ball?"

"With pleasure. And now I must rejoin Lady Ann. Good day to you." She gave him her hand, onto which he pressed a fervent kiss, and went into the store. She took book after book down from the shelves and opened them, but could not even see the words. She only saw the look Chance had given her as he told her to get into the carriage, the hard profile he had presented her as they drove back. She seethed with anger. I *will* not love such a man, she decided, slamming shut the book she held so forcefully that the sound caused all the people in the store to turn and look at her curiously.

One of these was Mr. Rembling, just paying for his purchases at the counter. She met his gaze for a moment and casually looked away. She knew he did not associate her with the Mr. Portland he had been involved with the evening before, for Mr. Bynge had said Lord Chance had not revealed her true identity to him or to Thatch; nevertheless, she felt exposed and guilty. She found Ann and they left as soon as Ann's purchases had been paid for. Vanessa wondered if she was doomed to encounter all the participants from last night before the day was over. No doubt, she thought rather wildly, she would be requested to stand up by Mr. Thatch at the ball tonight!

20

The Cookes' ball was very like every other ball they had attended this Season, thought Ann somewhat wearily. The packed, overly warm room lit by thousands of candles, the same people one saw at every other ball, the shimmering jewels and gowns, the heavy scent of flowers, the pretty, shy girl whose come-out this was smiling dazedly at the milling guests. I really do not care for all this sort of life, Ann thought, longing suddenly for home and quiet days and the sweet, long country evenings and peace. She wondered if Giles would be content with life away from London. She turned to smile up at him as he stood behind her chair, scowling as usual at the other guests as though daring them to approach him.

She knew he would not dance, and while he would not object if she stood up with anyone else, he would grumble audibly about wasting her strength on such foolishness. Surely he would be as glad to get away from all this, as glad as she.

Vanessa felt strung as tight as wire, her heart beating erratically, each new male arrival a cause for anxiety. Was it Thatch—or Lord Gale—or Chance— Not that any but the last would associate the girl in lilac gauze, her silver-blond curls entwined with lavender ribands sewn with tiny silk violets, with the brown-wigged young man of the night before. But Chance was the person who was most likely to appear, for the Cookes were very old friends of Lord and Lady Carrisbrooke and would expect Chance to honor them by making an appearance, just as Ann had been expected to do so, which was why they were here despite the fact that both girls would have preferred to stay at home tonight.

As it was, Vanessa found all her partners interested in hearing more about her rescue of the hapless Miss Wilmott, who had clearly spread the story all over town, as Chance had predicted. Vanessa damped their curiosity as best she could and changed the subject adroitly. She hoped Mr. Bynge would soon make his appearance. At least he would not ask her embarrassing questions. Her partner led her back to Mrs. Clarence, bowed, and went away.

"A very pretty-behaved young man," observed Mrs. Clarence languidly. She too was weary of balls and the further into the Season they went, the warmer it became, which always caused her physical discomfort.

"Yes, lovely," murmured Vanessa disinterestedly. Then she looked up and was barely able to suppress a gasp. There, grimly bearing down upon them, was Lord Chance. She felt the blood flood up over her bare throat and into her face, and it took every ounce of steel in her makeup to keep her head up. She *would* not quail before him, nor look ashamed. She silently cursed the betraying color which she could not control and which she was sure he would not miss.

He bowed to Mrs. Clarence and murmured a courteous "Good evening." He then turned to Ann. "My dear, I see you are in very good looks tonight. Will you dance?"

"I think not at the moment, Peter dear, though I thank you," Ann said with an indulgent smile, thinking how kind he was when he must surely be eager to lead Vanessa out. Peter, however, only turned to bow coldly to Vanessa; then, with a nod to Giles, he went away. Vanessa sat frozen, the color now draining slowly out of her face leaving it white and set.

Ann stared at her brother's retreating back in disbelief at his rudeness. She turned to Vanessa. "Good heavens, whatever has happened?" She saw Vanessa's expression and sighed. "Oh, dear, you two are at daggers drawn again. How very exhausting for you both."

Vanessa could not reply, though she knew Ann was teasing her, not understanding the seriousness of the rift that had now developed between her brother and her friend. Mr. Bynge presented himself at that moment and Vanessa gratefully gave

him her hand and allowed him to lead her to the floor. She
held her head high and flashed a beguiling smile upon Mr.
Bynge, who was immediately ravished and nearly inarticulate
with pleasure.

Peter had paused to greet Mrs. Clayton-Trees and her
daughter, and Mrs. Clayton-Trees was making the most of
the encounter, hinting broadly that her daughter was free for
this dance. Peter was looking about for an excuse to take
himself away when his eyes lit upon Vanessa flirting with
Mr. Bynge. Some perverse impulse that he preferred not to
examine caused him to turn back, bow to Miss Clayton-
Trees, and request the honor of leading her out. Miss Clayton-
Trees, radiating triumph, took the arm he extended to her and
they walked onto the floor. He made himself extremely agreeable to her, though he found her an even more tiresome
creature when she was being pleasant than when she was
displeased.

Vanessa managed to take in the greater part of this charade
without ever staring at them blatantly and proceeded to become even gayer with Mr. Bynge. She was very relieved
when the set was over. She refused to dance the next set,
though she noticed Peter on the floor with the Cookes' daughter.
After that, blessedly, he disappeared. She hoped fervently
that he had gone away altogether.

Mrs. Clarence, meanwhile, had turned to Giles and said,
"You do not dance, sir?"

"I have never learned how, Mrs. Clarence. I find it boring
and a waste of time."

"Ah, such a pity. You will make quite a number of young
ladies present most unhappy."

"They would be far unhappier dancing with me, madam, I
assure you, for I would only trample their toes," he said with
one of his rare smiles.

"Then do sit here next to me and tell how your play
progresses."

"Gladly, though I have nothing good to report. I have been
stuck fast in the second act for two weeks now. You see, the
problem is—" He launched into a long explanation.

Ann turned away, having already heard the problem with
the second act several times. She had hoped he might make
the attempt to dance with her tonight, the first ball they had

both attended since their betrothal, but she should have known that he would not. Although she was tired of the social round, the music caught her and her foot began to tap in time to it. She longed to be on the floor.

"Lady Ann, good evening." She looked up to find Mr. Rivers smiling down upon her. "I can see you would enjoy dancing tonight."

Her face lit up happily. Somehow Mr. Rivers always sensed her mood: when she had too little energy for dancing, he was content to sit beside her for a talk, and when, as now, she wanted to dance very much, he would lead her out. She turned to Giles, but he had not even noticed Rivers' arrival. I doubt he will know I have left his side, she thought sadly. Mr. Rivers, seeing the look in her eyes, pressed the hand she had laid upon his arm. She turned back to him.

"You are very perceptive, Mr. Rivers. How did you guess that I would like to dance?"

"Since there is nothing more important to me than your pleasure, I have made it my business to make a careful study of you in order to serve it. Also," he added candidly, "I saw your foot tapping."

She laughed delightedly. "At least you are honest, sir."

"I could never be less than open with you, my dear," he replied seriously, looking deep into her eyes.

She became flustered and dropped her eyes shyly, scolding herself for behaving like a schoolgirl at her age. She felt it very keenly that *she* was not being honest with him. She really should tell him about Giles, she thought, for with every meeting he allowed his intentions fuller expression. She had no right to allow him to go on, and yet she knew that if she told him, he would retire back into the country with his children and she would never see him again. Oh, it was so difficult! She felt she could not bear to lose his friendship altogether.

"Now you are fretting yourself about something and one should never fret while dancing," he scolded her gently, "especially while dancing with me. My grasp upon self-confidence is not nearly firm enough to withstand a frown from you."

Ann laughed and gave herself up to the pleasure of moving to the music—a pleasure she enjoyed very rarely.

Several dances later Vanessa's partner trod upon her hem, ripping away several inches of the ruffle. She excused herself to her abjectly apologizing partner and made her way out of the ballroom. On the stairs she heard her name called and turned to find Camilla Chamfreys hurrying up after her. Camilla had been looking for an opportunity to speak to Vanessa and, seeing the torn hem, had followed.

"Why, Miss Chamfreys, I did not see you all evening. How do you do?"

"Very well. I see you have torn your ruffle. Perhaps I can help you with it."

"How very kind of you."

They made their way to a bedroom that had been set aside for the lady guests to freshen themselves. There were several women in the room, repairing sagging coiffures, splashing cold water over hot cheeks, mending tears in their gowns. Camilla pushed Vanessa into a chair in a corner and dropped to her knees before her.

"Miss Chamfreys! What are you doing?" cried Vanessa in some embarrassment, attempting to pull the girl to her feet.

Camilla laughed. "Please allow me, Miss Pymbroke, it is one of my few useful accomplishments." With that she took a small case from her reticule, extracted a threaded needle, and began to reattach the ruffle with tiny, precise stitches. "I saw that great cloddish fellow you were standing up with and am not surprised he tore your gown."

"You certainly are a very fine seamstress, my dear," Vanessa commented admiringly.

"Oh, before Mama and Papa became so very famous, they quite often had to make their own costumes, so Mama taught me very young to help her. She was very particular." There was a short silence while Camilla tried to think of some way to bring up the subject of the trip to Medford Yatter, her whole purpose in following Vanessa upstairs. Vanessa, who suddenly saw a perfect opportunity to use the information she had gleaned from Miss Clayton-Trees, pondered how best to impart it.

"I was sorry you did not accompany us yesterday to visit Mr. Robin Chance," she said at last.

Camilla's eyes flicked up and then down to her work

again. "I doubt Mr. Chance would welcome a visit from me."

"Why, I think he would be very happy to see any of his friends."

"I imagine he must lead a very merry life down there, a handsome young vicar, son of an earl, devastating all the local ladies," said Camilla bitterly.

"That was not my impression," commented Vanessa dryly. "What a very strange idea you have of him, to be sure. He is not at all a flirt or a womanizer, I think, though I suppose if that is your impression of him it explains why you would not receive him before he left?"

"He did not call, though I was very sure he would do so after . . ." She swallowed and could not continue.

"After the Dewinters' ball?" finished Vanessa. Camilla nodded miserably. "But he did call, my dear, several times, he told me so himself, and is still very unhappy at the memory of being denied each time."

Camilla looked up, her brows knotted in a perplexed frown. "He—called? He told you he had called? But that is not possible!"

"Do you know, Miss Clayton-Trees told me a story the other day about the ball. It seems she wore a green domino, and Mr. Chance came up to her and identified himself, thinking she was someone else. Her curiosity was much piqued, of course, and later she saw him approach another green domino. She realized it was you when she recognized your mother and was so amused she went to tell your mother the story."

After a long silence Camilla said, "How very thoughtful of Miss Clayton-Trees to entertain my mother. I am grateful to you for telling me of this. I shall know what to do."

"I made sure you would," Vanessa replied, patting her cheek. She stood up and pulled Camilla to her feet. "Thank you for mending my ruffle, my dear. Shall we go down now?"

The next morning Camilla made sure to be downstairs before her parents and summoned the butler to her. "Willes, it has come to my attention that a Mr. Chance called to see me some time ago for several days in succession."

"Yes, miss, that is so."

"May I ask why I was not told?"

"Madam instructed me to deny you, miss. I assumed it was with your knowledge."

"Ah, I see. Thank you, Willes."

Camilla went straight up to her mother's room, tapped, and entered. Mrs. Chamfreys, wearing a much-beruffled bed cap that became her exceedingly, sat up against her pillows sipping her morning chocolate. Her abigail moved silently around the room tidying the dressing table and folding away clothing.

"My darling child, how energetic of you to be up and dressed so very early. You should get more rest after a ball. I think you look somewhat pale this morning."

"May I speak to you alone, Mama?"

"Oh, dear, you are going to be serious, I see, and it is so early, too." Mrs. Chamfreys pouted charmingly, but Camilla only returned a stony look. Seeing her daughter's lack of response, Mrs. Chamfreys gave in with a sigh. "Oh, very well, tiresome child. Leave us, Betty."

When the door had closed behind the maid, Camilla came straight to the point. "Mama, did you instruct Willes to deny me to Mr. Chance when he called?"

"Oh, good heavens, the little parson again! How boring to—"

"Did you, Mama?"

"Yes, yes, yes. Now *can* we be done with the subject? You really should not disturb me like this in the mornings, Camilla. After all, though I did not dance, the ball was tiring for me last night, and I have a performance tonight. I must have peace if I am to perform well."

"What a clanker that is," retorted Camilla disdainfully. "You know perfectly well you could perform just as well if you spent the entire day in battle."

"Ah, yes, when I was younger, but at my age—" Mrs. Chamfreys paused to press a frail-looking wrist to her forehead theatrically.

"I am not impressed, Mama. Six and thirty is hardly teetering on the brink of senility," replied Camilla. "I would be glad to learn why you should have my friends denied at the door."

"Now you are being dramatic, my dear. I have not denied your friends."

"And yet Willes tells me you instructed him to tell Mr. Chance I was not at home when he called."

"Only Mr. Chance."

"Without discussing it with me or even informing me of it."

"Oh, that would have been foolish of me. I know young girls very well. They adore to create scenes. Better just to nip the affair in the bud before it goes any further and you begin to imagine your feelings are engaged," admitted Mrs. Chamfreys with charming candor.

"There was no 'affair,' Mama; we had only met a few times."

"I suppose you are prepared to deny that you did not tell Mr. Chance you would be wearing a green domino at the Dewinters' ball?"

"Yes, I did, but I cannot see any great harm in that."

"Only that you were deceitful to your mother. You should have confided your plans to me. It was also deceitful to pretend to me that you did not know who he was."

"You have been listening to that dreadful sneaksby Miss Clayton-Trees, of course," said Camilla scornfully. "Very well, if you will have it so, I deceived you, but you have deceived me as well, so I think we are quits on that score."

"I will not have you speaking to me in that tone of voice, miss," flared Mrs. Chamfreys, "and I will never allow you to marry that parson, and so I warn you."

"Mr. Chance has not asked me to marry him, but if he should, I will not feel it necessary to take advice on the matter from anyone," said Camilla loftily.

"You are being ridiculous. You are not of age and your papa and I will not give our consent to the match. I doubt very much a vicar will go so far as to marry you without it."

"Your virtuous attitude is a little surprising in view of the fact that you eloped with Papa at sixteen."

"That has nothing to do with it, impertinent minx! It is your life we are discussing. I had no such chances as have been given to you. There is nothing to stand in the way of your making the most brilliant marriage, I have prepared you for it for years, your papa and I have worked hard to make it possible for you—"

"Mr. Chance is the son of an earl, Mama," Camilla reminded her, crossing to the door.

"But only the second son," wailed Mrs. Chamfreys despairingly.

Camilla paused, her hand on the doorknob, and turned back to look at her mother straight in the eye. "I mean to have him, Mama, if he asks me," she said softly but with a familiar steely ring to her voice. She left the room, closing the door with extreme gentleness.

Mrs. Chamfreys burst into noisy tears, for she knew that tone in Camilla's voice very well, too well to doubt that she would have her way in the matter. And her papa would never be able to stand up against her; he had never denied his daughter anything in her life. Mrs. Chamfreys' only, faint, hope was that the parson would not propose.

21

Peter sat stolidly chewing at a beefsteak, glowering at a morning newspaper propped up before him. A footman entered silently to lay a note before him. As he turned away, the footman caught Strother's eye and raised an eyebrow at him. Strother winked almost imperceptibly. The footman grinned and left the room. Strother eyed his master covertly. M'lord was in a nasty temper. His valet had confided as much to Strother this morning. "We are very broody today. Some female giving him fits, if you ask me. There, he's ringing for his breakfast. Best tread carefully. He threw a hairbrush at me this morning when I made so bold as to suggest he was looking peaky from too many late nights."

Strother tread very carefully indeed as he served Peter his breakfast, not caring to risk the precious Spode china to his master's uncertain temper.

Peter deliberately finished his meal and motioned the butler to remove his plate before he picked up the note, broke the seal, and opened it. It was from Ann, asking him to call upon her this morning, and adding, thoughtfully, that her hostess was spending the morning in bed and that Vanessa had gone riding.

Wants to ring a peal over me for last night, no doubt, thought Peter glumly, and of course I was rude, though I suppose I cannot tell Ann the reason for it. He again pictured Vanessa, sitting there so serenely, looking for all the world like a delicate bit of porcelain from Dresden, her deep-blue eyes taking on a tint of violet from her lilac gown, and later flirting with that stupid Bynge as though nothing at all unusual had happened to her just the night before. He swore horribly just beneath his breath, his fingers clenching his sister's note into a crackling ball. The butler eyed him nervously and hurried busily out of the room. Peter flung the note from him and rose. Get it over, he thought, let her give me her scold and be done with it.

When he arrived at Mrs. Clarence's, he was shown into the drawing room by Hay, who said Lady Ann would be down directly. Peter stood glowering into the fire for nearly five minutes before the door opened and he swung around impatiently.

Vanessa stood there, the shoulders of her habit damp. They stared at each other in shock. Peter recovered first.

"Ann asked me to call. I understood you had gone riding. I—"

"It began to rain, so I came back." She turned to leave, then stopped and slowly turned toward him again. "I have been remiss, Lord Chance, in not thanking you for all your efforts in my behalf two nights ago."

"I would very much prefer you did not thank me," he replied coldly, turning away to the fire.

"Guilty conscience?" she asked.

He swung about, eyeing her suspiciously. "Perhaps you will not mind explaining what you mean by that?"

"I feel sure you will not find it necessary to delve too deep into your memory to find the answer yourself. Good day to you, sir." She turned again to the door.

"One moment if you please, madam. I will be much obliged to learn what reason *I* might have for a guilty conscience. It was not I who behaved so scandalously, nor I who created a situation that caused several people a great deal of trouble to rescue you, not to speak of a sleepless night."

"I may have behaved unwisely, sir, but never with malicious intent to cause anyone torment or anxiety. Can you say the same?"

"I cannot imagine what you are ranting about."

"Oh, can you not? Then tell me why, after going to so much trouble on my behalf, you did not think it necessary to come and tell me that the matter had been settled? Tell me why you allowed me to keep the appointment when you knew well before the hour that it was unnecessary? And why, knowing that, you not only allowed me to go there, but deliberately kept me waiting a quarter of an hour? No doubt you enjoyed a leisurely breakfast, all the more delicious to you as you contemplated the torment you were putting me through?'' She had the satisfaction of seeing him wince and knew she had made a palpable hit. "That, sir,'' she cried triumphantly, ''was done with malicious intent, and I dare you to deny it!''

Since he could not deny it, Peter blustered, ''You may not have intended harm, but what of poor Mr. Bynge's anxiety, what of the pain you would have caused your family and friends had Thatch gone through with it?''

''You suppose Thatch a better shot than I?'' she asked hotly. ''I may tell you, sir, I am acquitted to be a very fine shot!''

''So is Thatch,'' he snapped harshly. ''You are very cavalier with your life.''

''It is my life! No one asked you to interfere!''

''I beg your pardon for contradicting you, but Mr. Bynge did.''

''He had no right,'' she replied stubbornly.

''No right? No right! After you used him? Presumed upon his simpleminded naïveté to get you into White's in the first place, then put him into a position where he was forced to second you in a duel, and to top it all off, you told him who you are. If you were so sure of yourself, so concerned for his feelings, you should never have told him that. Can you seriously suppose that after learning it he would not do everything in his power to stop it? At least he had the courage to face the fact that it must be stopped, even if he could not do so himself.''

''I am happy to note that you give him a bit of credit. I will add that he also behaved like a gentleman through it all and afterward.''

''While I did not? Well, I am not some green, infatuated boy who falls all over himself for your favors. And you are no longer the hoydenish schoolgirl who earns the admiration of her friends by foolish pranks. It is more than time, Miss Pymbroke, that you learned to behave more responsibly.''

While all this was going forward, Ann had come down to

find several servants riveted by the loud words issuing from the drawing room. They had all hurried guiltily away at her appearance and she approached the drawing room in time to hear Peter's speech about Mr. Bynge being forced to second her in a duel, and for a moment Ann was so intrigued she listened shamelessly. Then, recalling herself, she had reached out to silently close the drawing-room door and retreat back up the stairs. Second Vanessa in a duel? What in God's name was he talking about? What had Vanessa been up to now?

Below, Vanessa was so stunned at Peter's last remarks she was speechless for a moment. Finally she stuttered, "Y-y-you are detestable! How *dare* you give yourself the right to speak to me so?"

"I assumed the right when I was put in the position of having to rescue you from your own folly."

She drew herself up. "I will bid you good morning, sir," she said awfully, and turned to march stiffly out of the room.

Forgetting all about his appointment with Ann, Peter delivered a violent kick at the firedog and charged out into the hall, snatching his hat from Hay, who had hurried up to hand it to him as he went out the door. As he stalked blindly away, the quarrel echoed repeatedly in his mind. Her accusation, his, all came back to him, word for word, over and over. Then he began refining upon his own words, rephrasing them, sharpening, making them more telling blows, until at last he was inventing entirely different rebuttals that would have been far more effective. His rage built to a white-hot blindness until it exploded as he pictured himself shaking her like a doll, shouting, "*Now* will you see your idiocy? *Will you see!*"

He stopped in shock, dazed at the vividness of his imagined physical assault upon her. Why was he so angry? She deserved censure certainly for her irresponsible behavior: telling him all that farradiddle about looking for a wealthy husband, throwing herself at runaway horses, prancing about the streets in men's clothing, accepting challenges. Why, then, could he not simply censure her and be done with it without allowing himself to give way to so much rage? Was it really a matter of a guilty conscience, as she had said? How like her to accuse *me* of ill behavior after all I have been through for her sake, all the agony of mind—but I did want to punish her. I could have kept her from going to the assignation and I did deliberately keep her waiting there, but only to teach her—

Despite all his self-serving denials of any blame on his own part, Peter's old habits of mind reasserted themselves and he began to view the matter more rationally. If it had been some other young lady throwing herself at that horse, would he have behaved as he did? Yelling at her and calling her stupid, angrier than he had ever been in his life until the matter of the duel had come up.

He felt a thrill of pure horror as he pictured again her tiny figure dangling from that great brute's halter, followed almost at once by a flash of anger, and paused to wonder at it. He tried to picture, for instance, the Cookes' daughter in the same situation, but only saw himself being calming, helpful, and masterful. Masterful?

Was that it? Did he resent her courage and confidence, her self-sufficiency? Yes, he concluded, he did, but still— Should that create so much rage against her? What if she were lacking in all those qualities, as no doubt the Cookes' daughter was? He tried to imagine a Miss Pymbroke like that—submissive, blushing, modest—and came to the conclusion that she would rouse about the same amount of interest in him that Miss Cooke did. And he was interested in Miss Pymbroke, so the only conclusion he could draw was that it was for those very qualities that enraged him so when they manifested themselves.

Why should he care if she endangered herself? If she had caught his interest because she was daring and courageous, why should he not be more admiring? He saw suddenly the fragile body sprawled lifelessly upon the grass at Burney's Field, an obscene stain of blood spreading across the breast, and he caught his breath with the pain this vision caused.

And then he knew with an almost fatalistic acceptance that he had fallen in love with her. He had been outraged by her at their first meeting because he had fallen in love with her and wanted her to be beyond reproach. Something in her manner had upset him then, and that should have alerted him. He was exceedingly tolerant about everyone's behavior but that of the Chances. They must be beyond reproach. At first sight of her, he had unconsciously wanted her to be one of those

Chances, and had feared she would behave with her other partners as she had with him.

The fury he had expressed when she was in danger was clearly a part of his love for her. That she could put in peril that spirit, that beauty, that self he wanted for his own, made him want to punish her.

He tramped on, hands clasped behind him, chin sunk into his chest as he contemplated the hopelessness of his position. After today there could be no hope she would ever speak to him again, much less anything so unimaginable as to love him. He had found her only to lose her at the same moment.

Vanessa, meanwhile, had gone to her room to pace back and forth, lashing her anger with every step. The wretch, she fumed, the despicable wretch, to come here so filled with his self-righteousness, telling me how badly *I* have behaved! How dare he? There was a soft tap at the door, but she did not hear it.

Ann opened the door after a moment and peered in, watching her friend marching briskly up and down the room, muttering angrily to herself, her brow knitted ferociously.

"Vanessa? Vanessa, darling, what ever has happened? Vanessa!"

Vanessa halted and turned. "Yes?" she snapped.

"Vanessa, my dear?"

"Oh, Ann, I did not—I— What is it?"

"Perhaps I should go away?" suggested Ann gently.

"No, no, forgive me. I was thinking of—my mind was so preoccupied with— Forgive me." She put her hand over her eyes as though to blot out all she was seeing.

"Vanessa, my love, I heard. I did not mean to, I assure you, they said Peter was waiting for me and I came down. What has happened between you? Why were you both so angry?"

"It was nothing. You know we seldom agree."

Ann looked at her reproachfully. "I should not have asked. I am sorry. I will not trouble you with my foolish questions." She turned to the door.

"No. Ann, please, I am so miserable. He is—I am sorry, dearest Ann, but your brother behaved so dreadfully to me and put me in such a temper. I dislike saying such a thing to you—" cried Vanessa piteously.

"Darling! What has he done?" Ann came to take her hands, all her sympathies roused.

"He—he said I— Oh, Lord, I cannot tell you, it was so dreadful. Only forgive me, Ann, but I must tell you he is an odious man and I hate him—I hate him! I shall never speak to him again."

Ann looked at her long and wonderingly. "Good heavens! You are in love with Peter."

"No! Never—I will not—" Vanessa stopped her wild denials abruptly and pulled herself together. "You are being ridiculous, Ann."

She looked so unhappy that Ann soothed her. "Yes, my dear, I suppose I am. Do you think you could tell me what the quarrel was all about? Please do not if you would prefer it, but I must admit a devouring curiosity."

In fits and starts, with many diversions for bitter acrimony upon Lord Chance's character, the tale was told. Ann tried to conceal her dismay, not at the idea of Vanessa in men's clothing—that was too entirely like something she would do—nor even at Peter's dreadful behavior, for she was convinced she knew the source of that, but with the very real danger Vanessa had put herself in, however innocently and unwittingly.

It was clear that they were both in love with each other and wondered what the outcome of it could be with two such opposite natures in conflict, but for some reason she felt a vague sadness that she could not pin down for quite some time.

Alone again in her room after calming Vanessa's turbulent feelings as best she might, she thought for a time that it was because they were unlikely to settle their differences, much less recognize their true feelings for each other. Could two such disparate temperaments ever resolve their differences?

The more she thought about it, the less did those differences seem to matter. Indeed, they were more alike than otherwise, both strong and self-confident, both filled with courage of a rare quality. The only real difference was in their upbringing: Peter's life a steady progression toward the responsibility, careful thought, and decisive action demanded by his father; Vanessa's glamorous but rootless life, one of a girl forced to make her own decisions at an early age without a mother to dilute the headstrong volatility encouraged in his daughter by Mr. Pymbroke.

Peter and Vanessa both felt passionately about the things that mattered to them, and while that might make their friendship stormy, it need not be a deterrent to eventual happiness. In fact, without the passion, a marriage would be dull— Her thoughts halted with a jolt.

Now Ann recognized the real source of her sadness. It was in recognizing their passion—the quality so sadly lacking in her own romance. Giles had never displayed it to her, neither in friendship all these years, nor in his proposal, nor since. That he did not feel passionately about her, however dear he held her, was a fact that she now faced bleakly. And honesty eventually compelled her to admit that there was nothing resembling passion any longer present in her feelings for Giles. It had been there, that she was positive of, but without any nurturing, it had slowly died. Much to her amazement, this admission did not have any great devastating effect upon her.

22

Giles' hair stood up from his head in tangled disarray because of the many times his fingers had plowed through it in frustration. He had resolved the difficult problems of the second act only to be faced with more, for the manner of resolving the second act had created insuperable problems with the third. He finally pushed back from his desk and rose wearily, noticing by the mantel clock that it was near eight in the evening, and he realized he had not left the room all day. No one had interrupted him, for his servant had strict instructions not to enter the room while he was working unless the house was on fire.

Giles wandered out into the hall, thinking perhaps to ask his man to put together some sort of meal for him, but he saw a letter on the hall table and all thoughts of food fled his mind. Even from where he stood he could recognize the handwriting and his heart began to beat wildly. In two long strides he was across the hall and snatching it up with trembling hands. Oliver! He has not forgotten me!

He returned to his study and closed the door before he tore the seal away and spread open the letter. Ah, how the man could write! Oliver, waxing lyrical upon the beauties of Rome, Florence, Naples, fired Giles' imagination and envy. Then, less happily for Giles, Oliver wrote of all the interesting and amusing people he was meeting, especially of the young Italian count who was taking him about. Giles felt such a pang of jealousy burn its way through his chest as to make him feel physically ill. He put the letter aside for a moment to

180

recover, telling himself that he must not allow himself to indulge in such feelings ever again. He had vowed this to himself when he had made his decision that it was his duty to marry Ann. After a few moments he picked up the letter and continued to read. Slowly a look of dawning joy changed his countenance. Oliver wanted him to join him in Venice for a visit! He insisted Giles must have the inspiration of Venice for his poetry.

Ah, yes, I do need it, and Oliver will help me with the third act. I shall go—I must go, Giles thought with such an uprush of happiness that the room seemed stifling. Still holding the letter, he snatched up his hat and left the house. I shall speak to Ann at once. She will see how important this will be to my work—and only for a few weeks—the last chance before . . . As soon as I return I will put the announcement in the *Gazette*—she is sure to understand how necessary—

He ran lightly up Mrs. Clarence's front steps and rapped the knocker. When Hay opened the door, he looked rather disapproving at Giles' request to see Lady Ann. After all, m'lady was alone, without a chaperone. Still, he had best see. He asked Giles to wait. It had not occurred to Giles that she might be out for the evening, and he had an anxious moment before Hay came back to lead him into the back drawing room, where Ann sat reading.

"Well, Giles, this is a nice surprise. I am so glad I decided not to go to Mrs. Terhune's musicale or I should have missed you."

"You are not ill—"

"No, only tired of parties. I shall be glad to go home, I think. Are you not weary of London, Giles?"

"Yes, as a matter of fact, I am. That is one of the reasons I am here now."

Some unusual excitement in his voice caused her to look at him more closely, and she saw that his eyes sparkled, his mouth was relaxed, as though he had just smiled.

"Oh," she said slowly, "what has happened?"

"I have had a letter from Oliver. You remember my friend from Oxford. He is in Italy and—and he wants me to join him in Venice for a visit."

She noticed the slight hesitation before he finished his

sentence, the almost breathless joy with which he made his announcement. "And you will go?" she asked calmly.

"I really think I should, you know," he began eagerly. "Oliver says it will be so inspirational for my poetry, and he could help me with my play, I know. You will not mind, Ann, will you? Just for a few weeks, and while I am away, you could go back to Chance Court to rest before the—the wedding. It will do you so much good." He went on to explore all the benefits to both of them there were in this plan, with many revealing comments on his friend Oliver interspersed: his wit, his charm, his good looks, his talent.

Ann saw a Giles she had never known before, his eyes soft but as though lit from behind, the ardency with which he spoke of his friend—and she knew she would never see him looking that way while speaking about herself.

"And then, when I return, we can—well, go ahead with our plans." He ended rather lamely and could not quite meet her eyes. For fear, she thought, that I will see how unwilling he is. She took a deep breath.

"I have wanted to speak to you about those plans, my dear. I have been thinking a great deal about it all, and I have decided I made a mistake in accepting your offer. I do not think we will suit, you know, despite our close friendship all these years, or perhaps because of it. In any case, I hope you will release me from my promise. I am—I am crying off," she added with a little smile to lighten the whole thing and make it easier for him, though her heart beat a little faster from nervousness at this decisive step she was taking.

He stared blankly at her. "Do you mean you are— Are you saying you want to break off our betrothal?" he finally asked disbelievingly.

"Yes, that is what I am saying. It is not your fault, dear Giles, and of course you will remain as dear to me as you always have been. As I said, I have been thinking it over very carefully. Will you forgive me and stay my friend?"

As she spoke, she saw the hope and relief dawn in his eyes and knew she had made the right decision. It was somewhat painful to see the evidence he could not conceal of his happiness to be released, but the pain was only from vanity, she knew. There was also a lifting of oppression in herself, an oppression, she realized now, that had been with her since his proposal, though she had refused to acknowledge it when it first settled over her spirits. She remembered now his strange abstracted air as he had asked for her hand, one almost of shock or surprise at the situation in which he found himself. At the time she had put it down to his lack of romanticism, his straightforward way of expressing himself verbally. She had even chided him gently for not speaking to her of his love before asking for her hand. Even that hint had not evoked a response, for he was incapable of dissembling, especially to her, who knew him so well and would have recognized the falseness of it.

What had propelled him into the proposal? she wondered. Perhaps someone had said something suggestive, someone who had recognized the feelings she thought so well-concealed, and he had felt compelled by duty and his real love for her to do as he thought she expected of him. Not that his reasons mattered any longer. Had he been in love with her when he asked her for her hand, her own dwindling passion for him would have flared to life again, but he had been too honest to pretend what he could not feel, and her love had turned to ashes, smothering her in oppression.

Her mistake had been in accepting him, in allowing herself to pretend what *she* no longer felt, in not understanding that her acceptance had been only a token to the last, fading glimmer of the old dream. And now she could not even shed a tear for the death of that dream. She was too relieved.

Giles was never able to recall what he said to Ann. He found himself striding buoyantly down the street, heedless of his direction, his mind whirling with happiness at his release, intermingled with visions of himself beside Oliver in a gondola, Oliver's strong-boned profile and golden curls outlined against the ancient stones of the palaces lining the Grand Canal, Oliver's cynical green eyes glittering with amusement, seeking out Giles' own to share a silent joke.

He had no idea where he was or how far he had walked when he was suddenly halted by a hand on his arm.

"Whoa there, Dalzell. Are you giving me the cut direct?"

"What? Oh, Chance, I was— Sorry, I did not see you." Giles looked about in some confusion at being hauled so abruptly from his dreams. He was in front of Carrisbrooke House.

"Just out for exercise, are you?" Peter inquired kindly, taking pity on the man's confusion. Artists, he thought tolerantly.

"Yes, that is—" And then, unable to contain his joy, he told Peter of Oliver's letter and the invitation. He told Peter much more than he realized by his manner and his tone, and Peter knew then that not only was Giles Dalzell not in love with Ann, but he never could be.

"Do you mean to go?" he asked curtly.

"Yes, of course! Nothing could be more fortunate. You see, I have been working on this play, but there are so many distractions here. It will help me to get right away. Oliver, you know, has had two of his plays produced and he will be able to advise me."

"Does Ann know of this?"

"Yes, I have just come from her and she—"

"She does not object to your going off just at this time?"

"No. You see, the thing is she—well, it all happened so suddenly. Oliver's letter only came this morning, but I was too busy to look at the post. It was there all day—the letter, I mean—and I never suspected!" Giles looked awed at this realization that so much joy had been at hand for hours without his even suspecting it.

Peter, thinking only of how much unhappiness this must mean for Ann, was torn between the wish to tell Giles to take himself off and never come near his sister again and the knowledge that he must go very warily in the matter if he was not to make things worse for her. His eyes smoldered with anger and contempt that he made no attempt to disguise. "I hope you will at least delay sending a notice of your betrothal to the *Gazette* until you return. There would be bound to be gossip at the announcement followed at once by your disappearance for weeks."

Giles did not miss the anger in Peter's voice and his own happiness evaporated beneath it. He had been behaving like a fool, he thought. He pulled himself up and looked Peter directly in the eyes and said, "There will be no announcement at all. Ann has asked me to release her. Naturally, I did so."

"Naturally," replied Peter bitterly.

"I am sorry that you are so angry with me, Chance. I owe

your family too much to want to cause any of you grief, as you must know. I thought I was doing the right thing, what was expected of me, when I proposed to Ann. It had never occurred to me before to do so because I did not dream she— Well, I thought of us as brother and sister. However, she told me that she has decided we would not suit, and I make no doubt she is right. She needs a great deal more in a husband than I could— Well, enough of that. I will naturally go down to Chance Court and tell your parents what has happened before I go to Italy.''

He spoke with such simple, direct dignity that Peter could not help being impressed. He agreed with Giles' course of action as being entirely proper and bid him good day, afraid to say more before he had thought the matter over without anger.

He set off at once to see Ann, but suddenly changed his mind. He was not calm enough to do her any good by facing her with all this tonight. He would go to Robin first and talk it over with him. Robin had a way of seeing things in the proper perspective. By driving full out he reached Medford Yatter shortly after ten o'clock and found Robin sitting before the fire with a book. Robin rose at once in surprise and pleasure, embracing his brother in warm welcome.

"Glad to find you still awake. I hope you do not mind this late visit.''

"You know how glad I am to see you at any time. You will stay the night, of course. Excuse me for one moment while I tell the housekeeper to make a room ready.'' He came back after a moment and said, "There, now, you will sleep well tonight, dear fellow. The air here is so much better than in London. Well, I can see you are heavy with news. You look very serious.''

"I'm damned worried, if you want to know. I ran into that fool Dalzell this evening, his head so far up in the clouds he didn't know where he was.''

"Surely he is not a fool, Peter. He is a published poet, and not a bad one, to my way of thinking,'' reproved Robin mildly.

"Sorry. Not a fool, no. Something worse, I fear. Oh, Lord—'' He ran a hand distractedly through his hair, then rose to pour himself a glass of wine from the tray on a side table. He carried it back and stood staring morosely into the fire, his foot on the fender. After a few moments he began to tell his brother what he knew and what he suspected about Giles, and of the broken engagement. When he was finished, there was a prolonged silence.

At last Robin sighed. "How strange and unknowable are the ways of the Lord. Naturally, I had always assumed he and Ann would make a match of it someday, though I should have suspected something was wrong for it to have taken so long to come about. Are you sure about his feelings, Peter?"

"You had only to see him, his eyes shining—I have never seen him like that. Certainly never when he was speaking of Ann. Surly sort of fellow for the most part. What must we do?"

"What had you in mind?"

"Well, I am not sure. What do you advise as a minister of the Church?"

"The same as I would advise as her brother who cares very much for her well-being. Leave it alone."

"But she will have surely realized, just as I did, what his true feelings are, what he is. I fear she is not strong enough to bear such dreadful knowledge after loving him all these years."

"We are not made to bear more than we have the strength for, Peter, and Ann, for all her weak constitution, has great strength of will and mind. She would not appreciate our meddling in this. Besides, she knows Dalzell better than anyone else, and it is my belief that that is why she broke off the betrothal. She may not have acknowledged it to herself, but I am sure that somewhere in herself she must know the truth. She has had several young men in love with her and knows full well how a man in love behaves, how he looks upon his beloved. She cannot have failed to notice that Dalzell, for all his devotion to her, has never looked upon her in that way. I believe, now that I come to really think about this, that she would have broken her engagement eventually in any case. Ann could never bear a marriage based upon pity or duty, and she would come to see the truth before long."

"I should like to take a whip to that—that—" Peter ground out in complete frustration.

"We are all as God made us, Peter," admonished Robin gently, "and Dalzell has always been a friend of ours and a good brother to Ann. He truly cares for her, you know. He cannot help it if he has not the capacity to fall in love with her.''

Peter thrashed about in his mind for a way to refute this reasonable summation of the case, but could find none. Finally, he stumped across the room to the tray, replenished his glass, and gulped down the wine, trying to drown his feelings of inadequacy. He could not help his sister, he had not so far been able to help his brother in his unhappiness, nor had he even been able to help himself. The Chances, it seemed, were all unfortunate in affairs of the heart.

23

Camilla had spent several days thinking of what she must do. She had been polite but unforthcoming to her mother, who studied her every expression nervously, attempting to guess what she was planning. Camilla had thought of going to her father at once, telling him everything, and enlisting his permission and support in standing up to her mother, but had decided against it. To give her mother time to undermine her father's resolution would be a mistake, especially when Camilla had no firm assurance that Robin still felt the same about her. Miss Pymbroke's impression that he was still very unhappy at not having been received after the Dewinters' ball might just be pique at the insult.

Camilla had been very sure of his feelings during the time they were together at the ball, but some weeks had passed since that night and he might very well have changed his mind, or met someone who interested him more. For some reason she was obsessed by the conviction that Medford Yatter was inhabited by delightfully beautiful young women, all of whom had conceived a passion for their new vicar upon first sight.

Before she could decide anything, she must see him. This need became so overwhelming that it swamped all the rules of permissible conduct instilled in her by her upbringing. She would go to Medford Yatter tomorrow and confront him. To this end she requested and was given permission to borrow her father's carriage, claiming that after church she had sev-

eral calls to make; she informed her abigail to be prepared to
leave the house early in the morning as they were attending
services at a church an hour out of London. The next order of
business was to decide on her costume. She spent most of
Saturday afternoon on this project. Gowns, shawls, pelisses,
bonnets, and spensers were laid out on every available surface,
and many different effects and combinations were tried and
discarded before Camilla, to her weary maid's relief, at last
settled for a blossom-pink muslin with several rows of scal-
loped ruffles around the hem, a pelisse of fawn-colored sarcenet trimmed with mohair fringe, a straw bonnet with pink
ribands, pink kid slippers, and Limerick gloves. The very
glass of fashion, but still subdued enough not to offend the
congregation at Medford Yatter, and softly feminine enough
to appeal to any gentleman, Camilla thought.

On the next morning, followed by her maid, she entered
the church at Medford Yatter, looking composed and demure,
but quaking inside with nerves. She was very much aware of
being the focus of every eye, while with her own modestly
downcast, she was yet able to note that only three young
women were in the congregation, two on the plain side,
though not antidotes, and one fairly pretty girl with yellow
curls and meltingly lovely blue eyes. The usher seated Camilla quite near the front and she folded her hands to wait,
with heavily beating heart, for what fate had in store for her.
There was a stir and Robin entered, preceded by the choir
chanting a psalm and the altar boys. One glance at him and
she felt her what little confidence she had managed to retain
drain from her. He looked so remote, disconcertingly distanc-
ing in his white robes; his eyes seemed to be serenely contem-
plating some vision she would never see. It was difficult to
equate him with the eager lover she had last seen. It was
altogether most sobering.

The opening rituals of the service seemed unbearably slow
to her as she knelt and rose to her feet and knelt again, or sat
with eyes riveted on the back of Robin's head as he moved
about the altar on the Lord's business. Then he was mounting
the pulpit for the sermon and she found it hard to breathe.
Now he would see her! What would he think—do? He began
to speak simply but with moving sincerity about forgiveness,
his eyes roving over his parishioners, until they came at last

to her—and passed on! He did not recognize her! Then his eyes swung back to her with a jerk. He faltered, looked down at his notes, swallowed, and then went on smoothly.

What was he feeling? He did not yet know about her mother's scheming. Perhaps he was angry with her now for appearing without warning in such a way. Should she have written to him instead, explaining all, and asking him to call when next he came to London? She knew that would have been the proper way, but it had seemed too slow, too tame to her. Oh, it *would* be all right, surely, when she had explained it all to him. Would it not? She felt a lump forming in her throat at the thought that it might not any longer be all right. He might very well give her his forgiveness when she explained it all to him, but the long separation might have so cooled his ardor that he no longer had any interest in reviving it, or—oh, dear, heaven forbid—he had come into the clutches of Miss Demure Yellow Curls, who would have been gazing at him so adoringly each Sunday.

The final blessing was given and the final amen, and the choir sang their way down the aisle again. The congregation fell in behind to inch their way to the outer door, where their vicar waited to greet them. All except Camilla, who motioned her maid out, but remained firmly in her pew, eyes fixed on her gloved hands clasped in her lap. She knew this would cause a great deal of gossip and speculation, but she had no intention of entertaining them all with her meeting with Robin. He would come to her. The wait seemed endless before she heard his steps returning. She rose, stepped out into the aisle, and turned to face him, trembling. It is not going to be all right, she thought with a fleeting sick dismay, seeing the seriousness of his expression.

"Miss Chamfreys," he said expressionlessly.

"Yes, Robin. Is it all right that I came?"

"Why did you do so?"

"I came to—to tell you—to apologize for—"

"There is no need for you to do so, Miss Chamfreys; indeed there is not," he replied gravely, giving her not the least hint of his feelings.

Her heart seemed to wither for a moment, but she would not give in so easily. "You spoke quite movingly of forgiveness in your sermon," she reminded him.

"Oh, I see. You came for my forgiveness? But of course, you have had that all along, Miss Chamfreys, I do assure you."

"That is very kind of you, but forgiveness was not my sole purpose in coming. I wanted to explain—"

"Truly you owe me no explanation at all, Miss Chamfreys. I hope I am not so green in these matters as not to understand that young ladies can be flighty and have changes of heart—"

"Oh," she interrupted him, flaring into temper, "do stop calling me Miss Chamfreys in that daunting way and stop being so insufferably magnanimous! I vow, you sound like your brother—all those precious carefully rounded periods! I have come here to tell you what really happened and I shall tell you whether you care to hear it or not. It was that dreadful Miss Clayton-Trees. You approached her that night thinking it was me and gave her your name. Later she recognized Mama and told her all she knew and guessed. Mama did the rest. She gave Willes orders to deny me if you called. I only found out a few days ago and I came as soon as I could. And I will have you know, *Mr. Chance*," she added with pointed emphasis, "that despite all you have been given to understand about young women being flighty, it will be well for you to learn that while there may well be such women—indeed, it would not surprise me to learn of the existence of equally flighty young men—I, sir, am not given to such flights or sudden changes of mind!" She finished slightly breathless, bright patches of color flaring on her cheekbones, her dark eyes flashing angrily.

He stared at her admiringly for a moment before he said, "I think it is I who must ask for forgiveness."

"Then it is all right that I came?"

"It is wonderful that you came, you brave, sweet girl."

They looked and looked at each other, made unusually shy by the intensity of their feelings. At last he held out his hands and she confidently laid her own within them. He pulled her closer and held her hands clasped against his chest, then bent his mouth to hers, kissing her gently, almost fearfully, as though his feelings were so strong he dared not unleash them. After a moment she murmured, "Should we be doing this here?"

"What better place to express love?" he asked, smiling. "But you are right, the sexton may come in."

"I am not sure I can face anyone now. I expect they are all still out there, waiting for me to emerge."

"There is a side door leading to the house. Come this way." He led her down the aisle to a door beside the altar that opened into the robing room, quickly divested himself of his robe, and then took her out through a side door, along a path lined with beds of daffodils, dancing and bowing in the light breeze. It was a sparkling, sunny, perfect spring day, made for lovers.

In his drawing room he seemed to lose the restraints he had felt before and pulled her roughly into his arms and kissed her with an almost savage intensity. She met him with equal ardor, her arms tight about his neck to hold him as close as possible. It was not until nearly thirty minutes had passed thus blissfully that all the past weeks of unhappiness were at last assuaged and they could bear to release each other.

"Are you hungry, my darling?" he asked tenderly.

"Ravenously," she laughed.

He rang for his housekeeper, and when she appeared, he introduced her to Camilla and requested that she ask Cook to prepare them a rather hearty luncheon and show Miss Chamfreys upstairs to refresh herself before they sat down.

"Oh, good heavens, my maid!" gasped Camilla, suddenly remembering. "Could someone step around to the front of the church to fetch her? I asked her to wait there for me."

The housekeeper, her last suspicion fading at hearing the lady was properly accompanied by her maid, assured her it would be done at once. She led Camilla upstairs, said hot water would be brought up immediately, and disappeared to carry out her orders. Camilla laid aside her bonnet and pelisse, smoothed her hair, and when a maid appeared with a jug of hot water and towels, washed her face and hands before returning eagerly to the drawing room.

Robin came to meet her. "What a very becoming gown, but you are always so beautiful I suspect you would look just as well in a piece of sacking." He cupped her face in his hands and studied the perfect oval, the delicately flushed cheeks, the lambent depths of her dark eyes, and began to press small kisses randomly over forehead, eyelids, cheeks, chin, ending at last upon the soft, waiting mouth. They were lost again until a discreet tap on the door reminded them of the world about them.

"I believe our meal is ready, my love," he said, releasing her reluctantly and pulling her arm through his. "Come along or I shall have shocked Mrs. Brumble into fits."

Mrs. Brumble, the housekeeper, was far from fits. She was in a state of most pleasurable excitement. She had already seen the fashionably dressed young woman who had stayed behind when the congregation left, and she had wondered about her, though she had not been able to stay behind with the others on the church porch to gossip about her with her friends, for she had had to hurry back to the house. Therefore, she had not seen or been informed of the maid who accompanied the young lady, and had until now been bristling with indignation at the brazenness she displayed. Now that that problem had been disposed of, her feelings about Camilla veered about sharply. She did not know who the young woman might be, but that she was quality was perfectly clear, with her refined manners, elegant carriage, and uppity maid, who was even now awing the maids in the kitchen, where she condescended to drink a cup of tea. Mrs. Brumble felt that here was a young lady worthy of her dear Mr. Chance, and she could stop worrying about that yellow-haired chit who ogled him so shamelessly every time she had the chance. Mrs. Brumble knew how susceptible young men could be when they were lonely, and he had no real friends here as yet. The problem for the dear man was that though there was no side to him at all, he was socially so far above anyone in the village that they were somewhat in awe of him.

Mrs. Brumble bustled in and out of the dining room with various plates of food, viewing with satisfaction the pair, who ate everything put before them with healthy appetites while never taking their eyes from each other the whole time. Oh, yes, she thought with a nostalgic sigh, I know the signs. Didn't Brumble and me use to look upon each other just so, hearts in our eyes, when I was eighteen and slim as a willow just like her? With nothing left to serve, she retired again to the kitchen and began a subtle interrogation of Miss Chamfreys' abigail.

Robin pushed away his plate and reached for her hand.

"Now, my darling, we must decide how best to set about this thing."

"Oh, could I not just stay here? I thought if I were compromised—"

He laughed. "With your maid and Mrs. Brumble in attendance to ensure respectability? No, no, sweetheart, that would never work."

"I am silly," she admitted, suddenly wise for his good name. "What a dreadful thing to conceive of doing to you, a vicar! As it is, I suppose I have given the village enough gossip to dine out for the next month."

"We have enough problems without concerning ourselves with that. I will of course come up to London tomorrow to speak to your papa, but how will your mother receive the news?"

"Please do not be concerned about her either. It is my papa you will speak to, and when he consents, she will have nothing to say in the matter. I will talk to him first, of course."

"Oh, I fear she will have a great deal to say, and from what I have observed, your father gives her her own way for the most part."

"Yes, darling Papa is the best-natured fellow alive. He saves all his temperament for the stage, I think. But he has never denied me anything. The only time he stands up to Mama is when he thinks I am right. I will tell him all about us." She blushed happily at this delightful pronoun.

Unable to restrain himself longer, he pushed back his chair and came to snatch her up into his arms. After several moments of this close embrace, she said somewhat reproachfully, "Darling, do please *kiss* me."

Later Robin took her for a walk through the village, introducing her to the unusual number of people who found it necessary to take the air just as they were coming back down the street from the furthermost reaches of the village.

Miss Chamfreys, demure and friendly, made a most favorable impression on all but three disappointed damsels, two plain, one with yellow curls, who, though disdaining to parade the street with the hope of an introduction, yet had many disparaging comments to make about Miss Chamfreys.

Camilla and her maid arrived back in London before five

that same afternoon, and Camilla wasted no time in requesting a private interview with her father. Mr. Chamfreys, quite hopelessly under the dainty thumb of his daughter, gave in almost at once and, having made his decision, stood up very well to his wife's rage when she returned from a visit to Lady Danforth to be confronted by a *fait accompli.*

By the time Robin appeared upon the doorstep the next day, Mrs. Chamfreys had resigned herself and was busily planning the most elegant wedding she could conceive of. After all, an earl and his countess for one's in-laws was not to be sneezed at, and while Camilla would have no title, she would, when she chose to do so, move in the best circles, be intimately allied to one of the finest families in England, and have anything that a fashionable young matron might require.

"Yes," she imagined herself saying to her friends, "Camilla is visiting at Chance Court, the dear countess insisted they come to stay—" and though wild horses could not have dragged such an admission from her, she could not suppress the thought that it had been known for second sons to come into the title, though God knew she had no wish for anything dire to happen to dear Lord Chance!

Having settled, at Camilla's insistence, that the marriage would take place at the end of June, the problem of where it was to be held came under consideration. Mrs. Chamfreys was adamant that it must be as fashionable as possible or she would be ashamed, and she held out for St. Paul's. Robin ventured to suggest that his mother might prefer to have him marry in their church at Allchance village. But Camilla would not give way in the matter to either of them. They must be married in Robin's own church at Medford Yatter with his own congregation as witnesses. This would not only set the seal on his own acceptance, but hers as well. In the face of her obduracy, the rest finally gave in and it was set. Robin sent a note of their betrothal to the *Gazette*, penned a hasty letter to his brother, and took himself off at once to Chance Court to inform his parents of his new happiness.

24

The next morning, as Robin had requested her to do, Camilla went to pay a call upon Ann to inform her of events. She went as early as the dictates of society allowed in the hopes of finding no other callers. She was shown in by Hay and Ann came to her in the drawing room almost at once.

"Miss Chamfreys! How very delightful to see you. Please sit down."

"I hope I have not come too early?"

"Not at all. We finished our breakfast a quarter of an hour ago and Vanessa went off to ride with Lord Evelyn, her latest conquest. Mrs. Clarence is having her breakfast in bed this morning. I fear we have worn her out with all our partying this Season."

"Well, you look particularly well today, so I think it cannot have harmed you."

"Oh, do I? I thank you. I do feel in fine spirits today for some reason."

"Good—for me, I mean, for I have come to tell you some news that I hope will not be distressing to you."

She hesitated shyly while Ann waited politely. At last Ann said, "Please do go on, Miss Chamfreys. I know it must be good news from your expression, and I am always prepared to hear good news."

"Well, actually it is for me—and for your brother—your brother Robin, of course," she added hastily, blushing prettily.

"Oh, Miss Chamfreys, do you tell me that you and Robin—?"

"Yes," Camilla burst in, needing to be the one to say those wonderful words, "we are betrothed!"

"Miss Chamfreys! Camilla!" Ann ran to throw her arms about Camilla and embrace her enthusiastically. "This is indeed good news. I wish you happy, my dear, indeed I do!"

Camilla burst into tears of happiness and Ann joined her. After a moment they released each other to grope for handkerchiefs.

"Oh, dear, how silly to cry," said Ann, mopping her eyes, "but I am so glad. Poor darling Robin looked so wretchedly unhappy when last I saw him. Here, darling, sit down beside me and tell me how it all came about. What had happened between you and how did you make it up?"

Camilla was only too happy to oblige her and ever so gratified by Ann's keen interest in every minute detail of who said what, and what was replied, and then what happened. Camilla had nearly reached the end of her recital when the door opened and Vanessa came in, looking impossibly beautiful in a dark-green riding habit despite the faint shadows beneath her eyes.

"Vanessa, dear," cried Ann, "you are just in time to hear the good news. Robin and Camilla have made it up and are to be married. It is to be the end of June!"

Vanessa did her best to respond with the appropriate enthusiasm and kissed Camilla warmly. "I do wish you happy, dearest Camilla, as you must know."

"Yes, I do know. It is all due to you, Vanessa. I shall never be able to express my gratitude to you, for had you not told me about Miss Clayton-Trees, we might never have made it up between us."

Then, of course, she began at the beginning again and told the entire story to Vanessa. Ann looked puzzled. "But I do not understand how you came to know all this about Miss Clayton-Trees, Vanessa."

Vanessa confessed then the story of dressing up as a young man and fooling Mr. Bynge, of returning home to overhear a sentence or two from Miss Clayton-Trees to her aunt that had intrigued her, and then deciding to inveigle the rest of the story from Miss Clayton-Trees. Naturally she did not speak of the subsequent, disastrous events connected with her masquerade.

"Oh, you clever thing," exclaimed Camilla. "I should never have had the courage to do such a thing."

"Oh, I think you would have. After all, it took a great deal of courage to go to Medford Yatter as you did," replied Vanessa.

"It is only that you and I do not think of such larks as Vanessa can dream up," consoled Ann.

"Thank goodness she does, for had she not, I should never have known. Oh, what a meddlesome creature that Clayton-Trees woman is, to be sure. I shall never be able to speak civilly to her again," declared Camilla.

"Well, I am only grateful that some good came out of the wretched business," murmured Vanessa darkly, her face desolate with unhappiness.

Camilla did not notice, for she contemplated her own happiness. "Oh, do you know—I have just realized. Perhaps we three shall be sisters one day before too long and I—"

Vanessa rose and hurried out of the room, murmuring that she must change out of her habit.

"Why, what is it? What did I say that—"

"Do not regard it, Camilla. She and Peter are at swords' points again. He found out about her escapade, you see, and did not approve."

"Oh, dear, I am so sorry I spoke as I did. I thought for sure they would be making an announcement themselves very soon."

"Well, I think they might have done, but when Peter learned— Well, they quarreled bitterly."

"Oh, how very dreadful," Camilla exclaimed in genuine sorrow, for in her own happiness she wanted the whole world around her to be glad. "But it will work out, surely. She must still love him very much or she would not be so unhappy."

"Yes, I think she does."

"And what of him?"

"Well, knowing Peter as I do, I can only believe that he feels the same or he would never have behaved so badly about it."

"That seems contradictory," said Camilla in some puzzlement.

"Peter can be harsh toward those he cares for. He expects more of them."

"Oh. Well, I suppose I see. But he should also be more forgiving. Oh, Ann, you should have heard the divine sermon Robin gave Sunday on that subject. He is a most affecting preacher." She went on to expatiate for quite a half-hour on the wonderfulness of Robin before she collected herself and rose to leave.

Ann went upstairs with the intention of comforting Vanessa, but stood irresolute outside her bedroom door as she realized she really had no comfort to give that was of any practical use. She could not hold and caress her, for that was a form of comfort Vanessa rejected. In school, after some more than usually severe punishment for yet another infraction of the rules, she always avoided physical comforting, for she said it only made her cry and feel sorry for herself. At last Ann turned away and went instead to Mrs. Clarence's room.

She found Mrs. Clarence lying against a great hillock of pillows, reading a novel and eating comfits from a beautifully painted box.

"Come in, my dear. How lovely of you to visit. I am being entirely self-indulgent this morning, as you can see. How Pymbroke would scold if he could see me—my brother, you know. We were so different as children. He was always most scornful of my 'sloth,' as he called it. Vanessa is very like him too, though she never scolds me. She has his temper, however," she added significantly, for her abigail had made sure her mistress knew all about the quarrel between her niece and Lord Chance.

Ann sighed. "Yes, I fear so. She and Peter have had another misunderstanding, as I suppose you have heard. She is miserable."

"Well, she loves him, of course, and he criticized her severely. Your brother does not mince his words, Ann dear."

"No, but he loves her very much, I think."

"Oh, without a doubt. I have thought so this age. Have one of these, my dear, they are ever so delicious." Mrs. Clarence held out the pretty box.

"Thank you, but I have never cared for sweets."

"How fortunate for your figure. I have always been a victim of my sweet tooth—and now I am paying for it. But then, I am old enough not to care for my figure anymore. Is Vanessa moping?"

"She just returned from riding with Lord Evelyn."

"Perhaps he consoled her."

"I should doubt it very much. His sort of practiced love-making works best on sweet young things just out of the schoolroom."

"Ah, well, you must not worry too much about it all, dear Ann. These things have to work themselves out in their own way."

"Speaking of things working out, I have not told you the good news I came to report. My brother Robin and Camilla Chamfreys have made a match of it."

"There now! How perfectly delightful that is. Such a beautiful girl and she will make him an excellent wife. She knows how to conduct herself properly and is not at all like her ambitious mother. Though Mrs. Chamfreys is a most compelling actress. Most compelling."

"I am glad you like Camilla, for I do, very much, and I shall enjoy having her for a sister."

"You are looking better these days, my dear," said Mrs. Clarence with another of her lightning changes of subject. "I vow, I was quite worried about you there for a time. You seemed so pulled somehow, not at all the look of a newly betrothed girl."

Ann flushed and looked away in some confusion. She had not told Vanessa and Mrs. Clarence of her broken engagement, not from secretiveness, but from a disinclination to discuss it with anyone yet. Now she was embarrassed by her unforth-comingness. It seemed sly somehow not to have taken them into her confidence after all their kindness to her.

"Mrs. Clarence, I fear I have not been as open with you as you deserve. I hope you will forgive me and not think me deceitful for not telling you before, but I—I—"

"You cried off!" finished Mrs. Clarence with a note of triumph in her voice.

"Well, I—yes, I did."

"There now! I had a feeling you would do so. At least, I hoped that you would."

Ann looked at her in some astonishment. "Did you so? But why, Mrs. Clarence?"

"You did not suit, in my opinion. He cared for you, but he was too ungiving and you were too much so. There must, in my opinion, be more equality in that matter before there can be true happiness in marriage. And forgive me for saying it, my dear, but you were not in love with each other."

"Well, he was not with me, true, but I thought I was with him."

"I thought the same, for a time, but now I cannot agree. You are intensely loyal by nature. You were infatuated with him as a schoolgirl, I would imagine, and remained too true to it. I do not believe that can be a good basis for lasting love. The lasting sort begins with breathless exultation on both sides and, with mutual understanding and reciprocal tolerance becomes a comfortable devotion that lasts forever. Marriage shows up all the faults eventually, when loyalty becomes worn out by the inequality between the couple. But I imagine you worked out something of this yourself or you would not have broken it off."

"Yes, I suppose I did," Ann replied in some bemusement at all the older woman had said.

"Of course. That is why you are looking so much better. You have thrown off the weight of that long-dead infatuation which had become more of a burden to you than a pleasure. How did Mr. Dalzell take the news?"

Ann laughed. "With great relief. He is off to Venice to join his friend Oliver and reinspire his muse."

Mrs. Clarence chuckled comfortably. "Poets! You are well out of it, love. Poets make poor husbands, I have heard. Look at poor Annabella Milbanke. I doubt she has had more than five full minutes of happiness with that monster of depravity, Lord Byron."

Ann laughed again, kissed her, and went along to tell Vanessa about Giles. At least it would take Vanessa's mind off her own problems for a time, and that was a form of comfort.

Camilla arrived home to find her mother serving a glass of wine to Lord Chance.

"Ah, Camilla, here is Lord Chance come to call upon you

and you out for hours, naughty girl," cried Mrs. Chamfreys playfully.

Peter rose and came to kiss Camilla's cheek. "My dear Camilla. May I call you so now that we are to be relatives? How very glad I was to learn from Robin that you had agreed to give him the happiness of your hand in marriage."

Camilla nearly laughed aloud. He *did* speak in rolling periods! She wondered if he were quite so precise when angry. She recovered herself and thanked him prettily. "I have just come from your sister, sir. Robin asked me to call and acquaint her with our news."

"I am sure she was pleased to hear it."

"She was delightfully kind. What very nice relatives I am to have. Not every girl is so fortunate."

"I think you will also like our parents very well. They are extremely kind and open-natured, you will find."

"Oh, I am quite sure they must be," cried Mrs. Chamfreys enthusiastically, "to have produced such well-behaved children. Yes," she said rather crossly to Willes, who had entered and was waiting to be noticed.

"It is Lady Danforth and her daughter calling, madam."

"Oh, bother! Well, show them into the back drawing room and I will join them. Do forgive me, Lord Chance, a very old friend and I must not neglect her."

Peter bowed and begged her not to stand upon any ceremony with him now that he was family. Much gratified, Mrs. Chamfreys gave him a blinding smile and hurried away.

"Your sister is looking very well, Lord Chance," said Camilla, settling herself on the sofa.

"Oh, surely it can be Peter now?" he said teasingly.

"Yes, of course," she agreed with a smile.

"I am happy to hear you say Ann is looking well. I have not seen her since she broke her betrothal to Giles Dalzell. I have been somewhat remiss." His eyes looked grim as he remembered why he had been so.

Camilla looked at him in astonishment. "Why, I had not heard of their betrothal!"

"No, she did not want it announced, and a very good thing, as it turns out. I must tell you we are all relieved that it is over."

"Well, I must say I found him very agreeable. Somewhat obsessive about his work, of course."

"He is a good-enough fellow, just not right for Ann."

"No. I have to agree with that. Well, if it is not agreeable to her family, it is a good thing they decided to end it. I must say she does not seem to be pining. On the other hand," she said carefully, feeling her way, "I thought Miss Pymbroke looked far from well."

Peter looked up sharply. "She is ill?" he snapped.

"No, not ill, I think—only unhappy." Peter looked away, his eyes hooded, and did not reply. After a most uncomfortable silence, she ventured, "You may consider me intolerably interfering, but it seems to me that you also are unhappy."

"I have known more cheerful periods in my life," he stated grimly.

"Would you prefer that I not speak of it any further?"

"No," he said at last.

She knew at once what he was feeling. Though the subject might be painful, there was a need after a lovers' quarrel to meet again, or at least speak of, or hear spoken of, the beloved, just as one compulsively probed an aching tooth with the tongue. Had she not gone herself to Mrs. Clarence's dinner party to see Robin for the same reason?

"May I tell you what Miss Pymbroke did for me?" He nodded and she related to him Vanessa's encounter with Miss Clayton-Trees. "Then she came to me and told me what happened to cause the trouble between Robin and me. You may not approve of her dressing in that way, but had she not made it her object to learn the truth, Robin and I would most likely never have been reconciled. There was no benefit in it for herself, only for people she cared about, and some small amount of risk for her. Of course, I admit the risk was attractive to her, but nevertheless, I admire her and feel myself very much in her debt."

Peter was sorely tempted to tell her the rest of Miss Pymbroke's adventures, the ones that had turned out less happily, but felt it would not be a gentlemanly thing to do. The story was Miss Pymbroke's to tell, not his. Apart from that, there was his own less-than-honorable behavior in the affair, as Miss Pymbroke had so eloquently pointed out and as he would be bound to confess if he were going to discuss it at all. And the more time passed, the less reprehensible did her conduct appear whereas his own had come to seem more so in his own eyes. He worried at the subject continuously, until he had become very sore in his spirits. Ah, I will not think of it anymore, he would think, it is all hopeless. But he did think of it all the same.

He became aware that Camilla's dark eyes were upon him, awaiting some comment on her story. He cleared his throat. "Very commendable, of course," he said, and heard in his mind Ann saying warningly, "Pompous." Then he said, "Camilla, my dear, I know you mean to give me comfort. I can understand why you want to help, but I fear it is too late, far too late," and he immediately wished he had held his tongue, for it sounded, even to his own ears, weak.

It did not sound so to Camilla—only human. She heard the hopelessness and longing he was loath to reveal as unmanly and liked him all the better for it. "You are wrong, Peter. It is not too late, for she loves you very well and I think you return her feelings. So anything is possible. You must just decide if it is worth standing down from one's declared position, worth sacrificing a bit of one's dignity and pride for."

25

Mrs. Clarence, accompanied by Ann, was taking the air in her open landau. The park was thronged with carriages and riders, creating an almost festive atmosphere in the warm May sunshine.

"It really was too bad of Vanessa to refuse to come out with us on such a day. She would benefit by the air, to my way of thinking. I find her looking somewhat peaky," said Mrs. Clarence.

"She said she had to write to her father."

"Yes, I know, but I place very little reliance on that. She said the same yesterday when I asked her to come shopping with me. She is skulking about in the house so she will not come face-to-face with your brother, is what she is doing. But unless she means not to go about at all anymore, there is simply no way she can avoid a meeting."

"Perhaps when more time has passed, it will be less painful for her."

"Nonsense. If it is painful, she should face up to it. A certain amount of unhappiness is good for the character. It helps one to grow."

"Why do you not have a talk with her, Mrs. Clarence? I am sure it would be of help to her."

"No, my dear, I make it a policy never to interfere. In any case, I should not know what to advise her, and I believe in such an event one should do nothing. Besides, Vanessa is like her papa. Not easy to advise, those two. Ah, here is the gentleman in question."

Ann looked around to see Peter coming up to them, mounted on his black mare. "Good morning, Mrs. Clarence. Ann, my dear. You are both looking very fine this morning."

Mrs. Clarence surveyed him closely. "I thank you, sir, though I fear I cannot in truth return the compliment. You do not look as though you have been sleeping well. Perhaps some warm milk at bedtime would be helpful."

"Thank you," he replied gravely, "I shall have to try it." He turned to Ann and looked searchingly into her face for a moment. "I have heard your news. Forgive me for not coming to you at once. But I see there was no need for a shoulder to cry upon."

Ann smiled. "No, my dear, there was not. All is very well with me."

"Yes, I can see that. Well, give you good morning, ladies." He tipped his beaver and trotted away.

"Ah, lovers, how tiresome they can be with their tiffs and their makings up," sighed Mrs. Clarence. "Now, here is a much more cheerful sight."

Mr. Rivers was approaching them now, also mounted, with, on either side, his children on their ponies. He led his children up to the carriage and introduced them to Mrs. Clarence, and then his daughter, Elizabeth, to Ann. She was a fair, pretty child of six with a great deal of composure, who responded without shyness to the introductions, as did Dalby.

"Very pretty-behaved children, sir," said Mrs. Clarence. Mr. Rivers acknowledged the compliment, his pride in them evident in his eyes.

"Lady Ann," said Dalby, "do you not have a pony to ride?"

"No, dear, I do not."

"You may ride my pony, if you would like it," he said kindly, "he is a real goer."

"I can see that. He is lovely, and it is most generous of you to offer."

"Oh, it is nothing," he said grandly. Then more diffidently, "I was sure you would come to see me, but you did not."

"No, that was very remiss of me," she agreed solemnly.

"When will you come? Will you like to come now?"

Ann looked up at Mr. Rivers, who was much amused, and they both laughed. "Yes, Lady Ann, we would be honored if you and Mrs. Clarence would come back with us now for a visit.''

Ann turned to Mrs. Clarence. "That would be most agreeable," said Mrs. Clarence with vast amiability.

So they all turned out of the park and clattered off to Mount Street together. When they reached the house a groom who waited there came to lift the children down and lead the ponies away, while Andrew Rivers assisted the ladies down from their carriage and escorted them into the house.

Refreshments were ordered, and while Elizabeth, with Mrs. Clarence's encouragement, brought out a rather soiled bit of embroidery work upon which she had clearly labored over for a long while, Dalby brought Ann his drawing pad filled almost exclusively with extraordinarily rudimentary depictions of horses.

"Will you mind if I lift you up into my lap so that you can show me the drawings more comfortably?" queried Ann, not sure if four-year-old boys were still amenable to being held.

"No, I will not mind," he assured her.

She lifted him into her lap and opened the pad to another drawing. Dalby leaned against her comfortably and explained that this one was Tinker, his pony, and this one Fairy, Elizabeth's pony, and the next was Papa's mare, Midnight. They all looked remarkably similar, but of course Ann made no mention of this fact.

After a time Dalby observed, "You are very soft." He pressed back against her experimentally. She looked up with some embarrassment to find Mr. Rivers laughing, and she could not help joining him. Dalby seemed pleased to have amused them, though he looked puzzled at the cause of their amusement. He demanded her attention be directed back to his pictures and took her carefully through each page. When the last picture was shown, he closed the book and turned to look up at her.

"Do you have a little boy?"

"No, darling, I do not."

"I could be your little boy sometimes, if you would like it."

"Thank you. I should like it very much indeed." She dared not look up, for she knew Mr. Rivers was observing them closely, and if he was laughing, she was sure she would blush. She was relieved when a diversion was created at that moment by the appearance of the children's nurse.

"Oh, you must not come for us now, Bickers. We are entertaining," chided Dalby with great seriousness.

Mrs. Bickerton then recognized Ann and her face lit up with adoration. She dropped a profound curtsy. "Oh, Lady Ann, what a pleasure this is, to be sure. Such an honor—"

"How do you do, Mrs. Bickerton. Dalby looks very well."

"Thank you, m'lady. So kind—" Her eyes glistened with unshed tears as she was overcome by the dreadful memories recalled by this meeting.

"Bickers cries frequently," whispered Dalby. Mr. Rivers grinned and Ann had all she could do not to giggle.

Mrs. Clarence, not wanting to cause any controversy between nurse and charges, stood up. "I really think we must be going now, Mr. Rivers."

"Yes, of course we must," agreed Ann. With some daring she held Dalby close for a moment and then set him on his feet again. "Will you walk us to our carriage, sir?" she asked, looking down at him.

For answer he put his hand confidingly into hers and they walked to the door. Ann turned and held out her other hand to Elizabeth, and after only the slightest hesitation she came forward shyly and took it. Ann pressed it warmly, hoping the child would not think herself neglected while her baby brother garnered so much attention. Next time, Ann vowed, I will spend more time with her.

"Will you come to visit me again?" asked Dalby anxiously.

"Yes, of course I will."

"When will you come?" Dalby liked to have things definite. His deepest dislikes were for words like "soon," "perhaps," "someday," and "we shall see."

"I shall come the day after tomorrow and take you and Elizabeth to the Zoological Gardens. Will you care for that?"

He seemed for a moment too overcome to speak, but he nodded eagerly. Elizabeth evidently felt something a little more expressive of their pleasure was needed, for she said, "We would both like that very much indeed, Lady Ann, if it will not be too much trouble for you."

Dalby found his voice. "You may kiss me, if you want

to,'' he said magnanimously. ''I do not much care for it, but ladies seem to like it.''

''They do indeed,'' she said, laughing happily, and swept him up in her arms and kissed his rosy little mouth resoundingly. She set him down and held out her hands to Elizabeth, who came, less shyly this time, to raise her face to be kissed.

At the carriage, Mr. Rivers helped them in and, when they were seated, asked Ann if she would attend Lady Gregory's ball tonight.

She said without hesitation, ''Yes! Yes, I will.''

He did not ask her to hold a set for him, for he knew that if she felt able to dance she would not refuse him. He kissed the hand she held out to him and stepped back, thanking them for coming, while the children waved and called out their good-byes.

As they drove off, Dalby called out, ''You will not forget the Zoo—zoo—gical Gardens?''

She turned to wave. ''No, darling, I will not forget.''

Mrs. Clarence viewed Ann's sparkling eyes and flushed cheeks with great good humor. There now, she thought happily, that is all most satisfactory. Most satisfactory indeed.

''Mrs. Clarence,'' said Ann suddenly, ''I did not even consult with you about this evening. Perhaps you will not care for going to the Gregorys' tonight.''

''My dear, wild horses would not prevent me,'' declared Mrs. Clarence with a rich chuckle that caused Ann to drop her eyes in confusion.

Later in the afternoon a ravishing bouquet of tiny white and yellow rose-buds in an ivory holder arrived for Ann. The note accompanying it said, ''Thank you, Dalby.''

She decided she would carry it tonight and chose a pale-orange muslin to go with it. Carrying the gown and bouquet, she went along to Vanessa's room to consult her about her choice.

Vanessa sat with uncharacteristic lassitude on the window seat, her forehead resting against the pane, staring vacantly out into the top of a tree. She jumped up at once when Ann entered, her face taking on a look of artificial animation.

''Oh, what a pretty bouquet. Who sent it?''

''A new young man who I believe I am falling in love with.''

"Ann! Oh, my dear, how wonderful! Who is he?"

"You have not met him as yet, but you will."

"Then—then it is serious. Has he declared himself already?"

"Not in so many words, but alas, even if he should, we can never marry," replied Ann in sorrowful tones.

"Good heavens, why ever not?"

"Well, you see, he is but four years old, and while I would wait for him, I fear he—"

"Oh, you, you—" gasped Vanessa, then erupted into giggles. She picked up a small pillow from the window seat and threw it at Ann, who caught it with one hand and flung it back; then quickly depositing her gown and bouquet on the bed out of harm's way, she was prepared when it came back at her. The pillow flew back and forth while they laughed helplessly, doing little real damage beyond tousling their curls. They finally collapsed breathlessly onto the carpet.

"Whoosh," gasped Vanessa, "do you remember those pillow fights at Madame Beauclerc's?"

"And how angry Madame was when one split and the whole room was covered with feathers?"

"I could never forget. Did we not spend the entire next day on our hands and knees picking them up? Now, tell me about this young man."

"Actually it is young Mr. Rivers. Dalby Rivers, the boy I found in the park that day."

"Whose father is so particularly attentive to you. Ah ha!"

"What do you mean 'Ah ha'?"

"Oh, nothing, just ah ha. You will carry them tonight, of course?"

"That is why I am here. Do you think they will look well with my pale orange?"

"Perfect."

"What will you wear?"

"Oh, I had thought I would not—"

"Please say you will come. I have missed you these past evenings. I enjoy it very much more when we go together." Ann put out a pleading hand to touch her arm and Vanessa surrendered.

"Oh, you wretch, you know I can never say no to you. Very well, I will go, though I must admit they begin to be boring."

"What will you wear?"

"You may choose, it does not matter."

Ann picked out a seafoam-green gauze and then, taking her own gown and the bouquet, went away, saying she would have a nap. Ann was determined to dance tonight and knew she must rest first. She dropped off to sleep almost at once, a smile curving up the corners of her mouth like a contented cat. She had made Vanessa laugh and got her to agree to come out tonight, and then, the afternoon had been so pleasant.

Lady Gregory's ball was no more distinguished than any of dozens that had taken place already this Season. The decorations were attractive but not outstanding; the music was, in fact, played by the same orchestra that had played at most of the balls this Season; and the refreshments up to the usual standards, but not memorable. The evening was for Ann, however, the most lighthearted she had experienced since her own come-out, when the world seemed filled with promises of happiness. She remembered Mrs. Clarence's remark about throwing off the weight of an old infatuation, and knew that all these years she *had* allowed an unrealistic dream to color her every thought and action and to hold at bay all those lighthearted times most young girls experienced when they first left the schoolroom and entered the world of adults. For her there had always been Giles' scowling presence overshadowing her enjoyment with his fear that she would overuse her strength and he might lose her, the only person he had ever trusted—until Oliver. She hoped Oliver would be worthy of Giles' trust, for Giles deserved it. She sent out a silent thought of love to Giles and turned up a face lit with radiant good spirits to greet Mr. Rivers, who had come to bow before her.

She gave him her hand. "I hope you will tell Dalby how happy I am to be carrying his token tonight," she said.

"I was especially commissioned to bring news of just that to him. You are very good to carry it, and also very good to offer to take them on an excursion."

"I should have consulted you first. I hope you did not mind?"

"Not if I may be allowed to come along."

"Good heavens, can you want to?" She laughed.

"More than anything in the world. Every chance to be with

you is heaven-sent, my dear," he replied, pressing the hand he still held.

Having forgotten it, she now tried to pull it away in some embarrassment, but he would not release it. Finally she desisted. "We shall cause a scandal, sir."

"I certainly hope so. There is nothing I would like better than to have everyone talking about us," he said with such an infectious grin that she could not help laughing. "You seem very different tonight. You are always beautiful, of course, but tonight you take my breath away."

"It is Dalby's gesture," she said.

"I am sure he will be very grateful to you for the honor," he said, bending his head to her hand and kissing, with great concentration, each of her fingers. His lips were warm and she felt a small pleasurable shock quivering up her arm. It did not now occur to her to pull her hand away. In fact, she would very much have liked to give him her other hand for the same treatment. As though sensing this as she thought it, he took her other hand and applied himself to it with the same care. After a moment she gasped and he raised his head to look at her, his eyes expressing everything he had not yet said. It was only for a moment, but it seemed to her to go on and on, until a woman's shrill laugh recalled her to the present. He pulled her to her feet.

"I think tonight you will dance. May I hope it will be with me?"

She curtsied. "Willingly, sir."

Mrs. Clarence watched him leading her out to the floor, feeling an enormous satisfaction with the way the romance was going. That is the way it should be for her, Mrs. Clarence thought, that delicate rapture at the beginning that leads to passion. Mrs. Clarence waxed exceedingly romantic for a time as she watched them, then her thoughts became more practical. How fortunate that two such eminently suitable people should find each other in all of London. Rivers was gentle and giving, yet a man who loved well. Having a son already, he would never allow Ann to endanger her life by bearing a child, while his own children were still young enough to satisfy Ann's maternal feelings. Ah, yes, it would be a perfect match.

She turned her attention to her own niece. Poor child, she

was suffering, that was clearly to be seen in her eyes if one but looked for it, though she did not sit out a single set. The problem is she has always had everything too much her own way, always been admired and approved in all she did. It will not hurt her to learn to modify her behavior to conform to the ideas of someone else—if she cares enough for him to do so. Chance was in the right of it, not to like her roaming the streets at night, men's clothing notwithstanding.

Vanessa went through the evening in a blur of boredom, though she did not lack for partners. It all seemed pointless and dull and she could not keep herself from watching the door. The one she watched for so anxiously, so fearfully, however, did not appear that evening.

If only he would come and allow her the satisfaction of snubbing him . . .

26

Peter strolled along Bond Street morosely. He had just come from Weston's, where he had had a fitting on a new coat he had ordered, and was aware that he had made himself disagreeable to the long-suffering proprietor over the fit of the shoulders. For a man who had been taught how to make himself pleasant while being firm, it was depressing to acknowledge that he was so little in control of his behavior. He was not aware that the brooding remoteness of his countenance caused many of his friends passing him in the street to turn aside without speaking to him. He knew he was behaving oddly, but could not seem to shake off his mood. He found that his love for Miss Pymbroke was far beyond anything he had ever experienced, or even imagined. When he had, in the past, thought of someday falling in love, he had pictured it as a light, frothy sort of business, not this wrenching ache that could not be assuaged. He had resolved several times to forget her and everything connected with her; he had eschewed all entertainments for a week to avoid any possibility of an encounter with her; he had deliberately not gone to Ann when she might have needed his support, for fear Miss Pymbroke would be at home. Yet it was all to no avail. Her face haunted his every waking moment and most of his sleeping ones, her words of condemnation seemed to ring endlessly in his ears. If he could deny her accusation of deliberate cruelty, be still able to maintain his righteous anger at her for endangering her life and putting herself in a position to create an enormous scandal, he knew he would not be in quite such a painful state, but he knew now that all his attempts to justify his actions were exercises in futility.

"Peter?"

He jerked his head up and stared at his sister as though he had never seen her before.

"For heaven's sake, Peter, what is wrong? That was the third time I spoke to you and now you look at me as though I were a ghost!"

"Oh, Ann, sorry, I was—thinking."

"Apparently," she replied dryly, "and not pleasant thoughts, it would seem."

"Not very, no," he said, his eyes bleak.

"Really, my dear, do you not think this has all gone on long enough?"

"I fear I do not understand you," he said stiffly.

"Pompous. You know very well what I mean. This ridiculous quarrel between you and Vanessa."

"I prefer not to discuss it, if you do not mind."

"But I do mind, I intend to discuss it. Dearest Peter"—she put an entreating hand on his arm—"I cannot bear to see both of you pulling yourselves apart over this stupid business. You look like death and she is losing all her precious eagerness and sparkle. Can you not show all the generosity of spirit I have always seen in you and be the first to apologize? No"—she held up her hand as he opened his mouth to speak—"let me finish, once I have gone this far. No doubt she behaved foolishly, but is it such an earth-shattering mistake that you would ruin both your lives for it? Have you never been guilty of foolish behavior?"

For some moments he said nothing, then he sighed. "Yes, I have."

"Oh, my dear," she said, her beautiful gray eyes filling with tears at the sadness in his voice, "now you are like my old Peter. You will know what is best to do. I am sure of it."

"You are a good sort of sister to have, you know," he said, patting the hand on his arm.

"You will come about, Peter, once you see your way." She smiled so happily that for a moment he felt his gloom lift imperceptibly. Yes, perhaps it might be so. "Do you go to Almack's tonight?"

"Good Lord, no," he said in surprise at her question.

"Oh, please change your mind. We shall be going," she added, only slightly emphasizing the pronoun.

"I do not believe I could bear—"

"Yes, you can, dearest, of course you can. You must, you know. Now I must fly, for I need several things if I am not to look sadly ill-dressed and bring shame upon you. I will look to see you tonight for sure and will count on you to ask me to stand up."

She hurried away before he could protest further. Oh, surely it will be all right now, please let it be so, she prayed as she shopped quickly for clocked silk stockings for herself and silver ribands for Vanessa. It had taken every ounce of persuasion at her command to convince Vanessa to come to Almack's with her tonight, but she had at last worn down her resistance and won her consent. She had again been forced to choose Vanessa's gown for her and had picked out a celestial-blue gauze embroidered with silver leaves, which had necessitated a hurried trip for the silver riband. She had intended on her return to send a note to Peter asking him to please drop in to Almack's this evening, even if only for a few moments, as she had something urgent that she must discuss with him. Thank goodness the fortuitous meeting just now had made it unnecessary to resort to such a ruse.

By the time they reached Almack's that evening, Ann was having some difficulty retaining her carefree enthusiasm for the affair in the face of Vanessa's indifference. Throughout dressing, dinner, and the drive she had kept up a cheerful, mostly one-sided dialogue on every subject she could think of to keep Vanessa in spirits. She breathed a sigh of relief as the carriage drew to a stop and they stepped out. At least she had achieved the almost impossible task of getting them both here; now she must just pray that a higher power would take a hand and make them both see some sense. Of course she had not been able to tell Vanessa that Peter would be here, lest she refuse to come at all. They paused in the doorway for a moment while Mrs. Clarence greeted Lady Jersey and Princess Esterhazy, two of the ladies who presided over the club. Vanessa in her celestial blue, and she in a new lemon-yellow sarcenet that set off her dark-auburn hair perfectly, made, she thought, an arresting picture, with Mrs. Clarence's dark-purple satin girth providing a setting for them. She looked about and at once saw Mr. Rivers. He had clearly been watching for her arrival, for his face lit up and he came hurrying across the room to meet her. Quite suddenly all her difficulties and anxieties about Peter and Vanessa vanished from her mind and she felt herself floating peacefully to meet him.

Vanessa's eyes raked the room, her heart thumping uncomfortably, but he was not there. She felt ennui swamping her and wished very much that she had withstood Ann's pleadings and remained at home. She admitted to herself that though she dreaded an encounter with him, she lost all interest in any affair she attended when she found him absent. The love she had acknowledged on that dreadful morning driving back from Burney's Field had grown, seemingly thriving on the memory of his grim profile and harsh words—and her own unhappiness. She had tried to root it out, but it remained firmly lodged, healthy and unheeding of her attempts. She had finally surrendered to it, aware that she was condemning herself to misery.

But not forever, she promised herself defiantly. When this Season is over and it won't seem as though I am running away, I will go back to the Continent and Papa and meet all sorts of interesting and exciting men and forget Peter Chance and his rigid standards and stiff-necked disapproval. Why had she given her heart to a man with such an attitude? Who would ever dream that madcap Vanessa Pymbroke would fall in love with Lord Peter Chance, whose reputation for impeccable respectability had become a byword in society?

Suddenly she imagined she heard his voice saying, "You are no longer the hoydenish schoolgirl who earns the admiration of her friends by foolish pranks. It is more than time, Miss Pymbroke, that you learned to behave more responsibly." Oh, God, she thought, of course he is right. I am three and twenty and out five years and can still think of myself as the madcap Vanessa Pymbroke! Papa should have spoken to me about this years ago, or I should have recognized it myself. How revolting—an aging imp! She felt herself slipping into self-pity as easy tears welled up and she swallowed convulsively.

No! I will not do this, she said to herself, straightening her shoulders with determination. I did nothing so terribly wrong, but certainly in the future I will not give in to these impulses without more thought. She raised her chin and found herself looking directly into the eyes of Lord Chance, who had just entered the room. Princess Esterhazy rushed to greet him joyfully, and Vanessa followed Ann and Mrs. Clarence to a sofa. She did not realize she had stopped breathing until the room began to swim and spots appeared before her eyes. Her heart had slowed, but each beat seemed to crash almost painfully in her chest. She took a deep, shuddering breath and forced herself to turn her head away and attempt a smile of greeting to Mr. Rivers through lips that seemed strangely stiff.

He smiled warmly in return. "Good evening, Miss Pymbroke. I hope you will give me the pleasure of standing up with me for a set this evening."

"Certainly, Mr. Rivers. Will the third suit you?"

"Very well, thank you." He bowed and turned back to Ann.

What a handsome, kind man, Vanessa thought. Why could I not fall in love with such a man, gentle and warm and approving? Perhaps, though, even he would not be approving of me either. Perhaps men do not care for women to be other than shy and submissive—and missish, she added with contempt, and I shall never sink to that! I would rather never marry at all. Which is just as well, since it begins to look as though I will never get an offer.

She checked and saw that Lord Chance was now talking to a woman of a certain age displaying a great deal of her powdered white bosom. Then Lord Evelyn was before her, declaring she had promised him the first set, and she stood up indifferently and allowed herself to be led out. He made love to her with intense zeal as they danced, but his words only made her laugh. What a fool the man was, she thought contemptuously, all the while smiling in case Lord Chance should be watching her. She slid her eyes in his direction. He was! She forced herself to become more animated in her responses to Lord Evelyn, and kept it up through the next two sets with Mr. Bynge and Mr. Rivers.

When Mr. Rivers led her back after their dance was over, she found Lord Chance in conversation with Ann and Mrs. Clarence. He turned to her and their eyes met fleetingly before they both looked away. Everyone began talking at once to ease the tension, only Peter and Vanessa remaining mute. After ten minutes of this, Mrs. Clarence decided to take a hand in the proceedings.

"There now, the music is striking up. Go along, all of you, and dance. I like to watch young people enjoying themselves. Lord Chance, do you lead Vanessa out. She needs the exercise, Lord knows, after moping at home so many days." She stared up at him with bright, challenging eyes.

He met her gaze for a moment, accepted the challenge, and bowed. He turned to Vanessa. "Will you do me the honor, Miss Pymbroke," he murmured, his eyes fixed upon her left ear. Without raising her own, which she could not have done under any circumstances, she nodded and they turned to the dance floor.

After a few steps, however, he said, "Will you mind if we walk on the terrace instead? It is quite mild tonight, so you would not be in danger of taking a chill."

Again she acquiesced with a nod. Her tongue felt paralyzed and her mind blank and she seemed to be propelled along with the help of some outside force. The warm dark terrace was patterned in huge blocks of light from the windows and she paced silently through the alternating squares beside Peter. They reached the end of the terrace and he paused at the balustrade. She waited will-lessly.

"Miss Pymbroke," he said at last, "I am once more in the unhappy position of owing you an apology."

Something broke inside her and she literally felt the blood speeding up in her veins, returning volition and thought. She could, at last, raise her head and look at him directly. He continued. "I did, as you said, behave reprehensibly to you. The realization of it has made me most unhappy."

"Please be assured then, sir, that I gladly accept your apology. I also have been unhappy."

"It grieves me to learn that I can have been the cause of any unhappiness for you."

The end of the set caused a large number of couples to stream out onto the terrace and the intimacy of the moment was over. They turned back. Vanessa felt that if she did not speak, and soon, everything might be lost forever. He had given—now she must.

"Lord Chance, I must tell you that I have come to understand that my thoughtless behavior was the cause, however unwittingly, of distress and anxiety to others. I am very sorry for that." He did not respond for so long that she feared her admission had done no good. The music for the next set was striking up and almost at once they were alone again. They paced on silently to the other end of the terrace. Again he paused and, after a moment, turned to her.

"Miss Pymbroke, may I call you Vanessa?" She was so surprised she only said, "Oh," and gaped at him.

"You see, I want to tell you something and it will sound less pompous if I say Vanessa."

"Then *indeed* you must," she replied, her mouth twitching with a suppressed smile.

He grinned, acknowledging her meaning. "Yes, I am aware of sounding that way, Ann often reminds me of it. I am making an effort to sound less so."

"You are doing very well," she said encouragingly.

"Vanessa, I love you very much," he said simply.

She felt her heart leap with happiness and seem to go gamboling about in her chest, turning cartwheels of joy. "Do you, Lord Chance?" was all she could manage to say.

"Yes, and I would be very grateful if you could call me Peter. That is, if you mean to respond positively to my declaration."

She gave him an absolutely blinding smile and said, "Then I suppose I must call you Peter."

He reached for her and she came eagerly into his arms. Paying no attention at all to another eruption of guests onto the terrace, they kissed with all the rapture and passion recommended by Mrs. Clarence as the most satisfactory way to begin a lasting love. At last, without breaking their embrace, they drew back to look into each other's eyes.

"I fear," she confessed, "that though I will try, I cannot promise to change a great deal all at once."

"I would not have you changed—at least only the least bit," he added. "I suppose honesty compels me to admit that I will not either, though."

"We will both have to take it on trust, I think. We will

both try, that is all we can promise: I to be less a thoughtless madcap and you, I hope, more—more—"

"Neck or nothing?"

She giggled. "Yes, exactly."

"I think you must already concede me a point on that score then, my darling, for never in my life have I dreamed of compromising a young lady by taking her onto the terrace during a ball and kissing her in full view of the entire company."

She considered for a moment and then said with judicious fairness, "I will concede that point, sir."

"Thank you, my love, my dearest love. Now, I do not mean to be unreasonably demanding, but you have neglected to tell me your feelings for me," he complained.

"Did I so?" she said wonderingly. "I had thought you must understand them very well, for I will have you know, sir, that it is not my habit to *allow* myself to be taken onto the terrace and kissed in full view of the entire company."

"Tell me," he demanded compellingly, bending to brush her lips with his own. She obediently murmured the words against his mouth, and then forgot everything for aeons.

The beginning strains of a waltz broke into their consciousness. He released her and pulled her arm possessively through his own.

"Come, it is a waltz and I have never danced it with you."

"Oh, but I would not dare!" she protested, "though I am now on the list, it is my first time here and I have not yet been given permission. The ladies who make the rules would ostracize both of us if we did so without it. Did you not know that is the rule? They must approve of you and then if you conduct yourself becomingly they very very condescendingly consent that you may dance the waltz."

He listened to all this, a smile growing on his face, then pulled her out onto the floor, bowed before her and looked at her challengingly, as he held out his arms. "Will you concede me another point, my dear love?"

About the Author

Norma Lee Clark was born in Joplin, Missouri, but considers herself a New Yorker, having lived in Manhattan longer than in her native state. In addition to writing Regencies, she is also the private secretary to author/actor/producer/director Woody Allen. Ms. Clark's previous books, *The Perfect Match* and *The Marriage Mart*, are available in Signet editions.

JOIN THE *REGENCY ROMANCE* READERS' PANEL

Help us bring you more of the books you like by filling out this survey and mailing it in today.

1. Book Title: _____

   Book #: _____

2. Using the scale below, how would you rate this book on the following features? Please write in one rating from 0-10 for each feature in the spaces provided.

	NOT SO								EXCEL-	
POOR	GOOD			O.K.			GOOD		LENT	
0	1	2	3	4	5	6	7	8	9	10

RATING

Overall opinion of book .... _____
Plot/Story .... _____
Setting/Location .... _____
Writing Style .... _____
Character Development .... _____
Conclusion/Ending .... _____
Scene on Front Cover .... _____

3. About how many romance books do you buy for yourself each month? _____

4. How would you classify yourself as a reader of Regency romances?
   I am a ( ) light ( ) medium ( ) heavy reader.

5. What is your education?
   ( ) High School (or less) ( ) 4 yrs. college
   ( ) 2 yrs. college   ( ) Post Graduate

6. Age _____   7. Sex: ( ) Male ( ) Female

Please Print Name_____

Address_____

City _____ State _____ Zip _____

Phone # (____)_____

Thank you. Please send to New American Library, Research Dept., 1633 Broadway, New York, NY 10019.